The Confession

Erin McCauley

Lisa,
My favorite aunty.
I love you so much.
Thank you for always
being there.
Love
[signature]

CRIMSON
ROMANCE
Avon, Massachusetts

This edition published by
Crimson Romance
an imprint of F+W Media, Inc.
10151 Carver Road, Suite 200
Blue Ash, Ohio 45242

www.crimsonromance.com

Dedication

TO GRAMS, FOR TEACHING ME TO DREAM. I MISS YOU EVERY DAY.

Acknowledgements

A special thank you to my pen pals, Tammy, Chassily, Joan, Diana, and Lori, for the support, guidance, words of wisdom, and happy hour brainstorming. I couldn't have done this without you. Thank you Cathy, for talking me off the ledge when I wondered if I was crazy, and for your never wavering support and friendship. Thank you Dad, for your medical wisdom, support and love; you'll forever be my hero.

Jennifer Lawler, thank you for taking a chance on me, and believing in my stories as much as I do.

Thank you to my personal dream team, Jennifer, Michael, and Cyera, for believing I could do it, even when I didn't. I am so blessed to be your mother. And to my husband, Chuck, for working so hard, so I could chase my dreams and for taking this journey with me. I love you.

Chapter 1

Aimee gripped the steering wheel, her stomach churning as she stared at the mansion in front of her and the reality of where she was sank in. She still couldn't believe she'd come all the way to California, and she didn't have any idea what to do now.

The towering front door opened, and a tall man in a T-shirt and tattered blue jeans emerged. His dark hair caught the light from the sun as he stepped off the porch, giving the impression of a glowing halo. She gasped when he smiled and waved at her. His strides were long as he crossed the walkway. It was then she realized he hadn't been waving at her but at an older man pushing a wheelbarrow across the yard. She continued to stare, mesmerized by the flexing of his tanned biceps when he pointed. He laughed at something the other man said and reached up to clasp him on the shoulder before turning back.

He stopped in mid-stride, looking across the driveway, apparently just noticing her car parked by the fountain. Their eyes met. His face transformed to an emotionless mask as he marched toward her. She wanted to put the car in drive and race for the gate, but at the rate he was approaching, it was already too late.

She rolled down the window, prepared to lie and apologize for the wrong turn that brought her here.

"You're early. Emily isn't quite ready, but you don't have to wait in your car." His words were polite, but his once active hands were now stiffly tucked into the pockets of his jeans.

"Early?"

"Aren't you here to meet with Emily?" His eyes narrowed.

She couldn't think of a thing to say as her mind tried to catch up with the conversation. He was acting like he'd been expecting her, but that wasn't possible. He stood in silence, waiting for her response.

It was the same question she'd been asking herself for the last twenty-four hours. Was she ready to meet her? "Yes, I suppose I am," Aimee stuttered. Her hands began to shake.

Opening the door to the car, she stepped out. Her knees buckled and she could barely feel her legs. Holding onto the open door to brace herself, she looked up and attempted to smile. Suspicious deep blue eyes locked onto hers.

"What did you say your name was?"

She sucked in a breath. Did he know who she was? That was ridiculous. He couldn't possibly know. She swallowed hard and licked her lips. "A . . . Aimee, my name is Aimee."

With his eyes still fixed on her, he reached out his hand. "I'm Mark."

She placed her hand into his, and felt the world shift beneath her. Electricity shot up her arm, the warmth of his hand radiated through every nerve in her body. She snatched her hand back as if she'd been burned.

She looked up at him, unable to identify the feelings racing through her. For a moment she thought she'd seen the same reaction in his eyes before his expression changed back to wary. He turned and walked toward the house. Should she follow? She concentrated on putting one foot in front of the other as she slowly walked behind him.

The house was massive, built out of light-colored brick, with numerous tall windows catching the morning sunlight. Her head tilted back as she drew closer. The second story was lined with French doors opening onto small Venetian balconies. She looked over her shoulder at the brick wall covered in ivy surrounding the property. She'd driven through an ornately carved gate that remained open at the beginning of a long rounded drive encircling a huge water fountain made completely of marble.

She stopped at the foot of the porch stairs. What if Emily didn't want her here?

"Are you okay?"

His deep voice broke through her thoughts. "I think so. I'm . . . I'm sorry. I guess I'm not exactly prepared for this."

"There's no reason to be nervous." He held the front door open for her. "She's an amazing lady, and very easy to work for."

It took a moment for Mark's words to sink in. She blinked and turned back to him. "Work for?"

He stared at her, his brow creased. "The job interview? Weren't you sent by the agency?"

Aimee followed him into the foyer, unsure of how to respond. If she told him the truth, he wouldn't hesitate to throw her out. After coming this far, she couldn't let that happen.

As she struggled for the words to explain, she couldn't help but notice the impressive entry. A grand staircase wove up two sides of the room, and a crystal chandelier hung from two stories above, resting over a huge marble-topped circular table. A large vase sat in the middle of the table filled with colorful flowers emitting an intoxicating scent.

Mark stood silently beside the table, his arms crossed, waiting for her reply.

Before Aimee could speak, an elegant, middle aged, blond woman descended the stairs, a warm smile on her face. "I hope I haven't kept you waiting long."

Aimee could only stare, her mouth slightly agape, legs weak, and her body trembling.

"I'm Emily. Emily Sinclair." She held out her hand.

Could she be? Could it be possible that this beautiful, regal woman was her mother? Aimee placed her hand into Emily's, looked into emerald green eyes much like her own, and returned the smile. At that moment, all the pieces fell into place and she knew exactly what she needed to do. "I'm Aimee. It's nice to finally meet you."

Chapter 2

Mark walked into the large kitchen, kissed Mimsey on the cheek, and reached around her to steal a cookie from the rack on the counter.

"You rascal, you know those are for the landscapers."

He winked and scooted his six-foot frame onto the kitchen counter before taking a bite of the still warm chocolate chip cookie. "You know I can't resist your cookies, Mimsey. I could smell them all the way down the hall."

Mark had been stealing her cookies for as long as he could remember. Mimsey was the cook, but she was as much a part of the family as he was.

She swatted him with the dishtowel she'd pulled off her shoulder. "Off the counter. You're dirty." Her entire body shook with laughter when he poked his bottom lip out. "You're too old to be using that pout face, Marcus Lee."

"Still works on you, Mimsey."

She swatted him again as he reached for another cookie. "How's the yard coming along?" she asked, bending to pull another sheet of cookies from the oven.

"It's going to be beautiful, but I'm worried about the timing. Emily's birthday is only a month away and there's still so much to do." Slipping from the counter, he leaned against it and crossed his ankles. "The rose garden isn't in, the patio isn't laid and she keeps coming up with more ideas."

"She always tries to stay busy this time of the year, you know that." Mimsey watched him as she lifted the hot cookies off the pan and placed them on the cooling rack. "You're doing a great job, and I have no doubt you'll have it completed by her big day. Look at how much you've already accomplished."

He grunted.

"Hopefully, when she hires her new assistant, the two of them will be so busy that she won't have time to keep coming up with all these new ideas. Then you can concentrate on the projects already started."

Mark uncrossed his arms and pushed away from the counter. "I wish she wasn't so hell bent on hiring someone immediately."

"It makes sense she'd need someone quickly, especially with the auction coming up, the party, and the all the work going on around here," she said, spooning dough onto another sheet.

"The first girl is up with her now. I don't think the interview will last very long. She was so nervous I don't think she even remembered why she was here."

"I hope you weren't mean to her, Marcus. You know how intimidating you can be to these young girls. Maybe if you smiled once in a while, you wouldn't be almost thirty and single."

Mark laughed. "I like being single. I have all the women I can handle right here with you and Emily." He winked at her.

Mimsey scowled.

"This time," he said seriously, as he fought to control the anger that began to surge through him as he remembered Emily's previous assistant. "I'm going to insist Emily run a proper background check, and possibly request a DNA sample before the new girl sharpens her first pencil."

"You need to let that go." Mimsey reached out and gently rubbed his arm. "You can't hold all that anger inside, it does you no good. What's done is done."

He knew she meant well, but he couldn't let it go. "I should get back to work."

"Marcus Lee, I mean it. You need to stop being so protective and trust that not everyone who comes into Emily's life has a hidden agenda."

"I can't do that. From where I stand, every person is guilty until proven innocent. I have enough evidence to prove that's a legitimate stand to take."

"Marcus . . ."

He leaned over and planted a kiss on her soft chocolate-colored cheek. "I know she needs some help. I get that. But it doesn't mean I'll stand by with my head in the sand this time. I will be polite and courteous, but I won't be foolish. I won't allow her to be hurt again."

He strode out of the kitchen and peered through the window overlooking the driveway. When he didn't see the girl's car, he headed up the stairs. Tapping lightly on the door, he walked into Emily's office. She sat behind a large antique desk, her head down, her hands moving a sleek gold pen across a notepad.

She looked up as he approached. "I was wondering when you'd show up."

He shrugged. "Are you trying to tell me I'm predictable, or overbearing?"

"Both." She smiled and set her pen down.

"Well?"

"She's perfect. She's highly qualified, professional, friendly, and available immediately."

Mark paced the room. "Are you sure? She seemed like a scared rabbit to me." He stopped and leaned onto her desk, palms flat, and his body tense. "Aren't you at least going to run a background check before you hand over the key to the safe?"

"I will request one, but the agency won't send anyone to me who hasn't passed a background check. I'm going with my gut on this girl and she's moving into the cottage today." She stood and walked around her desk. "Mark, stop worrying so much. You're going to give yourself a heart attack."

"Don't you think after your last assistant I have a right to be worried? She wasn't just one more in the extensive line of long-lost daughters, she was convincing. Not only did she almost walk away with a large sum of money, she hurt you. You opened up your heart, and she broke it."

"I know I need to be careful. I also know you're worried. Justifiably so, but I have a good feeling about Aimee. Didn't you sense something different about her?"

He did, but he wasn't sure if it was a good something. She made him feel things he didn't understand. Her beauty was undeniable, but he didn't think that was what drew him to her. He'd experienced a jolt when their hands touched. For a moment, he'd actually thought she'd felt it too.

She confused him. Something wasn't right, and it put his normal suspicions into overdrive. Her golden hair was stylishly cut in a way that screamed modern, professional, even successful, yet she wore jeans and tennis shoes to a job interview. She seemed ready to run when he'd approached her car, her bright green eyes showing a mix of confusion and fear, but she exuded an aura of confidence when she reached out to shake Emily's hand. Aimee seemed nervous about the interview when she arrived, but Emily didn't seem to have detected any of that. Something didn't add up.

"You hired her on the spot? You're not going to interview anyone else? Maybe call her by the end of the week?"

"She's perfect, and I don't have another week. If anything comes back on her background check, I promise I will allow you to personally toss her into the street. Deal?"

"Be careful." Mark wrapped his arms around Emily before turning to leave. Reaching for the door handle, he turned back around. "And don't make assumptions that she's as innocent as she appears. They never are."

Chapter 3

Aimee set her bag down inside the front door and entered the cottage nestled in the back of the property. It had a separate bedroom, a warm, inviting kitchen overlooking a large vegetable garden, and a comfortable living area with a bay window that allowed the afternoon sun to warm the small space. A vase filled with freshly cut flowers stood on the dining table and a large basket of freshly baked muffins sat on the kitchen counter with a note:

There are some basic necessities in the refrigerator, and fresh towels in the bathroom. Make yourself at home and please don't hesitate to call the house if you need anything. I look forward to seeing you in the morning.

— Emily

Aimee ran her fingers over the elegant, handwritten note before placing it gently back on the counter. She wasn't sure what she was doing. Her decision to take this job was impulsive and more than a little foolish. As a successful handbag designer, she had a business to run in New York, and the new season's sketches to complete. Orders would be piling up within the month, and after flying to North Carolina to be with her dying mother, she was already weeks behind. Instead, she would be planning an auction and coordinating a birthday party in San Francisco. It was crazy, but she couldn't think of any other way to get to know Emily.

Carrying her small suitcase into the bedroom, Aimee unpacked her things into the dresser drawers. She ran her hand tenderly over the old leather case she'd brought with her. Closing her eyes, she fought back the tears as she remembered the secret nestled inside. Her mother's secret. The secret that completely changed Aimee's life. It was like she could hear voices bellowing from inside the latched case. Voices raised in anger, and soft muffled cries of pain. Wiping a tear from her cheek, she rose from the bed and slid the case gently onto the top shelf of the closet.

Aimee's knees were shaking, her stomach in knots. After spending the last thirty minutes with Emily Sinclair she was again questioning her right to be here. The woman was amazing; smart, beautiful, warm. But behind the brightness of her eyes lie a shadow, an ache she seemed to believe she'd hidden, but Aimee saw it. It broke her heart.

Turning to leave the bedroom, she lingered in the open doorway for a moment, realizing she had nothing appropriate to wear if she was going to start work the next day. Having only packed jeans, two pairs of shorts, and one simple black dress when she'd left for North Carolina, she'd have to call Luther and have some of her things sent from her loft in New York. Then she would have to do some last minute shopping to tide her over.

She pulled her cell phone out of her purse and turned it on. Seven voice mails, five from her sister Joan, and two from Luther. Joan could wait. She had nothing to say to her.

"Aimee," Luther said the minute he picked up the phone, "where have you been? I've been calling you." She could easily picture him pacing through the store, throwing his hands up in dramatic despair. "Why haven't you checked in with me? I've been so worried."

"I'm fine, Luther. I'm sorry if I worried you. It's been a little crazy." She smiled at his loud expulsion of breath.

"How is the old battle axe, still alive and kicking?" He paused, his voice softening. "Sorry, I shouldn't have said that. I know she's sick and it can't be easy for you. She is your mother, after all."

"It's not easy, and a lot has happened. It turns out she isn't—"

He growled into the phone, interrupting her as venom dripped from every word. "What? How could she do that to you? Getting you all worried about her, call you to her bedside in the middle of the night, and for what? Just to get your attention? I always thought that woman could never surprise me, but then . . ."

"A lot has changed."

"What are you talking about? What has changed? Sounds like the same old games to me. Is she actually dying, or was that a staged act to spin a little upheaval into your world? Oh, she'd like that all right, sounds exactly like something she'd pull. The woman hasn't said a kind word to you your entire life, and still thinks you should be worshiping the ground she slithers upon . . ."

She couldn't help but smile as her best friend ranted and raged in her defense. Luther was her business manager and the one person in the world she trusted. But this time things were different. She wasn't ready to talk about it, even to him.

"It's a lot more complicated than only her illness, and a long story. I promise to tell you in detail, but I need a favor, and I need you to not freak out on me."

"You're not going to leave me hanging like this, are you? You can't do that to me. A lot has changed, she says, but can't talk now. You will just have to sit and wait until I'm damn good and ready to talk about it, she says. Just go about your life, Luther, like I didn't say anything—"

"You're freaking out on me."

"What is it? What is this favor?" The hurt was clear in his tone.

Trying to reassure him, she said, "I promise to fill you in. I'll tell you all the details I know, just not today. I still need to find a store around here and pick up some clothes for work, and I need you to send me some of my things."

"Clothes for work? Now what are you talking about?"

"I need you to go to my loft and send me some clothes other than jeans, including shoes, the works. I also need some of my sketch books, the ones I started drawing the new line in. And I need you to hold down the shop for a while."

"Aimee, what is going on?"

"Please, Luther. I'll explain everything when I can."

"You better believe you'll explain, dropping bombs on me like this, no warning, just boom, boom—"

She interrupted him. "You're freaking out again."

"Of course I'm freaking out. What did you expect with all this nonsense you spew at me? Work clothes for what? Are you suddenly opening a new shop in North Carolina?"

Aimee walked over and curled into the bench seat built into the bay window, looking out at the beautiful gardens. "No. It's not a new shop. I'll explain later, but I need them sent to the Sinclair Estate in San Francisco. Oh, and please address them to Morrison, not Roberts."

"Sinclair Estate? San Francisco? Why are you going by Morrison again? Aimee, what in the hell are you doing in San Francisco? I thought you were in North Carolina."

"Well, it looks like I'll be organizing an auction to start." Aimee could no longer make sense of the incoherent questions being thrown through the phone line. "I promise to explain when I can. I'll call you soon."

Aimee hung up with Luther still rambling on the other end.

Chapter 4

Mark stared at the empty screen on his laptop. "Once upon a time," he typed, emitting a small chuckle. He sighed, ran his hands through his hair, and hit the delete button. Leaning back in the lounge chair outside of his cottage, he kicked his feet up on the corner of the table and took a long pull from his cold beer. The setting sun transformed the sky into a vivid watercolor of oranges, pinks, and reds. Leaning his head back, he closed his eyes and let the silence of the fading day soothe him.

A gentle breeze blew over him, bringing with it a soft, feminine scent with a spicy touch of sex appeal. He knew it was her before he saw her. He sat up in the chair, his ability to relax vanishing with a single scent. What was it about her that got under his skin?

He watched her come around the old oak tree, carrying a shopping bag in each hand. She paused a moment to smell the blossoms on a rose bush, a faint smile touching her lips. She didn't walk quite as much as she glided, an air of elegance mixed comfortably with a sense of purpose. She hesitated when she saw him.

"Hello, Mark."

"Been out shopping, have you?"

She nodded. "I didn't bring much with me, I'm afraid."

"I doubt you anticipated starting your new position immediately. Emily is overwhelmed right now and probably didn't think about the fact you'd need a bit of time to get things arranged."

"It's all right. I'm having my things sent to me, and I was able to find enough to get me through." Motioning with the bags she held in her hands, she smiled at him and began to walk away.

"Why don't you put your bags away and join me for a drink," he said, hoping she would agree. He was anxious to learn something about her. With Aimee, his curiosity was almost as strong as his distrust of her.

"Oh, I don't want to intrude. It looks like you're busy." She nodded toward his laptop.

He smirked and looked at the blank screen. "Not busy at all. I would enjoy the company."

"Well . . ."

"I insist. I'll go open a bottle of wine and meet you back here." He stood up and headed into his cottage, giving her no chance to refuse.

Ten minutes later, Aimee sat down across from Mark and accepted the glass of wine he handed her. He watched her in silence, wondering what she was thinking. She seemed uncomfortable, looking down into her lap and playing with the stem on her wine glass.

"Is your cottage adequate?" he asked, breaking the silence.

"It's beautiful, thank you."

"Are you from the San Francisco area?"

"No, actually I'm from the East Coast. New York," she replied.

"That's a long way from here. What possessed you to apply for a job in San Francisco?"

"It was more of an impulsive decision."

She certainly looked sincere. Would someone really move across the United States on impulse? Could she be running from something, or worse, was she here to get close to Emily like the last girl had been?

"So are you originally from New York?" He attempted to keep his tone light.

"I grew up in North Carolina, but moved there after college."

"What did you do in New York?"

"I ran a boutique. How about you? Are you from San Francisco?"

His eyes narrowed. He knew she was trying to change the subject. It seemed like a harmless question. He wondered if he was coming across like an interrogator. He decided to let it go for now and try to keep the conversation light and friendly. "Born and raised," he said, looking around. "In fact, I've spent most of my life right here."

Aimee looked surprised. The silence lingered for a moment before Mark added, "Emily kicked me out of the big house and into the cottage right after college." He smiled at the memory. "She said I was overly protective and I needed my own life, even if I wouldn't leave to find it."

"You've never wanted to leave here, to have your own home somewhere?"

"No. Not really. I love it here."

"What about your parents?"

"My mother lived here as well until I left for college, then she caught the traveling bug. She's been jet-setting the globe ever since." He refused to give his father any thought.

"So is your family related to Emily in some way?"

He could swear she was actually holding her breath as she awaited his response.

"Not in the blood sense of the word, but she's family to us."

She nodded. Her expressive face told him a lot more than her words, and he wasn't sure why she was so cautious about asking the questions she obviously wanted to, or why he was so hesitant to offer her any more information than he was.

"Brothers and sisters?" he asked, hoping to keep the twenty questions game going.

"One sister, you?"

"Just me. Are you close to your family?"

"I was to my dad. Not so much my mother or sister. We have a . . . I suppose the best word would be strained. We have a strained relationship."

Her face appeared pained. He almost believed that the strain she spoke of was something she didn't understand and something she wished was different. "I'm sorry to hear that."

Changing the subject again, she said, "I'm sorry I interrupted your work earlier. I didn't realize there was another cottage out here when I first came through."

"You didn't interrupt anything. I was staring at a blank screen." She looked at him with confusion.

"I have this wild notion that I'll write a book someday. Or rather Emily 'sees great potential in my future as a storyteller.'" He laughed. "When I was a little kid I would make up stories to cheer Emily up. As I grew up, the stories became more elaborate. She loved them and thinks I should write them down to be published."

"Was she sad often?"

He stared at her, slightly taken aback by her question. The tone of his voice grew sharp. "Regardless of what it looks like from the outside, she hasn't lived a completely charmed life. She's gone through more than most, and more than anyone should."

"I . . . I'm sorry. I didn't mean to suggest . . ." she muttered, her face flushed.

He looked at her genuinely apologetic expression. He felt like a heel. "I shouldn't have snapped. I'm sorry."

"It's fine. I didn't mean to pry." Aimee quickly rose from the table. Thanking him for the wine, she mumbled something about her early morning and hurried back toward her cottage.

He knew he'd acted like an ass. He wanted to go and apologize but felt glued to the chair. He watched her leave, torn between his suspicions of her, and his baffling urge to pull her into his arms and chase the sadness from her eyes.

Chapter 5

The next morning, Aimee let herself in through the French doors in the back of the main house as she'd been instructed. The room was beautiful, with large comfortable sofas crowded with warm colored throw pillows, a big fireplace surrounded by bookshelves, and an abundance of green plants. It was inviting and full of bright sunlight.

"You must be Aimee."

She turned and nodded at the warm face of the woman welcoming her. The woman's skin was the color of melted chocolate, her hair the color of salt and pepper, pulled back into a bun, and her tooth-filled smile stretched from ear to ear. She wore a simple, soft gray dress partially covered by an apron with roosters walking across the bottom. Her eyes were gentle, but it was apparent those eyes didn't miss a thing.

"I'm Mimsey. It's very nice to meet you. Have you eaten breakfast? Emily and Marcus are just sitting down to theirs." Mimsey started from the room and, turning back to Aimee, bopped her head toward the door, inviting her to follow.

"I have eaten, thank you. Emily left some delicious muffins in the cottage yesterday."

"I'm glad you enjoyed them," Mimsey replied, her face conveying her obvious pride. "Come and join the others. I'll pour you some coffee."

They walked through the main entry, and in through the closed doors leading to the kitchen. Mark and Emily were seated at a small table in the corner, each sipping from a coffee cup and deep in conversation.

"Good morning, Aimee," Emily said, motioning for her to take the empty seat next to her. "Did you sleep well?"

"Very well, thank you." She looked over at Mark, his eyes watchful.

She mumbled "Good morning" to him as she sat down and thanked Mimsey for the steaming cup of coffee she placed in front of her.

She took a small sip of the hot liquid and listened to the banter going on between Emily and Mark. They were so comfortable together. Aimee wondered if she could have that ease with Emily. She wanted that desperately. Would Emily understand why she took the job as her assistant? Would she appreciate the thought behind it and not think of it as deception? She simply wanted to know her, needed to know her. So how come she still felt deceitful? Emily seemed to be such an amazing woman, nothing at all like Aimee had pictured. Not that she'd really known what to expect, but Emily's warmth and openness surprised her. Maybe she'd been living with disapproval for too long.

Mark waved his hands pointing to an invisible map as he discussed the day's plans for the grounds. "I'm thinking of using natural stone for the pathways. With the abundance of flowerbeds on either side of the path, I want it to look as natural as the surrounding area."

Emily's face lit up. "I love that idea."

Aimee scooted back in her chair and continued to sip her coffee while Emily talked about the rose garden being planted and the bench area she was having bricked in.

"I plan to sit in the sunlight, reading my autographed copy of Mark's book, surrounded by the scent of my roses."

Aimee stifled a giggle when Mark rolled his eyes. She pictured him sitting in front of his blank computer screen last night, and knew Emily's future plans for her rose garden would take longer than she thought.

She glanced over and noticed Mark looking intently at her, while Emily continued to discuss the different varieties of roses being planted this week. She bit her lower lip and looked back down, uncomfortable with his blatant scrutiny. She raised her eyes again and found him still watching her. His bright blue eyes never left hers, even when he responded to Emily. Aimee began to squirm in her chair as she felt the heat rise on her cheeks.

She turned her focus to Emily, trying to ignore the tension she felt. Last night hadn't ended well, and Mark seemed angry with her. She wished she hadn't asked the question she did, but was still unsure why he'd reacted with such venom. Still feeling his eyes on her, she became increasingly uneasy. She snapped her head up, fighting the urge to shout how rude it was to stare. He was no longer looking at her. She watched as both Mark and Emily appeared to have an entire conversation with only their eyes.

"Mark, Aimee and I are going to head up to the office, and then we're having lunch with Peter, so we'll just plan on seeing you at dinner," Emily said, her voice sounding slightly irritated. She rose and pushed her chair under the table.

He stood as well. "Make sure you check on that report. We really shouldn't be made to wait for something that important." He glanced over at Aimee. Turning back to Emily, he added, "I'll see you at dinner, and tell Peter hello for me." He nodded his head at Aimee, his face devoid of emotion. "Enjoy your first day."

Emily turned to face her. "Please don't pay Mark any attention, he's always grumpy in the morning."

Aimee smiled awkwardly, and looking over her shoulder saw Mark still watching them. She was sure that the silent communication going on between Emily and Mark had nothing to do with Mark's not being a morning person. She wasn't sure what to make of him. One minute he was smiling at her, his dimples melting any sign of animosity. The next minute he was watching her with accusing eyes. She could swear that he was silently warning Emily. Of what, she had no idea.

"I think it's a little more than his being grumpy," she murmured, unaware that she'd spoken out loud.

Emily chuckled. "Mark needs to work on his manners, but he's actually a very warm, loving man."

Aimee grunted, and followed her out of the kitchen.

They walked up the stairs, through another set of French doors, and into a sprawling office. A large antique desk sat between two enormous windows, and a smaller desk sat to the right side. The office was cool and elegant, with beige walls lined with gold-framed awards and photographs. There were no curtains on the windows, allowing the sun to shine through. Vases filled with fresh flowers sat on the corner of each desk. Another vase sat on a small table, set between a couch and two matching wing back chairs covered in a darker beige fabric with small white pin stripes.

"Who's Peter?" Aimee asked.

"He's the charity coordinator from the Talbot Cancer Foundation," Emily replied. "He's helping with the auction. He'll be working directly with us on this, and we'll be spending a lot of time with him."

Aimee stood in front of the photographs on the wall and walked from picture to picture. It was a who's-who of the entertainment world, all photographed with Emily. Aimee's mouth dropped when she came upon a picture of Emily with the President of the United States. Intermingled amongst the celebrities were photos of her with Mark as a young boy. In one of the photo's Mark stood beside a beautiful olive-skinned woman with flowing black hair and a mirror image of his smile.

"That's Mark's mother, and my best friend, McKenzie Lee. Stunning, isn't she?" Emily said.

"Stunning is an understatement," Aimee replied. "I think she might be the most beautiful woman I've ever seen."

Emily laughed. "You should have seen her in high school. It wasn't easy being her best friend."

"How long have you two been friends?"

"Since birth, we like to say, but honestly since about fifth grade. We did everything together. We still do when she isn't jetting off to remote areas of the world. She's as amazing as she is beautiful. I miss her. I'm glad she'll be home soon."

Aimee couldn't help but notice the look of pleasure that crossed Emily's face. Aimee's smile faded. She leaned in to get a closer look at one particular photograph. A young Emily stood in a long white wedding dress, her blond hair covered in a veil. A large diamond twinkled on her left hand as she clasped a bouquet of pink roses, her face alight with happiness. Standing beside her was a tall, handsome man in a black tuxedo.

"That's my Nathan. Handsome devil, wasn't he?" Emily looked lovingly at the framed picture. Walking over to her desk, she picked up another frame and handed it to Aimee. "This is my favorite picture of him."

Aimee took a deep breath and with shaky hands, lifted the picture for a better look. Surrounded by a field of green grass, Nathan leaned back on his arms, and smiled with love at the photographer. His left eye was covered by a patch of blond hair, and his bare feet were crossed at the ankles. "Did you take this picture?"

"I did."

"He loves you very much."

"Yes he did, but what makes you say that?" Emily asked, looking back at the picture.

"It's in his eyes. I can tell by the look on his face he's deeply in love with the person behind the lens. Maybe that's why it's your favorite picture. You see it too."

Emily's eyes grew misty. "I suppose I do." She gently took the frame from Aimee's hand and with one last glance, placed it back onto her desk.

"Where is he now?"

"I lost him many years ago." Emily walked behind her desk. Aimee could see her struggling with her emotions, but it was only a brief moment before they were back to business. "Let's get you caught up on this auction before our meeting with Peter this afternoon."

Aimee mumbled an "of course" and sat down across from Emily's desk, while she tried to silence the unanswered questions running through her mind.

Chapter 6

"So how was your first day in the trenches?" Mark asked, passing a bowl of fresh green beans to Aimee.

Aimee spooned the beans onto her china plate. Dinner was almost a formal affair in Emily's house. "It was good, I think. Peter was very helpful in getting me caught up on the auction, and I met with the caterer this afternoon."

"Aimee was amazing. Everyone loved her, and she handled herself like she'd been doing this for years. I think our poor Peter might even have a little crush," Emily said, winking at her.

Aimee felt the heat rise on her cheeks and looked over at Mark from under her lashes. She couldn't read his reaction, but he was once again staring directly at her.

"If you want Peter to focus on work, maybe you shouldn't hire such beautiful assistants."

Aimee dropped her fork, causing it to clatter loudly against the china plate. With an embarrassed "excuse me" she silently lifted her fork into her mouth and chewed. She glanced at Emily and found her looking curiously at Mark.

After a lengthy stretch of silence, Emily finally asked, "How did the patio in the rose garden turn out?"

"It looks good. If you'd like, I'll show you both the progress after dinner."

Both of them nodded, just as Mimsey poked her head into the dining room.

"I'm sorry for the interruption, but there is a call for Aimee on the house phone. She said it was urgent."

Stunned, Aimee looked up and realized all eyes were focused on her. "I'm so sorry. I don't know who it could possibly be.

Excuse me."

She rose from the table and followed Mimsey to the sitting room. She picked up the phone with a confused "Hello?"

"Aimee, where are you? What are you doing? You should be here taking care of mother. She is beside herself with worry. You just took off . . ."

"Joan . . .?"

Her sister continued to rant into the phone. "How could you do this to her or to me? What is wrong with you?"

"It's complicated, but—"

"What are you doing in California? You need to come home immediately."

She wondered how Joan knew where she was. It was evident that her mother hadn't told her the situation. She waited until she was sure her sister was finished before she said, "Is mother okay? Health-wise, I mean?"

Joan raised her voice. "No, she's not okay. She's dying, and you just ran out of here like the house was on fire, and we haven't heard a word from you since. You won't return my phone calls. I had to find out where you were from Luther. What's going on with you? I swear you are the most selfish—"

"That's enough with the insults. You have no idea what's going on, so don't presume that my actions are selfish. I can't come home right now. I *won't* come home right now. Don't call me here again. If you need to reach me for anything other than insulting me, you can leave a message on my cell phone and I'll call you back."

"Tell me what's going on—"

Aimee hung up the phone without letting her sister finish her sentence. She leaned her head onto the palm of her hand trying to get her emotions under control.

"Is everything okay?"

She whipped her head around and found Mark standing inside the doorway. He was leaning up against the door-frame, his arms crossed and his face expressionless.

"Everything's fine. I'm sorry for the interruption."

"Everything didn't sound fine," he replied.

"My sister has a tendency toward the dramatic, and our mother's been sick," she finally managed to say, her voice cracking over the word *mother*.

Walking further into the room, he tucked his hands into his pockets and looked down at the floor before he spoke. "I'm sorry your mother's sick. Is she going to be okay?"

She answered him honestly. "Actually, I don't think so. She's been sick for a long time."

"I'm sorry to hear that," he replied, his voice sincere. He walked over to her, and awkwardly placed his hand on her shoulder in an obvious attempt to console her.

Her skin sizzled beneath his touch. Recognizing his discomfort and uneasy about her own reaction, she stood, and walked slowly from the room. They met Emily in the hallway.

"Is everything okay?" she asked.

"Fine," Aimee replied. "I'm so sorry about the interruption and the personal phone call to your home."

"Don't worry about that. Are you still hungry?"

"I don't think I could eat another bite, but thank you."

"Mark, are you still willing to give us a tour of the work completed today? I would love to see it." Emily placed her arm through his and led him toward the back door.

Aimee followed behind them into the backyard. The sun was still shining, illuminating the vivid flowers surrounding them on all sides. They walked deeper onto the property, past the pool and away from the cottages. They approached the newly installed sandstone patio. Emily slid her arm away from Mark's, clapping her hands together in glee.

"It's so beautiful," she sang, spinning in a circle.

The patio was surrounded on one side by multiple rose bushes, their blossoms bursting open in an array of colors. The opposite side of the patio was still just a dirt-filled flowerbed awaiting the next day's planting. Wrought iron furniture with bright yellow cushions sat in a circle, inviting long conversations.

"Don't they smell marvelous?" Emily asked, leaning her head back and inhaling deeply.

"They do," Aimee replied, taking a moment to enjoy their scent. "Roses have always been my favorite flower."

"Mine, too," Emily responded, sitting down in one of the chairs and tucking her legs under her.

Aimee noticed the look of peace on Emily's face as her eyes scanned the rose garden. She realized Emily's expression mirrored her own feelings as she curled up in the chair across from her. Roses had always made her happy, and it felt right that she and Emily would share that.

After speaking to her sister, Aimee desperately needed to shake the turmoil she felt. Even after sharing a brief moment with Emily, she found herself mentally debating her decision to come here. Her thoughts were soon interrupted by the sound of weeping. She watched Emily remove something from her sleeve, place it on a rose bud, and with a mumbled "excuse me" walk quickly from the rose garden, tears running unchecked down her face.

"What happened?" she asked Mark. "What's wrong with Emily?"

She could see Mark fighting back tears of his own before he finally answered, "She saw a ladybug."

"A ladybug? I don't understand."

"Ladybugs are very symbolic for Emily." He paused, as if carefully choosing his words. "Ladybugs are protectors. They eat the insects that will harm her roses. She calls them the protectors of the beautiful."

"If they are good for her roses and protectors, why does seeing one reduce her to tears?"

He looked at her for a long moment, crinkling his brow in thought. "Sometimes, even the protectors fail to protect what's most precious, what's most beautiful." He bowed his head and inhaled deeply, before slowly rising from his chair. "If you'll excuse me, I have some work to do back at the cottage. Goodnight Aimee, I'll see you in the morning."

Sitting alone, surrounded by thousands of beautiful roses, she suddenly understood.

Chapter 7

Walking into the kitchen the following morning, Aimee was surprised to find the room empty. Emily and Mark weren't laughing and sipping coffee at the table in the corner, and Mimsey wasn't cooking eggs at the stove. Today was different from the day before, and in the silence was sadness. She poured herself a cup of coffee, and taking it with her, headed out of the kitchen toward the office.

She found Emily seated behind her desk, her head bent forward concentrating on the computer screen. Aimee said "good morning" and walked around to her own desk.

Emily smiled at her. "Good morning, Aimee. I apologize for my behavior last night. I think I was a bit over-tired and somewhat overwhelmed."

"No apologies necessary."

"It was just a silly ladybug," Emily continued. "I seem to have a love-hate relationship with them."

"There is no need to apologize or explain."

"Was Mark okay? He worries about me more than he should."

"He seemed fine. He obviously loves you very much."

"Too much, I'm afraid." Emily's eyes lit up as she leaned back in her chair. "You would think he were my son and not McKenzie's on most days."

"Well, that's not a bad thing. Having someone love you like he does should be seen as a blessing, don't you think?"

"He is that . . . a blessing. I like that word, makes me feel cherished."

"Well, it's clear that you are," Aimee said. "So you haven't seen Mark this morning?"

"No. He didn't come over for breakfast." She was silent for a moment. "He's an amazing young man, don't you think? I only wish he'd settle down and find a nice girl to fuss over. He'll make some lucky girl very happy one day." Emily smiled directly at Aimee.

Aimee shook her head. "Don't look at me. I don't think he's very happy I'm here."

"Just give him time. He seems to see a hidden agenda in everyone."

"Why is that?"

"Mainly due to past experiences. Mark doesn't do well with secrets or lies, and tends to believe that everyone in my life, with the exception of him, is living both."

Aimee looked down at her desk, her stomach clenching and her heart pounding. *Tell her!* her mind screamed. "Does he really believe all secrets and lies are bad? Isn't it possible that sometimes people keep secrets, or tell a lie, to protect someone from being hurt?"

"Wow, that's a big question for only one cup of coffee." Emily folded her hands in her lap. "I don't think secrets and lies are ever justifiable, and I believe Mark feels the same. If you really look at the reason why someone tells a lie, even if they believe they're doing it for the right reason, there are a million other pieces of evidence that prove it's actually just a selfish decision."

The tears welled up in Aimee's eyes and she took a deep breath. "Emily, I have to tell you . . ."

"Peter. What a nice surprise," Emily chirped as she suddenly rose from behind her desk.

Aimee leapt in surprise and inhaled sharply. She pasted a smile on her face and looked over at Peter, walking purposefully into the office. His legs were long, his shoulders broad, and his sandy hair was cut in a classic style, flattering his slightly heart shaped face. She wasn't sure how a man could appear elegant and rugged at the same time. His brown eyes appeared to watch her intently as she rose to greet him.

"We've acquired a couple of new items for the auction and I wanted to get your approval to add them to the catalog before it goes to the printers." He unbuttoned his suit jacket, placed his briefcase on the table and clicked it open.

They each took a seat on the couch and Peter handed them the new item listing.

"Wow. An original Andy Warhol painting, that's fantastic," Emily said with excitement. "What a wonderful donation."

They spent the remainder of the morning going through the list, while Aimee made notes of phone calls she needed to make, and deliveries she needed to finalize. They were still in need of a few items for the main auction, as well as items for the silent auction that would be held during the dinner reception.

"I hate to cut this short, but I have a lunch appointment this afternoon, and I'll be late if I don't get going. Will you two be able to handle this without me?" Emily said, rising from the couch.

"Of course, I believe I'm in extremely capable hands." Peter smiled at Aimee and stood up as well. "Aimee, would you like to continue our meeting over lunch? There's a fantastic little bistro downtown that serves the best coq au vin you've ever tasted."

"I . . ."

"You should go." Emily smiled at her. "He's not exaggerating about the coq au vin, and you can get yourself better acquainted with Peter as well as the auction items. I won't be back before three, so enjoy yourselves." She walked around the small table preparing to leave. "Aimee, did you have something you wanted to tell me earlier?"

Her heart sank. "It was nothing. Enjoy your lunch."

Emily grabbed her purse from the hook by the door, and with a final wave, said to Peter, "Just leave the updated list with Aimee after you two have gone through it, and we'll talk again this week."

"I will." He placed the papers back into his briefcase, closed the lid with a snap, and held out his hand. "So will you join me?"

She placed her hand in his and allowed him to help her up from the couch. "Of course, I just need a minute to grab my purse." She looked into his handsome face and returned his smile.

"I'll wait for you in the foyer then."

She headed downstairs and out the back door. Approaching her cottage, she spotted Mark walking toward her on the path.

"Aimee," he said nodding his head in greeting, his mouth in a straight line. He quickened his pace.

She returned his greeting and opened the door to walk inside.

She heard him speak again and turned around to see him stopped on the pathway, his back toward her, his head bent down. He slowly turned to her and lifted his head. He looked at her for a long moment, his piercing blue eyes clouded with unreadable emotion.

"Would you like to join me for lunch? Mimsey is fixing chicken salad," he finally muttered, as if the invitation was painful to ask.

Confused by her own feeling of disappointment, she frowned. "Thank you for the invitation, but I was just running out to a business lunch."

He didn't say anything, only tipped his head toward her again, turned, and continued walking down the path.

She shook her head in confusion, picked up her purse off the counter, and headed back to the house.

Peter stood patiently in the foyer as she came down the hall.

"All set?" He smiled, holding the front door for her.

He opened the passenger door of his deep blue Jaguar and with his hand resting on the small of her back, assisted her inside. She felt someone watching her and, looking up at the house, she could see Mark standing in the window, peering down at them. Unable to read his expression through the glare from the sun, she lifted her hand in a short wave.

Goosebumps rose on her arms when he quickly stepped back from the window. Wishing she had the ability to read minds, she shook her head in confusion, and turned her attention back to Peter.

Chapter 8

Mark pounded the shovel into the dirt, swaying it back and forth to loosen the soil. He paused, using his forearm to wipe the sweat from his brow. He glanced up at the smoldering sun. He realized he'd been attacking the flowerbeds for close to three hours but no amount of physical exertion could chase the vision of Peter's hand on Aimee's lower back from his mind, or squelch his overwhelming anger at seeing them together.

Shaking his head in self-disgust, he hoisted the shovel up and brought it down, embedding it deep into the dirt. He pulled his drenched T-shirt over his head and placed it over the shovel's handle. Lifting the hose, he twisted the nozzle, allowing the water to trickle out. He placed it against his lips and took a long swallow before lifting it above his head.

He stood for a moment under the cold flowing water, allowing it to cool his skin as well as his temper. His turned at the soft purr of a car motor followed by the closing of a car door. He twisted off the nozzle. Running his hands through his wet hair, he began to walk briskly toward the main house.

He marched through the back door and hurried down the hallway leaving muddy footprints in his wake. He stopped before he reached the foyer and watched Aimee as she stood in the front hallway laughing at something Peter said and thanking him for lunch. Jealousy coursed through him as Peter grasped Aimee's hand and lifted it to his lips.

"Where have you been?" he barked, surprised at his own reaction.

Aimee jerked around and jumped back from Peter, her brow creased in surprise and obvious confusion.

Peter looked Mark up and down and erupted with laughter. "Maybe the better question is where have you been? You're shirtless, soaking wet, and tracking mud down the hall. Mimsey is going to tan your hide."

Mark clenched his jaw and felt the blood surging through his veins.

Seeming to recognize the situation, Aimee stepped between them and gently urged Peter toward the door. "Thank you again for lunch, Peter. I'll make sure to go over the list with Emily and call you by the end of the week."

With a final wave, she snapped the door closed and abruptly spun around. "What is wrong with you?" She bit off each word, her voice laced with steel. "You were so rude to Peter."

He knew he was acting like a fool. He felt out of control and completely out of his mind. Without another thought, he reached forward, pulled her against him and crushed his mouth to hers. He could feel her surprise give way to pleasure as the rigidity of her body dissipated and she melted into him. He lost what little self-control he had left when she reached her arms over his shoulders and ran her fingers through his wet hair. He pulled her tighter to him, wanting to feel every inch of her body pressed against his.

He slowly pulled his lips from hers and ran his thumb over her swollen bottom lip. Her eyes were closed. Her head tilted back exposing her delicate neck. He lowered his head and began to gently suckle its curves. He felt the vibration from her soft moan against his lips. He buried his hands into her hair and again molded his lips to hers. He ran his hands gently down her back and slowly up her sides. Losing himself in the moment, he tenderly brushed his hands over her blouse enjoying the sensation of heat, silk and lace.

The doorbell rang. Startled, they both quickly drew back. He looked into her flushed face and read the uncertainty in her eyes.

"I'm sorry," he whispered, before he abruptly ran his fingers through his hair in an attempt to smooth it and opened the front door.

"Luther?" Aimee squeaked from behind.

Chapter 9

Aimee knew her mouth was hanging open. She blinked, trying to recover the focus she'd lost in Mark's kiss. She rubbed her hands over her face, blinked again, and looked up. It was definitely Luther standing on the porch, surrounded by suitcases and garment bags.

"Luther, what are you doing here?" Finding her legs, she walked toward him and wrapped her arms around his waist.

Putting on his dramatic wounded face, one he'd worn often over the years, he gently pulled away, pushed her arms down to her sides, and stepped farther back from her. "Oh, no you don't. This is not 'Luther, what are you doing here,' this is 'Aimee, what are you doing here?' What the hell is going on?"

Her eyes grew wide as she slowly turned her head and looked at Mark. He was watching them both intently. He reached around her and held out his hand. "I'm Mark."

Luther looked him slowly up, then down, pausing at his naked chest, and pursed his lips appreciatively. "Well, yes you are. Hello, Mark." He purred.

Trying not to laugh at the look of sheer puzzlement on Mark's face, Aimee said, "Mark, this is my friend Luther, from New York."

Luther put his hand into Mark's, and squeezed rather than shook. "It seems I have rudely interrupted you two." He looked Mark up and down again, then reached over and reconnected a button on Aimee's disheveled blouse.

Her cheeks flamed as she begged Luther for silence with her eyes. He smiled maliciously in reply.

"You didn't have to fly here, Luther," Aimee said, trying to break the eye contact between him and Mark. "They do have these conveniences called phones now."

He glared at her.

"Not that I'm not glad to see you," she added.

"And let you hang up on me again? I don't think so." He looked down at her, his expression growing serious. "Aimee, tell me what's going on! I didn't fly three thousand miles . . . in coach . . . can you believe I had to fly coach? It was horrible. Look at me, I'm a mess." He waved his arm up and down for emphases. She looked at his perfectly creased jeans, and his wrinkle-free baby blue shirt, and smirked at his extreme exaggeration.

Mark raised his eyebrows in confusion as he watched Luther smooth the bright pink silk ascot at his neck.

As if recognizing that he'd become sidetracked, he stood up straighter, looked into her eyes and said in a soft heartfelt voice, "Aimee, I've been so worried about you. When you said that your mother . . ."

She quickly reached out and grabbed his hand in a crushing grip before stepping around him onto the front porch and pulling him with her. "Excuse us, Mark, we need to get these bags off the porch," she managed to say before closing the door in his face with a snap.

She turned to Luther, her face red with anger. "Are you crazy? You can't just show up here. Who is watching the shop?"

His eyes became angry slits. "Oh, no you don't." He pursed his lips, and snapped his fingers in a 'Z' formation before placing his hand on a jutted hip. "You just drop a bomb like this? Just up and take a job in San Francisco with no explanation, and expect me to sit in New York and wait by the phone? I don't think so, girl."

"We can't talk about this here, Luther." She reached down and picked up a suitcase. "Grab one of those and follow me."

"I will not," he replied, looking down at the bags in horror. "Where is the staff? I know a mansion like this has staff to carry a visitor's luggage."

She turned around and glared at him. "Grab the bags, or I promise I will put you in a cab, not a limo, not a town car, but a cab, and send you back to the airport without any explanation, and without letting you even change your clothes."

He mumbled under his breath. The only word she was able to make out was "bitch" but he grabbed a bag and followed her around the house.

She held open the door to her cottage and turned back to see what was keeping him. He was walking slowly down the path, turning in circles as if trying to see everything at once, and continuing to mutter to himself.

"This yard is the size of Central Park," he said when he finally made it to the cottage, still struggling with the single bag he carried.

Once inside, she took the bag out of his hand and set it down next to the one she'd carried. She looked at her watch and then up at Luther. He was silently watching her. His eyes filled with warmth and concern, all evidence of his earlier anger faded.

"You didn't need to come all this way. I would've called you." She was surprised by the tears that welled in her eyes.

He pulled her into his arms. "Let it out, girl."

She relaxed against him and let her previously unshed tears flow. After she was able to regain her control, she took the handkerchief he held out to her and wiped her eyes. Taking his hand, she led him to the couch.

Choking back a new wave of tears, she finally uttered, "She lied to me. For my entire life she has lied to me."

"Sweetie, start at the beginning. I'm so lost here."

She told him about the box, and her mother's confession. "I think Emily could be my mother, Luther." She wiped a tear from her cheek and leaned into Luther's open embrace.

Luther led her to the couch and sat beside her, gently stroking her hand. "So what was Emily's reaction when you told her?"

"I haven't told her." She looked at his disapproving expression. "Please try to understand. I couldn't just barge in and say, you're never going to believe this, but . . ." She rose from the couch and began to pace. "I didn't . . . don't . . . know if this is even something she'd want to know. I needed to be sure that my telling her wouldn't hurt her any more then she already has been."

"You don't think she deserves to know, even if it may hurt a little?" he finally asked her.

"Of course I think she deserves to know. It's complicated." She blew out a breath of frustration. "I ended up in a job interview. Just one of those timing things, or call it mistaken identity, whatever. Then I saw her. Oh Luther, she is so beautiful, but so much more. She is just one of those people who draw you in. You want to know her. I needed to know her. I told myself that if I could take this chance to understand her, maybe I would know for sure how she'd receive this bombshell."

"And now?" he prompted.

"Now it's out of hand. She's been hurt and lied to so many times. She hates lies and just pulling up to this house and letting her believe I was here for a job interview was a lie." She stopped pacing and looked into his eyes, silently begging for his understanding.

"You didn't lie. You just omitted the truth. Fix it, Aimee. Tell her."

"But what if it's already too late for that? She feels very strongly about trust, and I've been less than honest. I thought I was just being careful, trying to save her feelings, but maybe she's right and I'm just being selfish."

"You're losing me again. I can see that not telling her this and letting her believe you're just an employee can be taken as dishonest, but what do you mean by selfish? You're not being selfish. In fact, it seems to me you're only thinking of her in this situation."

"Emily said that if you look deep at the reason someone feels they are justified in telling a lie, you will discover that it's a selfish decision. I think she's right. What I've done is selfish, now I'm waist deep in this lie, and not only will she never believe me because of it, but Mark will truly hate me." She let her hands fall to her sides and hung her head in defeat.

"And Mark's the hot, half-naked man that you were about to have sex with in the foyer?"

She laughed. The sound was a mixture of hysterics and frustration. "I wasn't about to have sex with him in the foyer." She looked at his disbelieving face and hung her head again. "I just really wanted to. What is wrong with me? He's the closest person to her. He's like her personal pit bull, even if it annoys her. He totally distrusts me, treats me like an inconvenience, and makes me feel things I've only read about. He barks at me, and then kisses me until I can't stand up on my own legs."

"And you want him." Luther interjected.

She looked at him, and rolled her head to the side as if dejected. "Oh Luther, I really do. I have no chance with him, not as long as I work for Emily, and he will never trust me again once the truth comes out. Not that he will ever believe it . . ."

"He won't have a choice. The truth is the truth."

She looked down at her watch again and cursed under her breath. "Unless it isn't. The truth, I mean. I have to go. I'm meeting with Emily fifteen minutes ago. I need you to stay put, stay out of trouble, and don't speak to anyone. You got it?"

"I want to meet her." He stuck out his bottom lip.

"I'll talk to her about dinner," she replied, opening the door. "Until I can come up with some way out of this, it has to stay our little secret, got it?"

He nodded his head and blew her a kiss. She turned to go and bumped into Mark standing outside her cottage.

"Mark." She placed her hand to her heart. "You scared me."

His eyes were hard, his face emotionless. "You left a bag on the porch." He placed it at her feet and walked stiffly away. His behavior left no doubt he'd heard her utter the word secret. Watching his retreating back, her heart sank.

Chapter 10

It was three hours later when Aimee walked back into her cottage to change for dinner. She found Luther sitting at the dining room table typing on her laptop.

"She is amazing, Aimee," he gushed. "Her Talbot Cancer Foundation has raised billions of dollars for cancer research since it opened. She is one of the biggest contributors to the fight against cancer. Not just financially, but she's, like, Florence Nightingale or something. She's driven people to their chemo treatments if they didn't have transportation. She visits hospice houses, hell, she even built three of them. She's put over a dozen children who lost a parent to cancer through college. And tons more of them work for the foundation or the hospice houses."

Walking up behind him and wrapping her arms around his neck, she leaned her chin into his shoulder to read with him. "Wait, back up a little, there." She moved closer to the screen, her eyes flicking left to right as she read the interview question that caught her attention. Emily had lost her husband, Nathan Talbot, when he was only thirty years old to cancer. The foundation was named after him.

"Do you think, maybe?" Luther asked.

"I don't know." Standing up, she walked into the kitchen. Filling a glass with cold water, she took a large swallow trying to control her urge to cry.

Luther turned in his chair. "She hasn't mentioned anything about her personal life to you at all?"

"No, she hasn't. She comes across very open, but she's actually guarded, justifiably so. She's been through so much. No wonder Mark is so protective of her." She placed the glass on the counter and walked over to sit in the open chair next to him. "Luther, I think I should go home. I don't think I should disrupt her life. What if she has already made peace with her loss? What if . . . what if it isn't true?"

"You're reaching." He took both of her hands into his. "Do you want my honest opinion?" Not waiting for her response, he continued. "Talk to Mark. If he loves her the way you say he does, maybe he will be the best person to tell you how to handle it."

"But he'd never believe me. And even if I managed to somehow convince him, he would be done with me. I don't think he'd ever forgive me."

"You're a hard girl to resist, Aimee Roberts, or should I say, Aimee Morrison. You practically had sex with him in the foyer and he doesn't trust you now."

She playfully punched him on the shoulder before laying her head down on the table.

"This is quite a mess, isn't it?" She mumbled.

"Well, girl, you've never been void of drama, and this is definitely topping even *your* list."

She lifted her head and looked lovingly at her friend. "So do you want to meet her?"

Jumping up from his chair, he clapped his hands together with childish delight. "Hell yeah I do."

She laughed. "Okay, give me a second to change." Kissing him on the cheek, she strode from the room.

Luther paced the front room, dressed and ready, waiting for Aimee. His back to her, she silently watched him wringing his hands, and talking to himself as she came out of her room.

"She's going to love you. Don't be nervous." She laughed, walking over to him.

He gave an appreciative whistle to the coral wrap dress she'd chosen to wear.

"I think Mr. Mark might just toss you onto the dining table during dinner when he catches a load of you in that."

"I doubt he'll notice. He didn't seem too happy to see me this afternoon when he brought your suitcase over. In fact, he looked angry. He changes moods faster than any woman I've ever met."

"Oh, he'll notice. He may be moody, but he certainly isn't dead."

She smiled up at him and, placing her hand in the elbow he offered, allowed him to escort her to dinner.

*

Mark could hear the laughter coming from the dining room the moment he opened the back door. He paused, trying to shake off his uneasiness at seeing Aimee again. He'd acted like a jealous fool and then all but mauled her in the foyer. He was ashamed of his behavior, yet knew he couldn't trust himself not to do it again. Then there was the question that continued to nag at him: Could he trust her? He found it strange her friend appeared surprised she'd taken a job with Emily. Then there was her "our little secret" comments this afternoon that he couldn't shake. How could he be so drawn to someone he knew he couldn't allow himself to trust?

He walked into the dining room unobserved. Aimee was leaning in, reaching for the bottle of wine. Her blond curls were pulled back from her face in a fancy clip, her green eyes sparkled like emeralds, and her tanned shoulders were bare. She took his breath away.

"You are fab-u-lous," Luther said, kissing the top of Emily's hand. She blushed, a genuine smile illuminating her face.

Luther pulled his hands back and sat up in his chair, finally noticing Mark. "Well, there you are. I've been getting acquainted with Ms. Emily and was just telling her what a fantastic first impression you make on visitors." Luther winked at him as Aimee's face flushed a bright crimson red.

"I'm sorry if I've kept you waiting. I had a couple of important phone calls to make."

He looked over at Aimee, unsure of how she'd react to him. She watched him for a minute before her eyes fluttered down, and she folded and refolded the napkin on her lap. The shy, hesitant girl he saw now was in strong contrast to the passionate woman he was kissing earlier. He realized he liked the variations.

"We're glad you've made it." Emily nodded her head toward the empty chair. "It has been so nice getting to know Luther. He thinks he might be able to get us an original bag from Amore' for the silent auction. Isn't that great? He knows the owner."

"That's great and very generous," Mark replied. Looking over at Aimee, he asked, "How did you and Luther meet?"

"We worked together," she replied. "We've been friends ever since."

"Ah good ole' Saks," Luther said, folding his hands together and placing his chin upon them, expelling a wistful sigh. "Those were some fun times. Aimee was my muse from then on."

"Your muse?" Emily asked.

"She is the most creative creature I've ever met. I think she could make a hat out of a spider web and people would pay top dollar for it."

All eyes turned to Aimee. "Luther is exaggerating. I was known for my window displays. That's all."

Watching his face, Mark thought Luther seemed surprised by her response. "Is she being modest, Luther?"

"I don't think she gives herself enough credit for anything she's done. Certainly not for her incredibly creative talents she likes to keep hidden under a bushel." He looked directly at Aimee.

"So what do you do now, Luther?" Emily asked.

"I work for Amore' Handbags on Fifth Avenue." His voice sounded distant, almost disappointed.

"Oh!" Emily said with glee. "Now I see how you know the owner. I think she's amazing. Some of her new designs have a waiting list almost three years long. I would know; I've been on the list for the plum clutch for almost eighteen months."

"Let me see if I can pull a few strings on that wait time," Luther said, winking at her.

Mark wasn't sure if he was overly suspicious after the "secret" comment, but he could've sworn Aimee looked proud at Emily's statement. Looking again, it seemed her eyes were begging Luther to be quiet, and he was beginning to wonder if the sudden draft under the table may have been caused by a kick being thrown.

"Did you work for Amore' Handbags as well, Aimee?" he asked.

Her face lost all color for a moment. Stuttering her reply, she said, "Not exactly, no."

"Not exactly?" he asked, receiving a disapproving glare from Emily. "What does that mean . . . exactly?"

"Mark, we're having a nice dinner, this is not an interrogation."

"I apologize. I didn't realize I was interrogating anyone." He turned his attention back to Aimee. "I was just curious about all this creative talent we keep hearing about. You've never mentioned it before. Are you an artist?"

"No, I'm currently an assistant." Aimee smiled at Emily. "My position keeps me very busy, although I am using my old window display talents in staging the venue for the auction."

"And doing a fantastic job," Emily added.

"Aimee can do anything. She has the magic touch, I always tell her. I think she was born with it." Luther tilted his head, batted his eyes and reached over to pat Aimee's hand.

"Has there been any news in regards to your mother?" Mark asked, surprised when she almost appeared panicked by his question. "Have you had a chance to call home?"

She slowly released a breath. "No changes. It's still touch and go."

"Is your mother ill?" Emily asked.

"She is. The doctors say it's only a matter of time."

"Oh, I'm so sorry, Aimee." Reaching over, she took Aimee's hand in hers and squeezed.

"It wasn't sudden," Aimee said. "I've had time to prepare myself."

"Are you very close to her?" Emily asked.

"We have a very . . . well . . . tumultuous relationship. I wouldn't say we're close."

"She's a bitch, and treats Aimee like crap," Luther interjected before sitting back, his arms folded across his chest in a defiant pose.

"Luther!" Aimee choked.

"I'm sorry, girl, but the truth is the truth, and that woman is the spawn of Satan."

Aimee's cheeks flushed, and Mark noticed she didn't attempt to dispute her friend's statement.

"I'm sorry you don't have a better relationship with her," Emily said. "I had such a wonderful bond with my mother. I think there's a connection between mothers and daughters that can never be broken. Even after losing her, I can still feel her and see her smiling like she was standing directly in front of me."

"When did you lose her?" Aimee asked.

Mark watched the uncertainty that crossed Aimee's face. He was beginning to wonder if his previous behavior had anything to do with her hesitancy in asking about Emily's life. It was almost as if she were afraid she'd be prying if she did.

"It was about fifteen years ago. Both of my parents were killed in a plane accident. As hard as it was to lose them both, I almost had a sense of comfort knowing they were together. Isn't that strange?" Emily asked.

"No, not at all, in fact it sounds . . . well, sweet. I can easily see how that could be comforting," Aimee replied, her eyes misty. "Excuse me for a moment."

Aimee pushed away from the table, rose, and walked through the swinging door leading to the kitchen.

Luther stood up and excused himself, following her into the kitchen.

Chapter 11

Mark sat at the bar and opened the folder. He felt guilty for hiring a private investigator, but he had to be sure about Aimee. Emily was already opening her heart to her, and, if he were to admit it, so was he. She pulled at him, kept him awake at night, and thoughts of her had him so distracted during the day that his work was getting further and further behind.

The first page of the report was about her life and family in North Carolina. So far, there was nothing questionable about what she'd told him. She'd lost her father two years ago to a heart attack, and her mother was very ill. Her sister, Joan, was staying with her mother after her third divorce. The ex-husband had a gambling problem as well as an addiction to cocktail waitresses. He didn't have to question why the marriage hadn't lasted.

He knew Aimee paid her bills on time and it didn't appear she had any loan sharks looking for her, or the same gambling addiction as her ex-brother-in-law. It helped in some small way to know she wasn't destitute, but even a millionaire could be lured by Emily's wealth.

He looked through old school photos of her. The private investigator was thorough; he had to give him that. When he flipped to her senior prom photo, he paused. There was something chillingly familiar about the photo. He stared at it, trying to remember if he'd seen the photograph in her cottage. He knew he'd never seen it before, so why did he still feel as if he had? He placed it to the side and looked through the remaining pictures in the file.

There were a few pictures of her with her younger sister. She didn't resemble Aimee in any physical way. She was tall and gangly, where Aimee was short and curvy. Her hair was dark, and her eyes brown, nearly cold in comparison to Aimee's warm green ones. She looked almost angry, even while posing with Mickey Mouse at Disney World. One photo of them caught his attention. Narrowing his eyes in concentration, he closely studied the details. Aimee was holding hands with a tall, dark haired boy in a football jersey who was holding a trophy, her face lit up with obvious pride. Joan was on the other side of the boy, looking at him instead of the camera, her expression showing a mix of desire, resentment, and jealousy.

He sat the picture down and took a pull from his cold beer. He wondered what it must be like to have a mother you didn't believe loved you and a sister who, it appeared, resented you. If Luther and these photos were accurate, Aimee had a completely different family life than any he'd witnessed or experienced. He wasn't sure why, but it made him sad and, not for the first time, he had the urge to comfort her. He chuckled to himself as he realized what a hypocrite he was. He was feeling sorry for her mistreatment as he went through files from a private investigator he'd hired to prove she was quite possibly a fraud.

He closed the folder and signaled the bartender to bring him another beer. Looking up, he caught sight of Aimee's reflection in the mirror over the bar. He blinked, and looked again, wondering if he'd conjured her up out of longing or perhaps guilt.

She glided into the room on Luther's arm. Her jeans were tucked into tall black leather boots, and a white blouse was cinched at her waist with a rhinestone encrusted belt. Her blond hair was loose from the clip she'd worn earlier and bounced gently as she walked. Tossing her head back, she laughed at something Luther whispered into her ear.

"Sir?"

He'd been so intent on watching her that he hadn't noticed the bartender place the beer down in front of him.

"Sorry," he said as he placed the bills on the bar. "Keep the change."

He'd lost sight of her. Turning on his stool, he scanned the room. He finally spotted her coming out of the restroom. She paused at the edge of the hall, apparently looking for Luther.

He was sitting at a table in the back corner of the room, his arm resting over the back of the booth, and he appeared to be listening intently to every word his new companion was saying. Mark looked back at Aimee, and saw that instead of joining Luther and his new friend, she was heading toward the bar. He swung quickly around, unsure if she'd noticed him, and hastily bent the folder in half before shoving it inside his jacket pocket.

"Mark?"

He turned toward the sound of her voice and smiled. "Hello, Aimee. I don't think I realized the full meaning of the term 'it's a small world' until now." He waved his arm in the direction of the empty stool next to him.

She sat down and crossed her legs under the bar before thanking him for the invitation. The bartender was standing quietly in front of her, hanging on her every word in anxious anticipation of her order. She requested a glass of chardonnay and turned back to Mark.

"Luther begged me to bring him out, and Emily suggested this place, so here we are. We've only just arrived and I've already been abandoned for the first pretty face he found."

He laughed and clicked his beer bottle to the edge of her wine glass. "To pretty faces."

She smiled and took a sip, her eyes watching him over the rim of her glass. He wondered what she was thinking. What was it about her that made him question all of his doubts and want to jump in head first? He wanted to know about her, not simply the facts, but the deeper side of her. What made her tick, what made her happy, what made her sad, what did she dream of? He shook his head. What a mess: private investigators, hallway rendezvous, heat and longing. None of this made sense.

A rowdy group of men, clearly just arriving after the big game, pushed their way up to bar bumping their stools from behind. He jumped as the heat from her hand burned through his jeans and into his thigh. Her face was mere inches from his. Their eyes locked, and his heart raced. They didn't move as the man who'd bumped her stool stood above her apologizing repeatedly. Neither of them seemed to hear him. Unable to resist, Mark ran his fingers through her hair. Applying light pressure to the back of her neck, he pulled her the last inch to him. He kissed her with all the emotion he felt, letting himself go in a sensation of belonging that he neither understood, nor knew how to handle.

Her hand clamped his thigh, her body pliant against him. He resisted the urge to pull her the rest of the way off her stool and completely onto his lap. Regretfully, he pulled his lips back from hers. Her eyes remained closed, her body still bent toward him, as if she were unable to move. He studied her face for a moment, running his thumb over her swollen mouth, and over the small mole that sat just above her top lip. She was so beautiful, it was no wonder he couldn't keep his hands to himself when he was around her.

Her eyes fluttered open, taking a moment to focus before she smiled and adjusted herself back onto her stool. "You have to stop kissing me like that." She took a sip of her drink. "It makes me lose track of where I am."

"Do you know which man bumped your seat? I'd like to buy him a drink."

She laughed before turning around to check on Luther.

"I know you two worked together at Saks, but that's really all I know. Are you roommates? How long have you been friends?" he asked, realizing he really wanted to know, not for any other reason than to know her.

"We're not roommates. I live alone, and prefer it that way, but Luther only lives about a mile away from my loft. I don't know what it is about him, but we've been friends since the first day we met." She sipped her wine and ran her fingers along the stem of her glass. "I was a little out of my element in the big city, having just left North Carolina. He still teases me about the way I dressed back then. I think his first words to me were, 'It's obvious you're not from around here, but it's a shame that you don't have a friend or a mirror.'"

"You became immediate friends after a statement like that?"

She nodded her head. "I appreciated his honesty, and he made me laugh, even if it was at my own expense."

"He must have been upset about your decision to move to San Francisco."

"He understands."

Her short answer made it clear that the reasons she'd moved wasn't open for discussion tonight.

"How did the call to your mother go?"

"I spoke to Joan. It was as expected. She gave me a guilt trip for being here and not there. She played the martyr card, even though I've seen through her for years, and went on and on about being the sole caregiver."

"Have you thought about bringing in a nurse?"

"I've hired more than one. They don't last a day before they're fired. Joan learned the martyr role from mother, and a nurse takes away some of her leverage." She sighed and took a sip of her wine. "I kept the call short, or at least as short as I could. I just didn't have the energy for it. That sounds so selfish when I say it out loud."

"Have you always had a rocky relationship with them?"

"Sadly, yes. I've never really understood it. My mother is so critical of me, I could become president or win a Nobel Prize and she would still criticize. Joan, well, Joan is just Joan. She hasn't been happy a day in her life. I don't think she knows how to be. She's just one of those 'glass is always half empty' type personalities."

"What about your dad? Was he critical of you as well?"

Her eyes grew bright. "Just the opposite, I couldn't do anything wrong as far as he was concerned. You've heard the term Daddy's Little Princess? That was me."

"I can see that being the case. I think I could easily be controlled by a three year old in a pink tutu."

"He was so amazing. I miss him every day. Just talking to him, you know?"

Mark nodded his head in understanding, and let her talk. He loved the sound of her voice, the way it rose when she was about to laugh and the way it purred when she reminisced. Sitting here with her, he found it easy to forget he had a file on her from a private investigator, tucked into the inside pocket of his coat.

Uncrossing her legs, she turned closer to him on the stool. "So tell me about your father. I've heard incredible things about your mother from Emily, but I don't think I've heard him mentioned."

His smile faded. "He's not a part of my life. He never was, and he never will be."

"I'm sorry. I didn't know."

"It's been a long time, but it still pisses me off when I think of him."

She looked down at her hands lying in her lap. A sign he'd come to learn meant she was uncomfortable. She looked up, searching his face intently. "Do you want to talk about it?"

"Not much to talk about. He was a leech, a gold digger, the worst kind of man. Hell, I wouldn't even call him a man. He played with my mother's heart and affections, married her, got her pregnant, and then threatened to take me away if she didn't pay him a large sum of money. It was all a game to him. He got what he wanted, and he went away, but my mother never fully recovered."

"Oh Mark, I'm so sorry."

"Like I said, it was a long time ago. I haven't seen or heard from him since. That, however, is a good thing. For his sake, I pray it stays that way."

She reached over and laid her hand over his. They sat silently, each of them lost in their own thoughts until Luther came to find her.

Mark watched her leave, wondering why he'd shared such a personal part of his life with her, and why he felt a sense of relief that he had.

Chapter 12

Sitting at her desk, Aimee attempted to concentrate on updating the week's schedule but her mind kept returning to the night before. She could still feel Mark's lips on hers, feel the warmth of his hand beneath her own, and see the pain in his eyes when he talked about his father's betrayal. It felt like one more piece of the puzzle fell into place last night. Mark had been through so much. He'd been deceived and had also witnessed his mother and Emily being betrayed by people they loved. It was no wonder he felt the need to protect these women, and himself, from people who would harm them.

She wished he didn't feel she were one of those people. The last thing she wanted was to hurt Emily or him, but if she were being honest with herself, she already had.

The phone rang, interrupting her thoughts. "Emily Sinclair's office."

"This is Janet Lewis, with the Lewis Employment Agency. Is Ms. Sinclair available?"

"I'm sorry, she isn't in the office yet this morning. Can I take a message for her?"

"I wanted to apologize to her personally for our candidate missing her appointment. I would have called sooner, but I only recently learned that she had an emergency and hadn't made her interview. Along with our sincerest apology, I wanted to offer our services if she were still in need of an assistant."

Aimee's fingers froze, the pen hovering over the pink pad as the message she was writing began to sink in. This was the agency Emily thought sent her to interview for the job.

Feeling appalled with herself, but knowing she had no other choice, she slipped the message slowly through the paper shredder.

"Ms. Sinclair is no longer in need of an assistant, but I will pass on your message. Thank you very much for the call."

She'd just hung up the phone when Emily walked into the office. She looked beautiful in a pair of charcoal gray slacks and a pink silk blouse. Her blond hair was pulled elegantly back in a smooth pony tail at the base of her neck, and her ears were adorned with small clusters of pearls.

"So what's on our schedule for today? Anything we can get out of?" Emily asked casually, sitting down on the corner of Aimee's desk, her eyes mischievous.

"We should finalize the auction listing and get that sent over to Peter as soon as possible, but it doesn't have to be today. You have a meeting with . . ." She directed the mouse to roll down the calendar on the computer screen. "Preston Talbot at one." She looked at Emily, wondering who Preston Talbot was, and what connection he had to Emily's late husband.

"Call Preston and ask him if we can move lunch to later in the week. Grab your purse and meet me out front." She drifted from the office without another word.

A few minutes later, Aimee was ushered into the back of a town car parked next to the fountain. Emily smiled when she scooted in next to her.

"Are you going to tell me where we're going?" Aimee asked.

"I am going to introduce you to a good friend of mine."

Sitting back against the leather seats, she looked skeptically at Emily. "But you're not going to tell me who or why?"

"Sure I am, eventually," Emily laughed, a rich warm sound that serenaded, and comforted, more than any sound Aimee had ever heard before.

The car pulled up outside a small building downtown that resembled a Greek temple. White pillars adorned the front step and double glass doors opened up to a spacious room with a wall of mirrors and free standing mannequins draped in elegant gowns.

A thin, short, white haired man in a three-piece suit walked over to greet them.

"Emily, darling, you look fantastic as always." He bent down and kissed her hand.

"Kevin, this is my assistant, Aimee. We're going to need something jaw-dropping for her as well."

Aimee was speechless as the world-famous designer, Kevin Johnson, walked over and took her hand, lifting it to his lips for a kiss. "She's beautiful. It will be an honor to dress her."

Still incapable of speech, she looked over at Emily with wonder. She gulped and muttered, "Kevin Johnson?"

"Come in." He waved his arm directing them to be seated on a soft brown leather sofa. An elegant woman wearing a white pantsuit, her neck adorned with long strands of pearls and gold chains, handed them each a crystal flute of champagne. "I think you'll like what we've created for you, Emily, darling. You will be a vision."

He clapped his hands together, and a tall, fair haired model glided through a wall of silk curtains. She wore a floor-length emerald gown, gathered at the left side of the waist with a square silver clasp. She posed, slowly turned a circle and floated back through the curtains. Model after model came into the showroom, each wearing a Kevin Johnson original. Some were short, most were long, all of them made with Emily in mind, in colors chosen to flatter her blond hair and porcelain skin.

When the last model had left, Emily chose her favorites to try on.

"Let's see what you have for Aimee," Emily said reaching over and gently squeezing her hand affectionately.

Aimee gasped, as the same fair haired models came through the wall of curtains. Each of them wore a different dress, this time chosen especially for her. It felt like a dream. She sat close to Emily, smiling appreciatively at the visions lined up before her.

"How do I possibly choose?" she asked breathlessly.

"Well, if you want my opinion, I think the long red dress with the slit would be fabulous on you, and you should try on the white wrap. Come on, let's go play dress up."

Emily's excitement added to her own, as they both jumped from the couch like school girls, anxious to see the dresses on. They each took turns modeling in front of the wall of mirrors and each other.

In the end, Emily chose the emerald green gown, and Aimee, the long red dress. Both of them were glowing with pleasure as they placed their boxes into the trunk.

After another hour shopping for the perfect shoes, they slid into a booth at Emily's favorite lunch spot. She was stopped everywhere they went, each person seeming to know her, and compelled to inform her of their guaranteed presence at the auction. She was gracious to each of them, sincerely thanking them for their support, and always introducing Aimee more as a friend than an employee.

They each ordered a salad, laughing at the fact that they would be eating a lot of them if they were still going to fit into their dresses by the date of the auction.

"I think it's coming together superbly. I can't thank you enough for all your hard work. I just kind of threw you to the wolves, and you handled it with ease," Emily said, tipping her glass toward Aimee's.

"It's been a great experience so far. It's for a wonderful cause." She took a sip from her own glass. "Is it hard for you? I mean, you have to always keep him so close to do this sort of work." She asked, wanting to know about Nathan Talbot, but treading lightly, unsure of her right to ask.

"You mean Nathan?" Realizing she did, Emily continued. "I do keep him close, but it's not hard. He was unforgettable to me. If I can spare just one other person the pain of losing someone they love to this horrible disease, then every dollar, every hour, every step is worth it."

"Does it get easier? The pain of losing him I mean?"

Emily shook her head, her eyes becoming distant as a single tear slowly rolled down her cheek.

*

"I can still remember the day we met . . ." Her voice was barely a whisper as she transported herself back in time, thirty-two years.

It was the night of her debutante ball. Her white dress was cinched at her small waist and flowed to the ground like a bell. Her long blond hair was pulled up in a pearl comb that had been her grandmother's. She felt like Scarlett O'Hara from *Gone with the Wind*, with her long gloves and hooped skirt, and her handsome escort, dressed in a white tuxedo, standing beside her. She was waiting in line to be ushered to her father for her time-honored introduction to society when she saw him. He was standing in line, just three girls ahead of her, on the arm of Sally May Covens. He'd taken her breath away.

Their eyes met and sparks flew. She'd known at that very moment that he would be hers.

After the girls were each presented, the music started and couples began to float onto the dance floor. She held onto the arm of her escort, but her eyes were scanning the room for him. When she spotted him, she realized he was also looking for her. They smiled, and her heart skipped a beat when he purposely led his date toward them on the floor. As they each took their positions for the upcoming waltz, he leaned in and whispered in her ear, asking her to escape to the terrace after the dance was finished. She nodded her head in acceptance and allowed herself to be whisked away by her partner, praying that the song would end quickly.

When the last note played, she gently curtsied to her partner and, excusing herself, quickly made her way to the terrace. As she walked through the doors she saw him leaning casually against the stone railing, a single pink rose in his gloved hand.

When he noticed her, he stood up tall and proud, his eyes seeming to take in every detail of her as she slowly floated toward him.

"This is for you," he said, handing her the rose.

She attempted to thank him but couldn't find the words to speak as she tenderly took the rose from his hand.

"I'm Nathan Talbot. And you would be?"

"I'm Emily. Emily Sinclair." She could feel the fluttering of her heart as she looked up into his handsome face.

"I wondered when I would meet you." Taking her arm he slowly guided her toward the stairs that led to the grounds.

"I don't understand," she mumbled, as she walked beside him. "Have we seen each other before?"

"No, but my mother always told me I would know her the moment I saw her," he said as he continued to walk with her under the stars. "I didn't believe her then, but I believe her now."

He turned toward her, and taking a step closer, leaned forward and gently kissed her. It was like a scene from an old movie, only it was truly happening to her. They never returned to the ball. Instead, they danced under the stars on the lawn next to the rose garden until the night ended and her father came to find her.

"We were married in that same garden less than a year later," Emily said, her eyes seeming to regain focus, almost like she were returning to the present.

"It's like a fairy tale." Aimee wiped a tear from her cheek. "I didn't think anyone actually had moments like that, where they just saw that person and instantly knew."

"I think times have changed. Your generation has expectations that tend to be unrealistic. You're always looking for something better, something more. You also seem to believe that every person isn't who they appear to be at first glance. Sometimes they are. I'm not implying that even with a fairy tale meeting there aren't some obstacles to overcome, but each obstacle is worth it. Each challenge brings you closer together."

Aimee nodded her head. "I wish I could've met him."

"He was the most incredible person I've ever known. He was strong and fearless, smart and outspoken, and honest to a fault. There will never be another man like him." She reached over and picked up her glass with shaking hands. "Have you ever been in love, Aimee?"

"I thought I was once. That old high school first love thing. He was the captain of the football team and I was the head cheerleader. Let's just say that he definitely wasn't who I thought he was at first glance. I gave him too much credit."

"What happened?"

"To sum it up, I wouldn't sleep with him, but my sister would, so he decided he would rather be with her, temporarily at least."

"That's terrible!"

"My sister has always been very friendly," she replied, trying to make light of the situation. She was surprised that after all of these years the hurt was still there.

"And you've never been in love since?"

"No, honestly, I haven't. I've dated, and there were a couple of times I thought, I can be happy with him, but I felt like I would be settling and I didn't want that."

"Never settle, Aimee. There is nothing in the world that comes close to being in love with that one person who loves you back the same way. I wish that for you. I wish that for Mark too, although that stubborn man is a whole other story."

Aimee laughed. "Mark has never been in love?"

Emily tilted her head as if contemplating her response. "No, I don't think he has. I worry that he will spend his entire life believing that she doesn't exist. I'm afraid he'll meet her, his one, and everything inside him that tells him it's her will be silenced by his own fear and skepticism."

"Do you really believe that everyone has a one?"

"I do. I just think it's up to each person to be willing to accept the signs when it happens. It's almost electric, like a physical reaction, a pull to that person you can't control."

Aimee remembered the jolt the first time her hand touched Mark's, and the way her body seemed to have a mind of its own when he placed his lips to hers. She shook her head in disbelief and a nervous giggle burst from her mouth.

"Are you okay?" Emily's brow crinkled in surprise.

"Not every electric reaction or physical pull means they are 'the one' right?"

Aimee found no comfort in Emily's smug, perceptive grin.

Chapter 13

"Where were you all day?" Luther plopped into the chair in front of Aimee's desk.

"I went shopping." She grinned, stomping her feet under the desk, and screeched like a school girl. "I met Kevin Johnson. *The* Kevin Johnson picked out dresses for *me*."

Luther shot forward in his chair. "Shut up!"

"I'm serious. It was amazing. Not just meeting him, although that was beyond comprehension, but Emily and I went dress shopping together." Sitting back, she blew out a breath. "I had the best day today. We tried on dresses, shopped for shoes, and over lunch she told me about the day she met Nathan."

"So, do you think . . .?"

Peeking around the flowers on her desk, she made sure no one was around. "If it turns out to be true that Emily is really my birth mother, I have no doubt he's my father. The two of them are like the real life Cinderella and Prince Charming."

"Wow, sweetie, that's so great. And sad, I guess. You won't ever be able to meet him."

"No, I won't, but somehow I'm beginning to feel like I already know him. The pieces I've learned make him larger than life. Every girl wants a father like that." She sighed. "I'd also like to believe my father, well, the man I always believed was my father, was real, real with me. Do you know what I mean?"

Luther nodded his head. "You want to believe all the love he felt for you was honest and genuine."

Gulping back the sadness that threatened to spoil her mood, she added, "I want to know, or believe, that he was the man I thought he was. That even though I'll never meet my real father, I still had an amazing father in my life."

"You did. You know that already. If you have any doubts, pick up the phone and make the call you should've already made. You deserve some answers."

She knew he was right, she needed the whole story. Something was holding her back from asking her mother the tough questions. At this point what did she have to be afraid of? She already knew that the impossible, the unthinkable, happened.

"I know you're right. If I tell you that I don't want to talk about this anymore, will you tell me I'm a coward and I'm burying my head in the sand?"

He smiled at her. "No, today I'll give you a free pass. You want to hold onto the happiness of your day and I won't ruin that." Standing up, he placed his hands on his hips. "Let's talk about my happiness for a minute. I didn't get to meet Kevin Johnson today, and I didn't get to break out any plastic in California. There's something so wrong with that. Take me shopping? You can make it up to me that you've been so very selfish. You know I can be bought, and I'm willing to give you that chance."

Signing off her computer, she rose from her desk. "I believe you were just whining about your plastic not yet being introduced to California. So why is it suddenly my bill? I would hate to take the joy from you or your credit cards."

"I'll sacrifice for your redemption." He placed his hand over his heart and exhaled a long, slow, dramatic breath. "I'm that good of a friend."

"You're too good to me. I don't deserve you." She took his hand as they walked out of the office.

"That's true, so true."

An hour later, they crawled out of the backseat of a cab in the Union Square shopping district. Luther twirled in a circle, his arms held out like he was one of the Von Trapp children in The Sound of Music, his grin stretched from ear to ear.

"How cute is this?"

Aimee looked around at the tall buildings, the bustling crowds, and the strategically place palm trees. "Cute?"

Grabbing her hand, he pulled her toward the Saks Fifth Avenue building. "You don't think it's cute? It's quaint, and charming, and all the people are smiling."

"No one is smiling as big as you are." She laughed at his expression. "You give new meaning to the term kid in a candy store. Why are you so excited? We have *the* Saks, actually on Fifth Avenue, and I think you must own stock in it with as much shopping as you've done there."

"Yes, but this is in San Francisco. It's totally different." He shook his head, looking at her as if she were a bit slow.

They walked inside and Luther sighed in contentment. Taking her hand, he pulled her toward the men's department, practically skipping across the floor. His sudden stop caused her to crash into his back.

"Look at these fantastic bags," he gushed. "If only they were as beautifully crafted, and as skillfully designed as an Amore'."

"You're still not getting a raise."

Sticking out his bottom lip, he lowered his head. "It was worth a shot."

"Aimee? Aimee Roberts, is that you?"

Spinning around, her heart skipped a beat at being called by her business name. "Lucy, how nice to see you."

Lucy Strand was one of the biggest gossips in New York, and one of her best customers. Even though it was close to eighty degrees outside, she was draped in a short mink coat over cashmere slacks and a silk blouse. She eyed Luther up and down, and dismissed him without speaking a word.

"What are you doing in San Francisco? I would have thought you'd be buried in work, what with fashion week right around the corner."

Aimee looked over to Luther, praying he'd step in with a sellable story. He raised an eyebrow at her and remained silent. Her mind was blank, and her palms were sweating. She knew she had to come up with something fast. Preferably something that would snuff out any gossip over martini lunches in New York.

"Luther and I decided we needed a little break and some sunshine, just a small vacation really. How about you? What brings you to San Francisco?"

"Ronald had a business meeting with a security alarm company for our new hotel. I saw an opportunity to get out of the dreary gray weather for a bit," Lucy said, still looking at her warily. "I'm a bit surprised by your timing."

"Nosey old busy body," Luther mumbled under his breath.

Aimee smiled reassuringly, hoping Lucy hadn't heard him. "I needed some sunshine, as well. It clears my head and gives me new inspiration."

Lucy made a small sound in her throat, and Aimee was beginning to worry that Lucy didn't believe her. "Well, we must get together for dinner tonight. I would simply love to hear all about your line for the new season."

"Tonight?" Aimee choked, panic setting in. "We can't tonight. We've already made other plans."

"So you have friends in the area?"

She suspected Lucy was trying to discover a more interesting reason Aimee was in San Francisco during the most crucial time of her season. Aimee was determined to make sure she left disappointed.

"It was intended to be a quick trip with Luther, but he seems to know everyone and ran into an old coworker of his who lives in the area." She smiled sincerely. "It was great to see you again, but we really should get going if we're going to do any shopping before dinner. Enjoy your trip and I look forward to seeing you back in the city."

"Let's plan lunch next week sometime." Lucy pushed.

"Next week won't work for me. Can we make it another time?" Aimee smiled, slowly stepping back in an attempt to end their conversation.

"You won't still be on vacation?" Lucy smelled gossip, and the gleam in her eye was making Aimee nervous.

"I have a bit of work to do here before I return back to New York." Aimee spun around and grabbed Luther's hand. "We really must rush. I'll call you just as soon as my schedule allows it. It was nice to see you again." Smiling over her shoulder, she pulled Luther closer to her and picked up her pace.

As soon as they'd stepped onto the escalator headed for the second floor, Luther began to laugh. "She's something else. It always amazes me to see people so needy for someone else's drama. It's like, get a life already."

Aimee tried to catch her breath. "You don't think she suspected anything do you?"

"Like what? That you're possibly working as an assistant for the woman you think might be your birth mother? Oh yeah, she's definitely onto your little charade."

Aimee glared at him.

"Relax." He rubbed her arm. "There's no possible way she has any dirt on you. The truth is too weird for even me to comprehend. She'd have to make it up and the one thing that can be said about Lucy Strand is that she prides herself on the accuracy of her gossip."

Taking a slow deep breath, Aimee stepped off the escalator behind him. "You're right. I'm being paranoid."

"Living a secret double life will do that to you."

"It's your fault. You made me come out shopping and let me bump into that woman."

He lifted his nose in the air, dramatically pretending to be insulted by her comment. "The fact you're blaming me for this is going to cost you double." He stopped at a display of light cashmere sweaters and began to sift through them. "Now that you're working for someone else you can see firsthand how hard it is to be a lowly assistant and not get any appreciation from your boss."

Aimee rolled her eyes.

"She abandons her company to work undercover for the rich and famous, and he's left to pick up the pieces." He lifted three sweaters into his arms. "It's a good thing you're coming into some money. Your credit card bill is going to be painful."

He turned on his heels and marched away from her. She never saw Lucy Strand standing only a few feet away, as she hurried to catch up with Luther.

Chapter 14

Beautiful blond women in flowing white dresses floated across an emerald green lawn, spinning in the arms of tall handsome men each holding a pink rose in a gloved hand. Masks covered their eyes, leaving only their joyful smiles exposed.

She descended the stairs, her pale gold hair held back with a pearl comb, her white dress a stunning creation of layered tulle. Scanning the yard, she searched for something, or someone.

Standing apart from the others, toward the edge of the crowded yard, was a man silhouetted in the bright moonlight. He was mysteriously familiar. He motioned to her, beckoning her to join him.

An overwhelming sense of urgency compelled her to reach him in time. In time for what, she wasn't sure. She lifted her skirt and rushed down the stairs toward him. Couple after couple danced and swung in and out of her path, a blur of white dresses and masked faces blocking her view. Pushing forward, she struggled to reach the end of the crowded garden.

From behind her, someone was calling her name, their voice like a soothing lullaby luring her back. She knew she was running out of time to reach him. Her urgency mounted. Having ignored the calls, the voice from the terrace was growing stronger, louder, confusing her. Which way should she go? Drawn to the sound calling her back, she turned around. There was no one there.

She twisted back. The garden once filled with dancing couples was now just a long stretch of green grass, and crushed pink roses. Realizing she was completely alone, she felt an overwhelming sense of loneliness and fear. He was gone. The moon shone down on a single pink rose. She raced over and picked it up. The beautiful pink rose was covered with dozens of ladybugs. Her chest tightened, the physical pain of her heart breaking was becoming increasingly strong, the agony building. Still holding the rose bud, she began to sob.

The voice, once sounding like a lullaby, became an insistent shout. "Aimee . . . Aimee, wake up!"

She awoke to Luther leaning over her in the bright room, his face conveying concern as she lay there shaking. He pulled her into his arms, rocking her and smoothing her hair back like one would a small child. "It's all okay. It was just a dream. I'm here."

"It was so real. I was so scared. I could see the people, smell the flowers. They all wore masks and white dresses and they were all dancing, and so happy. I needed to get to him, but I was too late."

"Needed to get to who?" he asked, still gently stroking her head.

"I don't know." Her breath hitched. "I don't know who he was, but somehow, I know that I knew him. I needed to be with him. But this soft voice kept calling me back and somehow I knew I needed to be there too. It was just a silly dream, so why do I feel so sad?"

"It couldn't have slipped your mind that you just heard this incredible fairy tale story about Emily and Nathan. The scene in your dream sounds a bit similar, only this time it's you, so we can assume you were racing toward your man. Your soul mate or whatnot, right?"

"Maybe . . ."

"But someone or something else is standing in the way. What do you think that is?"

"I don't know."

"Yes, you do, even if you don't want to admit it. The man in the moonlight is Mark, and the voice calling you back is your secret or maybe just your guilt over having one."

She turned around to face him on the bed. "Okay, Dr. Phil." She clucked her tongue mockingly. "Good grief, I'm certainly not dreaming that Mark is waiting for me in the moonlight. He hates me."

"Oh yeah, he hates you alright." He laughed at her. "Sex in the foyer, sex on a barstool. I wish I could find someone who hated me like that."

"I did not have sex with him on either occasion, stop being so dramatic."

"I saw you. He definitely doesn't hate you."

She let out a long sigh and mumbled, "I didn't have sex with him."

"Yet," he replied laughing as she softly slapped at him. His face grew serious. "What are you going to do now that you're sending me home tomorrow? You'll be all alone. Besides, you need me."

"I'll be fine, Luther, and so will you. I need you to keep things together for me at the shop."

"I still don't understand why I can't stay a couple more days." He sulked. "We still haven't discussed how long you're planning to stay here. We haven't talked about the new line, or even any real details about what happened to send you here. Have you talked to your mother? Tried to get some answers?"

She shook her head. "I'm not ready to face her."

"I know you're afraid, but you may not have a lot of time to stay that way." When she didn't respond he lifted her chin and forced her to look at him. "If you're afraid that this is all for nothing . . ."

"No, that's not it." Her eyes filled with tears. "I . . . I just don't want to be wrong."

Chapter 15

Aimee stood next to the open cab door as Luther tossed his bag into the backseat. They looked at each other in silence before he finally asked, "Are you sure you're going to be okay? There's still time to change your mind and come with me."

She reached out and took his hand. "I need to figure this out. If nothing else, I owe Emily a great auction and birthday party. I can't just abandon her right now."

"I know." He embraced her. "It was worth a shot. Selfishly, home isn't the same without you, plus all this worrying about you is hell on my appearance. I'm leaving with more bags than I came with, and the dark circles under my eyes were not the accessory I was going for when I bought this fabulous black cashmere." Stepping back from her, he ran his hands lovingly down the front of his sweater.

She laughed and stepping forward, laid her forehead onto his shoulder as he brought his arms around her again. "This is the moment that I wish you weren't so valuable to me at the shop. I do wish you could stay."

"Just make sure you call me this time. I won't ever forgive you if you keep me awake worrying about you. I need my beauty sleep." He placed a kiss on the top of her head and pulled back to look at her.

Reaching into his pocket he pulled out an empty gum wrapper. "Give me that." He said indicating her gum. "You're never going to live happily ever after with Mark if he catches you chomping and snapping that gum like you do. I told you to break that habit years ago."

She removed the gum from her mouth and put it into the wrapper he held. "I will not be living happily ever after with anyone but you."

"You poor, misguided, girl, how many times must I tell you to get over that fantasy?" He clucked his tongue. "We can never be. You're not the only one who dreams of tall, dark, and handsome men silhouetted in the moonlight." He climbed into the car and blew her a kiss before he closed the door.

She waved as the cab rounded the fountain and drove out of the gate. Turning, she slowly walked back toward the house. Before reaching the front door, she was surprised to see a sporty, silver Mercedes pull into the drive. She watched as a tall, attractive man with salt-and-pepper hair regally folded himself out of the small car.

He approached her, walking slowly and fidgeting with his tie.

"Can I help you?" she asked him.

He removed his sunglasses and tucked them into the inside pocket of his jacket, adjusted his cuffs before buttoning his jacket and smoothing it down with shaky hands. His face was pale, and she could sense his nervousness through his smile.

"Is . . ." he cleared his throat. "Is Marcus Lee at home?"

"I believe so," she replied. "Can I tell him who's here?"

He held out his hand to her. She reached out and shook his hand. "I'm Jacob Parson, his father."

She could feel the blood drain from her face as she stared at him in disbelief.

"I see you've heard of me." His attempt to lighten the situation was lost when his voice cracked. His eyes grew serious. "I understand he may not wish to see me, but I have to try. I just need a moment of his time if he will allow it."

She stood there silently, unsure of what to do. Her instincts were to ask him to leave, to tell him to turn around and go back the way he came.

"Please." His eyes, identical to Mark's, were sad and pleading.

She nodded her head and walking inside, held the door open for him to enter. She ushered him into the small sitting room off the foyer. "I'll tell him you're here."

She walked into the kitchen and found Mark sitting at the table alone with a cup of coffee and his laptop.

"Good morning," he said. "Want to join me for a cup of coffee?"

"Mark . . ." Her voice shook.

He rose from the table. "Is something wrong?" His brow creased.

She shook her head, trying desperately to find the right words that would ease this situation. Not finding any she said, "Mark, your father is here. In the sitting room. He wants to see you."

He stood as still as a statue. His blue eyes raged. The heat rose on his face changing his olive tone to one of hot molten lava. He clenched his jaw, the muscles simultaneously twitching on each cheek. The pulse at his temple throbbed, but he continued to stare straight ahead.

"What does he want?" he finally asked, his voice low, his words dropping like each was its own sentence.

"I don't know. He didn't say."

She fought the urge to touch him, wanting to calm him, but knowing any attempt would be futile. He straightened his stance, and marched from the room.

Chapter 16

Aimee jotted notes down in a binder as she walked through the civic center that would be the venue for the Nathan Talbot Foundation's charity auction. There were still so many details to work through. After giving her a thorough tour of the kitchen and prep area, she tried to concentrate on the additional questions the caterer was asking.

"I realize how much time you need to prepare," Aimee stated, hoping to squelch the caterer's panic bubbling just beneath the surface as the date drew closer. "Remember, doors will open at five and I need all the wait staff ready to go with hors d'oeuvre and champagne trays. All three bars must be double-manned for the entire event and ready to open at five. Dinner is at six-thirty sharp and I will have the final guest preference count to you on Friday, like I promised. Anything else we need to go over?"

She knew she'd put out the fire when the caterer breathed a sigh of relief. "I think that's it, thank you so much. I just want this to be a huge success for Emily."

"We all do." Aimee patted her shoulder reassuringly and walked into the main ballroom that would host the auction itself.

She pulled one of the folding chairs off the rack and placed it in the center of the room looking toward the front. The stage where the items would be presented, was sitting in pieces at the far end of the room. She tried to envision the completed stage, the wall of curtains behind it, the placement of the podium, and the floral arrangements set toward the edge.

Unable to focus, her mind drifted back to the main house and the raised voices that blustered from the front sitting room. She'd wanted to wait, to make sure Mark was alright, but the frantic phone call from the caterer had taken priority. Instead she'd sat and worried about him all morning. What did his father want? According to Mark, he'd been out of his life for, well, hell, he'd never really been in his life. Holding her cell phone, her fingers itched to dial. She knew he would want to be alone, and if he needed to talk, he would go to Emily. Why did it hurt so much to know she was the last person he would reach out to in this situation? They hardly knew each other, and he didn't trust her to check the mail, let alone with his personal feelings about his father. So why did that fact bother her so much? Why couldn't she stop thinking about the way his eyes lost focus, and his hands had clenched into fists at the mention of his father's presence?

Attempting to bring herself back to the job at hand, she pulled out her binder again, making a note to verify the count on the linen covers for the folding chairs. She also jotted down a call to the florist, and the security company she'd hired for the evening.

"Aimee?"

She whirled around surprised to hear someone calling her from the other room. "In here."

Peter walked into the room, dressed in a charcoal gray suit and a cobalt blue shirt. His tie was slightly loose, his eyes bright and his smile radiant.

"What are you doing here?" she asked, standing to greet him.

"I have a couple of things to go over with you in regards to the silent auction and heard you were here."

"You didn't have to drive all the way down here. You could've just called me."

"Yes, I could have, but then I would have missed an opportunity to see you. You've turned down all of my requests to take you to dinner, so now I'm forced to drive across town with any excuse I can muster just to see you."

She smiled, flattered by his attentions. So why was her first thought of Mark and how she wished he saw her the same way Peter did? "You know I can't have dinner with you. We're working together."

"Then I'll call Emily and tell her I quit." He reached into his jacket pocket and pulled out his cell phone.

She grinned, reaching out to slap his phone closed. "Don't you dare! I can't possibly do this on my own."

"Then I think you're going to have to have dinner with me. Are you busy tonight?"

She wasn't sure what to say. She knew any woman with a pulse would jump at the chance to have dinner with this gorgeous man. He was sweet, successful, friendly, and trusting. He wasn't a commitment-phobe and wasn't in need of medication to control his girlish mood swings. Again she wondered why it was that she wished the man begging her to spend time with him were Mark and not Peter.

"I can't tonight . . ."

"How about tomorrow?"

"Peter." She laughed at his perseverance. "I'm so busy this week, how about after the auction?"

"That's almost two weeks from now." He seemed genuinely horrified she would even suggest waiting that long. Judging by his expression, he was actually pouting.

"I'll see if I can free up some time before the auction, but don't count on it. We still have a lot of work to do." She smiled. "What did you need to discuss with regards to the silent auction?"

"Do you always have to have the last word?" he asked her, his eyes conveying admiration.

"Absolutely." Watching him, she realized that without intent, she'd just made herself a challenge. She pulled another folding chair off the rack and set it across from her.

She liked Peter. He was damn near perfect. He was attractive, employed, smart, funny, straight, single ... so what was wrong with her? Why wasn't she thanking her lucky stars that this Adonis of a man wanted her? He wasn't Mark. She felt the blood drain from her face as the reality hit her. She wasn't just crazy about him, and this was more than physical attraction. This was it. This was Emily and Nathan, earth-spinning, once-in-a-lifetime love. In a matter of two weeks, she'd fallen in love with the one man she could never have.

"Are you okay? You don't look well." Peter took her elbow to steady her.

"Fine, sorry."

"You just went completely white. Are you sure you're okay?"

Damn near perfect she thought again, feeling guilty she didn't return his affections. She nodded her head. She needed to keep it business, all business. "Come on into my office," she said, gesturing to the only other chair in the spacious room.

He continued to watch her closely as he sat in the folding chair across from her.

"So, what's the update on the silent auction?"

"We are short at least two items."

"Well that's not good." She began to doodle nervously in her binder. Taking a closer look at what she'd drawn, she grinned. "I have one of them taken care of. Let me see what I can come up with for the second." She rose from the chair and folding it, stacked it back on the rack.

"Well, aren't you going to tell me your idea?" Peter prodded.

She smiled broadly. "An original, one of a kind, Amore' jeweled clutch. I've got connections."

Chapter 17

Mark stood outside the door to the sitting room and inhaled deeply. He needed to get his temper under control before he opened the only barrier standing between him and his father. He had to admit he'd felt more comfortable when it was a large body of water and not just a sliding door. He told himself he would handle this calmly and show his father the front door, making it clear he wasn't welcome to pass through it again.

He opened the door to the sitting room, stepped inside, and closed it behind him with a snap. "What in the hell are you doing here?" His voice portrayed the bitterness and anger he felt.

"Hello, son," his father said calmly, rising from the chair he'd been waiting in.

"You don't get to call me that." Mark sneered.

"No, I suppose I don't have the right." His father lowered his head. He looked back up and quietly studied his son. "You look good."

The silence in the room lingered as Mark waited for his father to reveal why he'd come. The tension crackled around them like lightening in a storm. He wasn't sure if it was time or his lifestyle, but his father looked old, almost sickly. The memories he had of his father were of a tall, proud man, quick to laughter and quick to anger. The man standing before him seemed broken and a little lost. He wondered why he didn't feel any satisfaction in that discovery.

"What do you want? I can't imagine you came here out of curiosity regarding my appearance."

A single tear escaped from the corner of his father's eye. "I came to ask your forgiveness."

"Forgiveness?" Mark began to pace the room, his steps short

and rapid. Rage surged through him. He stopped and spun around to face him, his voice low, his fists clenched. "For what? Lying, blackmail, or maybe for breaking her heart? Or for using me as a pawn in your money-grubbing scheme? Maybe for abandoning me? What part of your long list of callous crimes are you asking me to forgive you for?"

"I've done a lot of things I'm not proud of." His eyes pleaded for understanding. "I was hoping maybe we could try to start over. I'm different now. I want a chance to prove that to you."

"I haven't seen or heard from you in, what, twenty-five, twenty-six years? You march back in here and expect me to welcome you?" Mark began to pace again, struggling to maintain his composure.

"I tried to see you, many times, but your mother—"

Mark cut him off, his voice lethal. "Don't. Don't you dare blame her."

"I'm not blaming her. The blame lies solely on me. I just wanted you to know that I—"

"That you what? That you finally grew a conscience? Congratulations. But you're about thirty years too late."

"Marcus . . ." He hung his head for a moment before looking back at Mark. "Contrary to what you believe, I've thought of you every day. I love you. You're my son."

Mark clenched his fists. "Love is not an emotion, it's an action. It's how you treat the people in your life and the actions you take to show them." He shook his head to clear the sudden vision of Aimee's face from his mind. "I think you need to leave now. You're not welcome here." He opened the door, stepped into the foyer, and held it for his father.

His father stopped at the open door and stood in front of him. "I have a bad heart. They don't know how long I have, but I was allowed another chance to set things right. Even if you won't allow me a place in your life, I'd like to know you were able to forgive me for all the wrong I've done to you and your mother before I leave this world. I know for you a lifetime has passed—"

"I'm sorry about your health. I really am. But you're right, I won't allow you a place in my life. You gave up that privilege a long time ago. If we're being honest with each other, let me also tell you that I will never forgive you for what you've done. You may think you've changed, but all I see is the same selfish man who walked out on his family with an envelope full of cash." Mark walked over and opened the front door. "Please leave."

His father walked slowly into the foyer, shuffling his feet, his shoulders hunched forward. "I'll be at the Four Seasons for the next two weeks while they run some more tests. In case you change your mind."

"I won't."

"I understand. For what it's worth, I wouldn't forgive me either."

He watched his father step down off of the front porch and climb into his shiny sports car. His father appeared defeated. Mark stood in the open doorway as the car rounded the fountain and drove out of the gate.

He expected to feel relief that he was gone. He thought he'd feel pride in the fact that he'd heard his father out, and hadn't caused him any bodily harm. He thought he'd feel vindicated when he tossed him out. He felt none of those things. He felt only emptiness.

Chapter 18

Aimee paced the front room of her cottage. Mark never made it to dinner, and Emily told her he wasn't answering his door or his cell phone. She was concerned. She knew it wasn't her fault, but a part of her felt responsible. She'd been the one to bring his father up the other night with her nosey questions, and she'd been the one to let his father into the house.

She tried to keep her mind busy, to not think about Mark. She called Luther and requested the handbag for the silent auction, as well as calling in some favors to get an all-expense paid trip for two to Paris Fashion Week as the other auction item. Now, the walls were closing in, and she was making herself crazy worrying about him.

Making up her mind, she grabbed a bottle of wine, slipped her shoes back on and walked the short distance to his cottage. After pounding on his door repeatedly and threatening she wasn't leaving until she could see for herself he was okay, he finally opened the door.

Even disheveled and angry, he was gorgeous. "I'd rather be alone if you don't mind," he snapped.

"I do mind. You can't lock yourself in here forever. Eventually you are going to have to talk about it."

She brushed past him into the cottage. Desire surged through her the moment her shoulder brushed his. Feeling off balance, she reached for the back of a chair to steady herself.

"Are you okay?" he asked walking over to her.

"I'm fine." Color flooded her cheeks. "I tripped."

He looked behind them as if locating the culprit, but said nothing. Taking the bottle out of her hand, he walked into the kitchen and popped the cork. Pouring two glasses, he tucked the bottle under his arm and headed for the living room.

She sat next to him on the couch and he handed her a glass of wine. Taking a large swallow from his glass, he topped it off and leaned forward resting his elbows on his knees, his eyes staring blindly ahead. She knew he was still in the room with his father, or maybe he'd drifted back in time to when he was a boy. The silence lingered, but she refused to walk away from him. She knew he needed to talk, and selfishly, she wanted to be the one he opened up to.

He unexpectedly scooted back on the couch startling her. He turned toward her, his blue eyes flashing a mixture of confusion, rage, and pain. She wiped the spilled wine off her hand, set her glass on the table and waited for him to speak.

"He said he wanted my forgiveness. Can you believe that shit?" She sat in silence knowing it wasn't an actual question he needed answered. "Twenty something years later, he walks in . . . hey son, got a bad heart, could die, will you forgive me now? That's such bullshit. I was actually surprised to learn he had a heart at all." He took another large guzzle of wine and poured himself more. "What did he expect me to do? Invite him in for dinner? Or take him to an A's game, just us guys, right daddy-o?"

He rose from the couch, nervous energy emanating from him as he paced back and forth in front of the coffee table. He continued to rage as he gestured with his hands, carelessly spilling drops of wine onto the carpet.

"Says he's different, can you believe that? Actually trying to tell the child he just up and left without so much as a backwards glance that he's different now. I wanted to punch him in his damn lying face."

Aimee could see he was starting to wind up again. She slowly stood and walked over to him, removed the glass from his hand and placed it onto the coffee table. Standing directly in front of him she looked into his eyes and spoke from her heart. "It's hard when every part of you wants to forgive, but deep down, you know it's impossible."

His fire died down, and now unable to speak, he nodded his head in agreement. She could sense his conflictions, and understanding he needed to get it all out, she asked, "So you really didn't punch him? Not even once? I would've never pegged you for a wuss."

She gave him the most innocent look she could muster. Mark began to laugh. Once he'd started, he couldn't stop. He bent over, leaning his hands on his knees as emotions left buried too long erupted from him. Watching, she could almost see the sadness leaving his eyes.

As the final chuckle faded, and he was out of breath, he looked up at her. "Thank you."

She took his hand and led him back to the couch. "Have you eaten today?" He shook his head and she clucked her tongue. "You have to eat something. I'll whip something up for you while you open another bottle of wine. You've selfishly emptied this one already and I need another glass."

He led her into the kitchen and reached into the cupboard for another bottle while she rummaged around in the refrigerator.

"It smells delicious," he said as she sat a spinach omelet down on the coffee table. "You're not joining me?"

"I already ate."

He took a forkful of his eggs and moaned with pleasure. "This is delicious."

"Thank you very much."

"No, thank you." His omelet loving smile faded, replaced by one with more meaning, more passion. His eyes flickered to her mouth as he slowly leaned in toward her and lightly kissed her lips. He drew back, still studying her mouth. She nervously licked her lips. He looked up at her face, lifted his hand to her hair, and pulled her close for a deeper kiss.

Her eyes fluttered closed as his tongue began to stroke hers. The pressure of his hands in her hair sent shooting bolts of pleasure throughout her body. He shifted, slowly coming over her as he gently lowered her back on the couch, his lips never leaving hers.

She wrapped her arms around him and slowly ran her hands underneath his shirt and along his muscled back. She could feel his moan as it vibrated through her palms. His hands left their tangled place in her hair and softly moved down the side of her face, over her shoulders and began a slow crawl down her chest. The heat from his hands seeped through the thin silk blouse she wore. Her back arched, creating more pressure as she drew closer to his hands. He slowly unbuttoned her blouse as his lips worked their way down her exposed neck and lingered at the base, gently suckling the curve before her shoulders.

He drew back her blouse exposing the black lace underneath. He kissed a path down her collarbone, driving her mad in anticipation. He kissed, and gently nibbled the swell of her breasts. Her body ignited with desire.

Softly, she whispered his name.

She felt his body stiffen. He slowly pushed himself up, balancing all of his weight on his arms. He looked down at her. She saw the cloudiness of passion evaporate from his eyes and physically felt him shut down.

"I'm so sorry, Aimee," he muttered as he pushed himself off the couch. "I shouldn't have . . . We can't . . ."

Aimee quickly scooted up to a sitting position and rushed to button her blouse. She could feel the heat climbing onto her cheeks as she shamefully peeked from beneath her lashes trying desperately to hide her face. He was pacing again, only this time she knew she was the cause. Humiliated, she bolted from the couch, grabbed her shoes from the floor, and dashed for the door.

Mark, reaching the door before she did, held his arm against it, using his weight to prevent her from fleeing. "I had no right."

"It's fine. I understand," she said, keeping her head down. She didn't, but tears were threatening to fall and she wanted to be gone before she embarrassed herself any further.

"It's not fine. Please let me explain." He reached over and

placed his index finger under her chin trying to force her to look up at him.

She knew she was acting like a petulant child, but she locked her chin to her chest so he couldn't look at her. So she could avoid looking at him. Had she thrown herself at him? Had she taken advantage of the situation knowing how vulnerable he was? She didn't think so, but she couldn't understand why he'd rejected her. She felt the first tear escape.

"It isn't right. Not like this. The timing . . ." He blew out a frustrated breath.

"Please let me leave." Keeping her head down, she turned and stared at the closed door.

"Why won't you look at me?" He moved his arm from the door and brought it to her shoulder, attempting to turn her around.

She couldn't look at him. She knew she'd see guilt and was afraid she'd see pity. She couldn't handle either one.

"Aimee . . ." He moved closer.

The heat from his chest radiated through her thin blouse. The warmth of his breath blew gently against her neck. His voice was soft and pleading for understanding. She was enticed to turn back into his arms. She knew she had to walk away before he noticed the heart she was wearing on her sleeve.

"We'll talk tomorrow, it's late." Her voice cracked, and the dam broke, setting free a torrent of tears.

Without looking back, she threw open the door and ran.

Chapter 19

Emily sat back in the booth at The Terrace Restaurant and sipped her glass of chardonnay. She tried to squelch the anxiousness she felt at seeing Preston. She pulled a compact mirror out of her purse and checked her reflection. Her hair was perfectly smooth, pulled back into a French twist. Her makeup was subtle, her eyes smoky, her lips lightly glossed. The diamond studs adorning her ears once belonged to Preston and Nathan's grandmother and were a gift from Nathan on their first wedding anniversary.

Preston and Nathan had been best friends as well as brothers. In the years since Nathan's death, Preston had honored the promise he'd made to his brother and watched closely over her. She wondered if Nathan ever considered how hard it would be on her year after year. She doubted he had, he'd never do anything maliciously to bring her pain. But seeing Preston did bring her pain, and the effort it took to cover the fact, always left her tired and sad for days.

She'd been able to maintain her distance from him to some extent, but the Nathan Talbot Foundation's annual auction brought them together each year. Preston would escort her to the auction and diligently stand next to her singing her praises as they socialized. He'd act like the host he believed himself to be in his brother's stead. And each year she'd swear that next year she was planning a masquerade ball instead of an auction. She never did.

She watched with trepidation as the maître d' slowly walked Preston toward her booth. He wore black slacks and a sea foam green sweater that made his hazel eyes vivid. He had only the slightest amount of creases on his beautiful face, and his hair was just slightly peppered. He appeared distinguished rather than older. His smile was bright and genuine. His stride was confident and powerful as he spotted her and increased his pace.

Her hands began to shake and she clasped them together on the table top. Her stomach churned, and her heart raced. Her eyes welled with tears as she blinked rapidly to hide any evidence of her reaction. Pasting on a bright smile of her own, she stood to greet her late husband's identical twin brother.

He pulled her into his arms and exuberantly lifted her off the ground. "You get more beautiful every day," he said, setting her down gently and kissing her cheek.

She wanted to hold on, to close her eyes and feel his arms around her. Nathan's arms. She wanted to bury her head in the crook of his shoulder and listen to him say her name in Nathan's voice. She wanted to cry at the injustice of it all. The living, breathing replica of what her husband would be like if he were with her today. How easy it would be to pretend.

"Preston, it's so nice to see you." She smiled and squeezed his hand affectionately.

Sliding back into her seat, she fought the urge to toss back her wine rather than sip it. He slid in across from her. Ordering a glass of wine and taking it upon himself to request another for her, he nodded his thanks to the waitress, laid the menu down, and turned his full attention to Emily.

"So how are things? It feels like forever since we've spoken."

"Things are good. The auction is coming together beautifully thanks to my new assistant. The yard modifications are more than I'd hoped for, and McKenzie should be home in a week or so. How about you?"

"I'm doing great. Business is good, better than good actually. Home sales may be down, and the economy is a bit of a mess, but the rich still want vacation homes, and they still call me to locate them."

Over dinner of grilled salmon for her and strip steak for him, they continued the small talk of business, McKenzie's latest venture, Mark, and home projects. Over coffee and dessert, she updated him on the preparations for the auction.

As they sat and waited for the waitress to bring the check, Preston finally asked the inevitable. "So are you seeing anyone?"

She shook her head and said as she always did, "I don't need to see anyone, I have all I need."

"It's not healthy to spend your entire life alone." He reached out and placed his hand on hers, rubbing soothing circles with his thumb.

"I'm never alone." She laughed trying to lighten the weight she felt inside her chest. "You can trust me on that one."

"You know what I mean, Em."

Her control began to slip when Preston called her Em in Nathan's voice. She missed him every day. It didn't matter that he'd been gone over twenty years. He was as much a part of her now as he was then. It was these moments, sitting across from his twin, when it became unbearable. It was so easy to lose herself in the fantasy that it was her and Nathan having dinner, or sharing desert, or that it was actually Nathan's hand lying on her own. She quickly pulled her hand back and reached nervously for her coffee cup.

"You're a fine one to be telling me about spending my life alone, Preston Talbot. What is that saying of people in glass houses?"

He laughed. "I don't want to spend my life alone, but my brother found you first and after all these years, he's still playing finders-keepers."

The conversation always came around to this. It was easier for her to pretend he wasn't serious when he made those comments, so she did. But she knew the truth. Preston had always wanted her, from the moment they'd been introduced. He'd told her as much a week after Nathan's funeral. She'd been honest and told him there would never be another man for her.

The waitress appeared again, and after signing the check, Preston's eyes grew serious. "I know how hard this time of the year is for you. With all the memories of Nathan, and the anniversary of your—"

She interrupted him, unable to hear the words he was about to speak. "I appreciate your concern, honestly I do. I'm handling it." She patted his hand. "So, are you going to be picking me up in the limo, or shall I call my fairy godmother and have her whip me up a pumpkin chariot?"

He shook his head and pursed his lips. "You win, I'll drop it. I think I'll bring the limo, that way you can stay out past the stroke of midnight."

Chapter 20

Mark let his body glide through the water of the pool using the momentum from his last push off the far wall. When he began to slow, he kicked his feet and sliced his arms through the water, regaining speed. He'd spent six years on the swim team between high school and college, but now he only swam when he needed to clear his head.

He took a breath and placed his face back into the water, picking up his pace. He turned to the side, blew it out, pulled fresh air into his lungs and continued. He lost count of how many laps he'd swam, but even his exhausted body wasn't helping to shut down his brain. He'd really messed up this time.

He couldn't stop seeing the look of hurt and embarrassment on Aimee's face. She'd done nothing wrong. Well, except not leaving him alone to sort out all the crap he was feeling about his father's visit. But that wasn't fair and he knew it. Deep down, he was relieved when she'd knocked on the door. She'd been a great listener and seemed to know exactly what he needed. Besides, he'd been the one to kiss her.

He didn't understand his strange internal conflict where she was concerned. He knew basically nothing about her, other than what little she'd told him, and what he'd learned from the investigator. Then there was the fact that he'd hired an investigator to gather information on her. That alone put them at odds. He knew what he was doing was wrong, but something was off with her. He knew she was hiding something. He just wasn't sure what it was.

So knowing he didn't trust her, why was it he couldn't stop thinking about her? Why did his entire body burst into flames at the slightest touch? Why did seeing her with another man, even in a working situation, make his fists clench and his stomach turn? Why was it that when he looked at her mouth, he had to kiss it?

After his father left, he hadn't headed to see Emily as he assumed he would. Instead he walked over and knocked on Aimee's cottage door. He'd needed to see her and he was disappointed when she wasn't in. None of this made sense.

He tried to convince himself there was nothing necessarily special about Aimee. Sure she was beautiful, sexy, easy to talk to, funny, and a great kisser, so what?

He dunked under the water, rolled, and propelled himself off the wall for another lap. He knew if he didn't exhaust his body, his mind would keep him awake. The last thing he was in the mood for was tossing and turning all night picturing a sexy blond with incredible lips. Not to mention the clear image of black lace over creamy pale skin . . .

"Mark?"

Startled, he gasped, pulling water into his lungs. He stopped mid-stroke and began to choke.

"I'm sorry," Emily said with the corners of her mouth twitching as she fought back a smile. "I didn't mean to startle you, or to drown you for that matter."

He plopped down on the stairs at the shallow end of the pool and coughed again. "No problem." He looked up at her and smiled. "You look exceptionally beautiful tonight. How'd it go?"

"Thank you, and fine." She sat down in the chair closest to him. "How are you doing? I heard we had a strange visitor, and now you're attempting to break the world record for number of laps swum in an hour's time."

She knew him so well. Sometimes he forgot she wasn't actually his mother. "I'm proud to report there is no blood whatsoever on the sitting room carpet, or the front porch."

"Mark, talk to me."

He looked into her concerned eyes and felt his heart warm.

"I'm fine. I must admit I was surprised he showed up here after all these years."

"What did he want, money?"

"You ready for this one? He wants forgiveness." He stood up and climbed out of the pool. Grabbing a towel off the chair, he dried his chest and wrapped it around his waist before sitting down in the empty chair next to her. He expected to feel the anger again. The gut churning, blood boiling sort that he'd felt earlier. He didn't. He felt only sadness, for the little boy who never had a father, and for the man who still carried that pain.

"Why did he come here now, after all these years?" she asked.

"It seems he had a bit of a health scare and has a second chance to make things right." Mark took a deep breath. "Can you believe he actually said that to me?"

She shrugged her shoulders. "What are you going to do about him?"

"Nothing, just like he did about me for close to thirty years. I don't have a place for him in my life."

"Does your heart agree with your hard head, Mark?" She reached over and took his hand in hers.

"Both are in complete agreement." He attempted a light hearted smile, but found it harder to produce than he thought. Emily didn't need to be worrying about him tonight. He knew how hard it was for her to see Preston, especially at this time of year. "Enough about me, how are you holding up?"

"I'm fine, really. Preston sends his love." She squeezed his hand and stood to leave. "I just wanted to make sure you were okay. We were all worried about you tonight. It couldn't have been easy for you to see him. Did you speak to Aimee? I know she was feeling bad about letting him in."

"Yeah, we spoke earlier." He lowered his head and readjusted the towel at his waist.

"Mark?" Emily knelt down and forced him to look at her. "Is

there something else you want to talk about? Is there something else on your mind? Or someone?"

She'd always been able to read him like a book. Part of him wanted desperately to talk to her. But he knew she wouldn't understand. She was a believer in true love. She'd never understand being torn between lust and distrust.

"Not at all, but thank you for checking on me, and I'm sorry I worried you by dodging the phone for a while. I needed to sort it out."

He stood up, pulled her to her feet and studied her for a moment. "Are you sure you're okay? Your eyes show me more than just tired, they have *that* look."

She kissed his cheek. "I'm good, I promise. Goodnight." She started to walk away, stopped, and turned around. "For what it's worth, the world is a better place when you let someone in. Trust your heart."

He stood rooted to the cement as he watched her walk away. He wasn't sure if she was still talking about his father, or if she knew something he didn't. Or something he refused to believe.

Chapter 21

Emily walked up the staircase eager for a hot bath and a full night's sleep. Her emotions were on overload as she tried to shift her thoughts from Nathan and concentrate on Mark. She wasn't sure how she could help him. The feelings he'd buried about his father were being forced to the surface and, for the first time in his life, Mark was in love. And fighting it with everything he had. He was a strong man with strong convictions. Sadly, he'd witnessed his mother's heartbreak as well as hers. It hadn't given him much faith in love.

Mark had been almost nine when Nathan died. He'd seen the joy that love could be and also saw the suffering that came from losing the one you love. It had taken two months for her to leave her room and close to a year before she'd found the strength to leave the house. During that time, she hadn't packed Nathan's things, nor let anyone else near them. For a time, she was inconsolable. A part of her had died with him.

It was Mark who pulled her out of the dark place she'd been. He spent hours curled up beside her on the bed telling her funny stories to cheer her up. He talked of faraway lands where Nathan and her little girl were together and happy. He'd tell of the messes they'd made for fun when she wasn't there to scold them, the giant lake they swam in every day, and the ice cream castle they lived in.

He'd been her savior then, and it was a role he refused to give up now. She just prayed the pain he witnessed in her grief for Nathan, and the sorrow he'd endured as his own mother cried herself to sleep, wouldn't stop him from embracing his own chance for happiness.

Lost in thought, she subconsciously walked to the far end of the hall and past her own bedroom. She was standing outside of the room she promised herself she wouldn't enter this year. Placing her hand against the door, she could almost feel the love on the other side. Warm tears wet her cheeks as she mentally tried to talk herself out of going inside. Tonight she'd mourned Nathan all over again. She didn't think she was strong enough to mourn another.

Tomorrow was the anniversary. As often as she tried, she'd never forgotten this day. Twenty-nine years ago tomorrow, after two years of failed attempts, she and Nathan had finally conceived their first child, a little girl.

After she'd been taken, her birthday became too painful, so Nathan insisted they cling to the happy memories of the day she was created. After she lost Nathan, both dates became agonizing.

She slowly turned the handle and swung the door open. She stood frozen as the memories flooded back.

She could see Nathan standing with a paint roller in his hand, a smear of cotton candy pink on his cheek. He was laughing, holding the roller out like a sword, threatening to cover her in pink paint if she didn't put her brush down. He'd walked over to her then, kissed her soundly and left a mark of pink on her cheek to match his.

His excitement for the arrival of their daughter grew daily as he meticulously crossed off the days on the calendar. He'd wanted to be the one to put her crib together, to hang the white lace curtains, and paint the pink walls. All the love he'd felt for his unborn child showed in every facet of her nursery.

Emily walked into the room, drawn by the dreams it once held. The tears flowed unchecked down her cheeks as she remembered the day they'd come home from the hospital alone. Someone had stolen their daughter. In the blink of an eye, she'd vanished.

Nathan's grief had been debilitating for him. For two weeks she'd awaken to find herself alone in bed. Each night she would find him sitting in the white rocking chair in the nursery, slowly rocking back and forth. His tears had been spent, but the sorrow was etched on his face.

She walked to the far wall and caressed the wooden letters Nathan had carved and painted. They hung from the wall, spelling out AMELIA. Once bright pastels, they'd eventually been painted a bright red but were now dull with time.

She sat on the edge of the twin bed that stood where the crib had been. She ran her hand over the once white eyelet bedspread now discolored with age. The originally pink walls were now a faded version of sunshine yellow. Hand painted vines crept up the two opposite walls as smiling black and red ladybugs climbed up the stalks, or rested on the leaves.

Each year, they'd updated her bedroom in preparation for her homecoming, knowing their little girl would be another year older. It had been their way of clinging to the hope that seemed so hard to hold onto.

Reaching over, she picked up the stuffed ladybug that rested on the pillow. Pulling it close against her chest, she curled up on the small bed.

After Nathan died, she couldn't bring herself to alter the room again. She couldn't be here without a lifetime worth of memories flooding back and ripping her heart open. The bedroom stood frozen in time waiting for a precocious six year old girl. Tonight it felt like a shrine to lost dreams. Her daughter had never come home.

Chapter 22

Aimee couldn't sleep. Tossing and turning for two hours had accomplished nothing more than messing up the sheets. The tea kettle whistled. Wrapped in her favorite chenille bathrobe, she poured the steaming water over a tea bag and bobbed it up and down mindlessly. She gazed out the window letting her thoughts wander.

What'd happened to her life? She'd been perfectly content running her store in New York, spending her free time alone or with Luther. She was never lonely and didn't spend her nights dreaming her Prince Charming would show up and sweep her off her feet. She'd worked through the grieving process and didn't cry about her dad every day. She'd lived her life for herself and liked it that way. Then, three weeks ago, her world turned upside down.

Now she cried every day. She missed her dad more than ever. She wanted to talk to him, to get his advice on how to handle this situation. As for Prince Charming, she'd proven she wouldn't recognize him, even if he did show up. Instead, she'd fallen for an emotionally bankrupt mama's boy, who was playing her like a violin.

"I had no right," he said. Give me a break, she thought. What man on the planet has ever jumped off of a half-naked woman, claiming he had no right? It was crap, and they both knew it. He just didn't want her. She practically threw herself at him and he pushed her away.

That was just fine with her. She was glad it happened like it did. She didn't want anything to do with Marcus Lee. To think that she'd been worried about hurting *him*. How do you possibly hurt a man without feelings? He seemed to have a never ending supply of love and concern for others, but he was clearly incapable of affection for a woman like her. Like her? She sighed and closed her eyes. Who was she kidding? It wouldn't matter if he did love her, they couldn't be together and she knew it. She'd messed that up the first day she drove through the front gate, and the way she'd handled everything since.

She sat down at the kitchen counter and sipped her tea. The song playing on the radio changed to a loved 'em and lost 'em ballad. She reached over and smacked the power button, silencing the words she was in no mood to hear.

She wished things could have been different. That she wasn't such a disaster or that her entire life wasn't in upheaval. Maybe if they could have met under different circumstances. Or never met at all.

Why couldn't she be smart and fall for someone like Peter? Hell, he was gorgeous, emotionally stable, and easy to talk to. He didn't seem to be dragging his life behind him like a lead weight. He was probably even capable of forgiveness, unlike the man she knew she'd need it from.

She blew out a breath. Everything in her life was in complete chaos. Needing to talk to someone who would understand, she picked up her cell phone to call Luther. It was almost three A.M. in New York, but it wouldn't be the first time she'd dragged him out of bed with a phone call. Before she could finish dialing, the phone rang in her hand. It was Joan.

"It's the middle of the night there, is Mother okay?" she asked, sitting back down at the counter.

"Will you come home?"

She could hear her sister crying. "What is it?"

"The doctor was here earlier. She doesn't have much time left. I know you're mad at her, but she seems really upset she may not see you. She keeps saying she needs the chance to explain. Aimee, what happened between you two?"

She wasn't sure if it was the lack of criticism in her sister's voice, or her genuine sadness, but she knew this time, it wasn't a dramatic ploy. It was time to go home and deal with things before it was too late.

"It's a long story. I'll catch the earliest flight I can and try to be home tomorrow."

"Thank you. I don't think I can do this alone."

Hanging up the phone, she dialed the airline. Joan needed her, and despite everything in their past, Aimee would be there for her.

She just wished she could avoid the inevitable conversation she would have with her mother.

Chapter 23

Push me higher, Daddy, higher. Aimee struggled to catch her breath as she pulled into the long driveway leading to her childhood home, past the large maple tree where the old tire swing still hung from its bough. She choked back a sob as memories of her father engulfed her. She lifted her foot from the gas pedal, allowing her Mercedes to coast forward under its own power. The vast lawn sloped toward the house as she rounded the bend. *Bet you can't catch me, Daddy.* Her ears rung with the sound of his laughter mixed with her own. She somberly remembered the sound of his large feet pounding the grass from behind as he scooped her up and tossed her over his shoulder, spinning her around making airplane sounds.

Parking the car, she took a minute to check her reflection in the rear view mirror. She paused for a moment, examining her face, trying to visualize what her mother would see. Her mother always found something wrong with her. It was a gift she'd developed early on. She hadn't understood her mother's criticisms growing up. She had a better understanding now. It still wasn't right and it still hurt, but there was little she could do to stop her mother from seeing her out of guilt-ridden eyes. Wiping a tear from her cheek, she pulled a comb out of her bag and ran it through her windblown hair.

Knowing nothing she corrected, or covered, or changed, would make a difference, she put away the comb, turned off the car, and prepared herself for the inevitable.

She reached above the porch light for the spare key. Standing outside the door, she was frozen in place, recalling the day she'd come home to care for her mother only three weeks ago. It felt like a lifetime had passed since that day. Her entire life changed in a single moment. She inhaled, willing herself not to cry as her mind returned there, visualizing the entire scene again.

*

The minute she'd seen her sister in the foyer, they had some cross words about her plan to stay in a hotel instead of the house.

"So where are your bags?" her sister had demanded.

"I left them in the car. I booked a room in town."

Joan's face changed to its customary scowl. "Why? You know Mom wants you here. She even called you herself. Are you really that selfish? Does it even bother you she's dying?"

Taken aback, Aimee wasn't sure how to respond. She'd been reeling from the shock of her mother insisting she come home. Her mother's illness had been progressing for years and the fact that she was nearing the end wasn't a surprise. That she had requested Aimee be with her in her final days had been.

Finding her voice, she finally said, "I was thinking about Mother. An extra person in the house would only add stress. This way, I could still spend time with her, but let her have some peace and quiet, as well." She hadn't spoken aloud her need for her own place to escape, too.

"Sure, don't worry about the fact it leaves me to take care of her."

"What happened to the nurse I hired?"

"Mom didn't like her so she fired her. She only wants us to take care of her. Grab your bags out of the car and cancel your room. She wants you to stay with her and it's the least you can do. You may be a high and mighty business woman in the city, but she is your mother, and it won't kill you to pitch in."

Being in no mood to argue, she'd silently walked past her sister and headed up the stairs. She'd slowly opened the door to her mother's bedroom and peeked inside.

Her mother was asleep, her chest gently rising and falling underneath the large stack of blankets covering her. A beautiful cream-colored silk scarf covered her head, her cheeks rosy from sleep, her hands clasped over the covers.

Watching her sleep, Aimee couldn't help but feel sadness for the relationship they never had and a loss for the love her mother never returned. Her mother stirred, causing Aimee to slowly back out of the room.

"Aimee, is that you?"

She stopped her retreat. "It's me, Mother. I hope I didn't wake you. I wanted to check on you before I unpacked my bags." She walked deeper into the dimly lit room.

"What have you done to your hair?"

Glancing at her reflection in the mirror over the dresser, she ran her hands through her new haircut.

"I cut it. It's all the rage in the city. Don't you like it?" Forcing herself to smile, she walked toward the bed.

"Just because everyone else is doing it, doesn't mean you should." Her mother shook her head in obvious disapproval.

Aimee took a deep breath and sat on the edge of the bed. "So, how are you feeling?"

"How do you think I'm feeling? I'm stuck in this bed. I don't have the strength to do anything for myself, and you're fine to just leave me here to rot."

"You know that isn't true. I came as soon as you called."

Her mother continued as if she hadn't spoken. "Joan's been here. Every day she's been here. I realize you have a business to run, but I think it's hurtful you don't care about me enough to come home."

She tried to ease her frustration by taking a deep breath. "Mother, you told me to stay in New York, remember? You said I would be in the way if I came home. I was only respecting your wishes."

"Joan gave up her life to come home and care for me. You just wrote a check and sent someone else in an attempt to ease your conscience."

Aimee bit her tongue to maintain its silence. She wanted to scream out the fact that Joan didn't have a job and needed a free place to stay. And that she'd hired a nurse because she was worried about her mother's care after being forbidden to come home.

Ignoring her defensive urge, she simply stated, "I was trying to help by sending a nurse to assist you. I'm sorry if I hurt your feelings. That was not my intention."

"Well you're here now." Her mother shifted the covers and slowly scooted back to a partial sitting position, slapping Aimee's hands away when she tried to help. "We have a lot to talk about." Her mother silently watched her, saying nothing. She seemed to be deep in thought. Her face angry one minute and distressed the next. After what felt like hours, but could only have been seconds, she said, "I'm not sure how to tell you this, or how I'll be able to make you understand that I did what I had to do. I want you to try to see it from my viewpoint."

"See what from your viewpoint? Tell me what?"

"I wish we didn't have to do this now. I'm not sure I have the strength to do it, but I'm afraid there won't be another time." She inhaled a large shaky breath. "Grab the box on the dresser and bring it here."

Aimee stood up from the bed and crossed the room toward the dark cherry wood dresser. An old leather case sat directly in the center. An uneasy feeling overcame her and she paused before picking it up. She looked over at the silver frame with a picture of her father smiling from atop a log on Myrtle Beach. She lovingly stroked the frame and, picking up the box, walked back across the room.

"Set it here," her mother directed, patting the covers next to her. Her mother closed her eyes. "Go ahead. Open it."

Aimee couldn't remember a time she'd seen her mother so nervous. Her feeling of uneasiness continued as she slowly lifted the lid. Inside laid an old baby blanket that had once been white but was now gray with age. Small, hand-sewn, red ladybugs crawled up one side. She lifted the blanket and looked curiously at her Mother's tense face.

She turned her head away. "Keep going."

Aimee laid the blanket down on the bed and lifted an old newspaper article from the box. "Baby Girl Abducted from Local Hospital" the headline read. She narrowed her eyes, and furrowed her brow. What is this? She lifted another newspaper clipping. "No Ransom Note in Sinclair-Talbot Kidnapping" She quickly scanned the article from the San Francisco Bay newspaper.

"A child was taken only days after her birth from the hospital nursery. There are currently no eyewitnesses. The Sinclair's, a prominent family in the San Francisco area, pleaded for the man or woman who took their daughter to bring her home. No ransom note has been received."

Glancing at the date, Aimee's hands began to shake. March 12, 1981. The month and year she was born.

Aimee felt out of breath as she reached deeper into the box with unsteady hands. More articles were folded neatly in a stack. She pulled them out and set them on top of the baby blanket. At the bottom of the box was a hospital bracelet. Aimee lifted the broken plastic circle. Written next to a picture of a faded pink teddy bear was a hospital identification number with the name "Baby Girl Sinclair."

Aimee held tightly to the bracelet, a fiery pain seized her chest. "Mother, what is this? Why do you have these things?"

Her mother turned to her, a look of remorse on her face. She reached across the bed, laying a frail hand on Aimee's leg. "It's you. You were 'Baby Girl Sinclair.' I had to do it. I loved him. You have to believe . . ."

Aimee leapt from the bed. She felt scalded by the touch of her mother's hand. She couldn't speak. In haste, she began to place the items back in the box, unsure of why. She closed the lid and, standing on unsteady legs, lifted the box from the bed. She looked down and realized her mother was still speaking. The room began to spin. Her chest felt tight. Tears began to fall down her cheeks.

She turned and darted from the room clutching the box protectively against her chest. She pushed past her sister coming up the stairway. Joan reached out to stop her, saying something she couldn't hear as she began to sob uncontrollably. She ripped her arm out of her sister's grasp and ran down the stairs. Grabbing her keys, she raced out the front door.

*

It took a minute to realize someone was shaking her arm. "Aimee, are you okay?"

She shook her head, attempting to bring herself back to the present. She wasn't sure how long she'd been standing there. "I'm fine, Joan."

"No, you're not fine. You're standing outside on the porch crying. I called your name multiple times and you didn't even hear me." Her forehead wrinkled and she seemed to be genuinely concerned.

"I'm sorry. I was lost in thought. How is she doing?"

Joan opened the door wider, holding it for Aimee to enter and closing it gently behind her.

"Mom's weak and sleeps a lot, but she's still with us."

Aimee nodded her head. She wasn't sure she was ready for this. She needed to know why her mother had done such a horrible thing. Standing back in her old house it didn't seem possible that this could actually be happening. She needed the truth, something to clarify what was real, and what wasn't. If it turned out she actually was Emily's daughter, then she'd have to figure out how to fix the huge mess she'd created with her own secrecy.

"I made us some lunch, are you hungry?"

Aimee was surprised by her sister's friendly attitude. She was almost nurturing. In all of her sister's twenty-six years, Aimee wasn't sure she'd ever seen this side of her, at least not toward her. Her face must have portrayed her astonishment because her sister added, "Aimee, mom told me. I'm so sorry. I can't even imagine what you must be going through."

Her mother told her? She wasn't sure why she was surprised by that, but she was.

"We have some time before she wakes up. Do you want to talk about it?" Joan asked.

She wasn't sure about that either. "I'm not sure what to say."

Joan nodded her head and patted her shoulder. "We don't have to talk now. How about some lunch? You must be starving."

She was no longer certain what planet she was on. Joan was concerned? Joan cooked her lunch? Was this the same girl who'd never said a kind word to her in her entire life?

Walking with her sister she couldn't help but notice her hair was too blonde, her makeup too dark, her lipstick too red, her shirt too short, and her pants too tight.

They truly were very different people. Aimee was the good girl. Always brought home good grades, was never late for curfew, and excelled in everything she put her mind too. Joan was the bad girl. She'd been suspended for smoking on school grounds, swearing at a teacher, and vandalism in the school library. Her grades were terrible, so bad that she almost hadn't graduated. She had the party girl reputation and seemed proud of it. Aimee had gone to college and started her own business. Joan jumped from job to job. She was the girl who fell in love hourly and married almost on the same schedule.

Growing up, she'd always believed she was more like her father, and Joan, more like her mother. She told herself that her mother favored Joan because they were more alike, and her mother seemed to completely understand Joan. She supposed the truth was as simple as her mother favoring her own child. It didn't make it right, or hurt less, but at least it made sense.

She pulled up a chair at the small table in the corner of the bright kitchen. Her sister set a large Caesar salad in front of her, topped with strips of chicken. She placed a basket of warm rolls in the middle of the table and sat down in the open chair.

Joan bit into a forkful of salad and chewed loudly. Aimee moved the lettuce around on her plate. She wasn't sure if she really wanted to talk to her sister about this, but she was anxious to find out exactly what her mother said.

"So when you said, 'Mom told me,' what did you mean? What exactly did she tell you?" Struggling with eye contact, she stared down at her plate. She broke off a piece of a warm roll to keep her hands busy.

"She told me what happened to make you leave the way you did."

Aimee looked up at her sister. "What exactly did she say happened?"

"She said she had to tell you that you were adopted. You know, so if you needed any medical information or whatnot, you would know after she was gone. That must have been hard to hear after so many years. Especially with how close you were to Dad. It must be painful to know he never told you."

Aimee was speechless. Why would her mother lie to Joan? Did she think the truth would stay buried forever? Hell, she was the one who opened Pandora's Box. Did she think she could slowly push all the pieces back inside?

"What she wouldn't tell me is why you were in San Francisco. She was really upset about it when I told her you were there, but she refused to tell me why. Did you go to look for your real parents or something?"

"Something like that." Aimee rose from the table and rinsed off her plate. She took a couple of deep breaths, trying to maintain her calm. She didn't understand why, but her mother lying to Joan upset her, as did the fact her mother would be upset that she went to meet her birth mother. Or maybe it was her mother's selfish fear that she would die in a prison infirmary with her name smeared all over the headlines while she was alive to see it. "I think I'm going to go see if she's awake. Thank you for lunch."

"Aimee . . ." Joan got up from the table and stood in front of her. In a soft tone she said, "I'm sorry. You hear something like this and suddenly everything is clear. I haven't always been very nice to you. I didn't understand your goody two shoes personality, or why you were Dad's favorite. But now I understand and I'm sorry for some of the names I called you and some of the things I may have done to you over the years."

Before she'd even asked the question she knew she would regret it, but she asked anyway. "What do you understand, exactly?"

"Well, that you can't help being a little uptight, it must be in your genes. It's something you probably don't have any control over. And it can't be easy after all these years to learn you weren't really Dad's favorite. He was such a great man, trying to make it up to you that your real parents didn't want you."

With a straight face Aimee replied, "He was a saint really. It's amazing how many years of hell he was able to endure and still maintain his sanity."

She walked out of the room, leaving her sister standing in silence with a puzzled expression on her face.

Chapter 24

Even after exhausting himself in the pool, Mark hadn't been able to sleep. The moments he'd dozed off, he'd been plagued by bad dreams.

In them, he'd been trapped behind a wall. He could see out, but like a two-way mirror, they couldn't see in. Both Aimee and Emily were sitting in a room crying and he couldn't get to them. Emily was wearing Nathan's ratty old bathrobe, and holding tightly to a stuffed ladybug. Aimee was wearing a white blouse, unbuttoned to the waist, exposing a lacy black bra. The wall dissipated and he'd rushed inside. It seemed they still couldn't see him, and his shouts of reinforcement went unanswered. As they continued to cry, their tears began to fall like large stones upon him. He could feel their sadness, as well as his own physical pain.

Sitting up in bed, he rubbed his eyes, threw back the covers and stumbled into the bathroom. He understood why Emily was crying, he'd dreamt of her sadness many times over the years, but Aimee? He stared at himself in the mirror over the sink. Shaking his head, he ran the cold water and splashed his face.

"You need to get a handle on yourself," he muttered to his reflection. "How long are you going to feel guilty about doing the right thing for both of you?" Judging by the bags under his eyes, he figured that his guilt, and his inability to sleep, was not leaving any time soon.

With his mind made up, he sighed, and headed for the shower. First order of business this morning was apologizing to Aimee. Second, burying himself in work, so he could guarantee he'd keep his hands off her in the future. Sounded like a perfect plan, so why did he doubt his own ability to stay away? It wasn't like he was in love with her. Hell, he hardly knew her. What little he did know intrigued him, but he wasn't the type of man that fell for someone because he was curious about her.

Or at least, he didn't think so. Maybe he did find her captivating, but so what? He'd been locked in this house too long. That was all this was.

He was having her investigated. She was keeping secrets, and he knew it. So she was sexy and beautiful, easy to talk to, and funny. He was sure there were a million women out there who were all of those things as well. He switched off the water and grabbed his towel to dry off.

He threw his towel over the top of the shower rod and walked into the bedroom. He stuffed his legs into a pair of well-worn jeans, pulled a T-shirt over his head and pulled his favorite flannel shirt off the end of the bed. He hurried back into the bathroom and running a comb through his hair, turned off the light and rushed from the cottage.

He stopped in front of Aimee's door. Determined to ease his guilt by convincing her he'd done the right thing, he knocked loudly.

When she didn't answer, he turned, and marched down the winding path toward the main house. She wouldn't avoid him today. One way or another, they would resolve this now.

He walked into the kitchen expecting to find her at the table sipping coffee with Emily. She wasn't there.

"Morning, Em. Have you seen Aimee? I really need to talk to her," he said, still scanning the room.

"She's not here. She went home."

He jerked his head back around. "What do you mean she went home?" He felt the panic bubbling as his heart raced. "She quit? Just like that?"

Emily furrowed her brow. "No, Mark, she didn't quit. What's gotten into you this morning?"

Realizing he was in fact, acting like a madman, he pulled out a chair and sat down. His legs twitched under the table. "I'm sorry. I didn't get much sleep last night and I really needed to talk to her."

He looked up when Emily didn't reply. She watched him over the top of her mug, her face emotionless. "I'd ask why you hadn't slept, but that would be a redundant question." She sipped her coffee casually, looked at him again, and let out a little humph sound. If he didn't know better, he would think that Emily was enjoying his suffering this morning.

He growled at her, rose from the table and poured himself a cup of coffee. Sitting back down, he sighed and asked, "Why did she go home? Is everything okay?"

"According to her very nice note, her mother has taken a turn for the worse. She needed to be there."

"I'm sorry to hear that."

"Do you want to talk about it?" Emily asked.

He paused, took another sip of his coffee and sat his cup down on the table. Looking up into her caring eyes he replied, "I think I might have hurt her feelings, and I just wanted to clear the air."

"Did you?"

"Did I what?"

She watched him closely. "Did you hurt her feelings?"

There were days he hated that she could read him so well. "Yeah, I did. I wanted to explain. It bothers me that she's there and I don't have the chance to do that."

"There's always the phone," Emily suggested logically.

"Some conversations need to be face to face, and this is one of them. If she is still talking to me when she gets back, I'll try to fix it." He stood up from the table.

"Mark . . ."

He turned to her.

"It's none of my business, but maybe it shouldn't wait. If you're this upset, I can only imagine how she must be feeling."

He knew she was right, and it bothered the hell out of him. He hadn't meant to hurt her, but he had. He didn't want to feel anything for her, but he did. He didn't want to talk about this over the phone, but he realized he was more afraid that if he didn't, she'd never come back. His stomach rolled, and his palms began to sweat. That was something he didn't want to think about. He *needed* her to come back.

Chapter 25

Aimee paused outside the door to her mother's bedroom. She inhaled and blew out slowly. Placing her hand on the knob, she paused. Her eyes welled with tears. She let her hand fall softly to her side. Turning around, she slid to the floor, pulled her legs to her chest and rested her forehead against her knees.

Why couldn't she open the door? The truth was already out; it wasn't like it could get much worse. She needed answers. Her mother was the only one who could provide them. This time she would face her without crumbling into tears. She pushed herself up from the floor, straightened her blouse, and turned the handle, determined to be strong enough to hear the truth.

Stepping inside, she let her eyes adjust to the dim room. The shades were closed tightly and a small lamp on the nightstand provided the only light. She stood quietly next to the bed. Her mother had drastically worsened in the three weeks she'd been gone. She no longer appeared frail, it was much worse. Her eyes were closed but she could see the dark shadows that surrounded them, as well as the hollows they rested inside. Every bone in her body was prominent, resulting in a skeleton-like appearance. Her skin was gray and her breathing labored.

Her eyes fluttered open. She didn't speak or smile, but studied Aimee in silence.

"Hello, Mother," Aimee whispered.

Her mother motioned toward her water glass. Aimee picked it up off the nightstand, and using the straw helped her mother take a small sip. Her mother smiled, although weakly, before clearing her throat and motioning to Aimee to open the shades.

The sunlight flooded into the room causing both women to blink their eyes. Once her eyes adjusted, Aimee couldn't stop her gasp at seeing her mother clearly. There was no color to the skin that now hung from her thin, weak body. She was literally skin and bones.

"I'm glad you're here." Her mother labored to pull herself into a sitting position.

Aimee walked over and helped her mother sit up, moving the pillows behind her for support. She weighed nothing at all. Her mother closed her eyes as if resting from the effort.

Her mother motioned Aimee to sit down in the chair next to the bed. "It's my time. I'm not scared. I'm looking forward to being with your father again. I've always wanted to be with him. I made some poor decisions making sure he would be in my life."

"We don't have to talk about this today." Aimee fought back the tears. Even with everything that happened, it was hard to see her mother fading away.

"Yes, we do." She turned her head on the pillow and looked intently at Aimee. "I need to explain before it's too late."

Aimee sat in silence, unsure of her own readiness for the conversation to come.

"When I met your father, he was in San Francisco on a business trip. He was the handsomest man I'd ever seen." Her mother smiled a genuine smile of remembrance. Aimee had never seen her mother look like that before. "I was a young girl, working in the café down the street from the hotel where he was staying. The first morning he came in, he was the only customer and he invited me to sit down while he ate his breakfast. He said he hated to eat alone. You and I both know that never changed."

Aimee nodded her head. She had sat down for breakfast with her father every morning until she'd left for college.

"Over poached eggs and toast, he talked to me about his business, a little about his hometown, but mainly, about the girl who'd broken his heart."

"I've heard the story of how you met, what does that have to do with me?" Aimee asked anxiously.

"Everything." Her mother took a deep breath and continued. "He'd asked her to marry him and she'd refused. She came from a prominent family and they didn't believe he was good enough for their daughter. In his mind, she'd chosen them over him. I knew his pain was fresh, and maybe deep down I knew his asking me to dinner was less about me and more about getting back at her, but I wanted to be with him. He made me feel good . . . special."

Aimee uncrossed her legs and scooted back in the chair. "So you went to dinner, fell in love and got married. I know all of this."

"No, you know the part we wanted you to know. I'm telling you the whole story. We went to dinner that night, and the next three nights after that. On the night before he was supposed to leave to go home, we made love. It was my first time." She wiped a tear from the corner of her eye. "I told him I loved him, and wanted to go with him. He told me he cared very much about me, but was still in love with her. He was a perfect gentleman about it, and hoped I understood. Of course I didn't."

She motioned for another sip of water. Aimee could see she was struggling to stay awake.

"You need some rest. We can finish this conversation later."

Her mother shook her head. "Please, Aimee, let me finish." She pulled the covers up a little higher, and neatly folded down the sheet over the top of the blanket. "I cried for days after he left. It was the most horrible feeling, being in love with someone and knowing they didn't want you. I knew I could make him happy. I was also just as sure that she never could. A month later, I learned I was pregnant. I was so happy. I knew it was a sign we were supposed to be together."

Aimee fought the urge to interrupt again. This wasn't making any sense. How had this all resulted in a kidnapping from a hospital nursery?

"I contacted him through his job to tell him my good news. He wasn't as happy about it as I was. I learned that upon his return home from his trip, the girl changed her mind, and they were engaged to be married. He told me he would do right by me and financially support me and the baby, but he loved her and couldn't lose her again. Of course I was devastated."

"This isn't making a lot of sense."

"It will." Her mother took a deep breath and closed her eyes for a moment. When she opened them, she stared forward, almost like she was reliving every moment of the past. "Knowing that we needed to talk face to face, and believing if he saw me again, especially carrying his child, he would realize we were supposed to be together, I flew to North Carolina. I was about seven and a half months pregnant by then. I went to his office and sat patiently in the waiting area beside a beautiful woman with red hair. That is the moment my life changed."

"Who was she? Was she his fiancée?"

"She was, and he hadn't told her. Imagine his surprise to see me, big as a house, sitting next to his fiancée. The scene wasn't pleasant. She cried and handed him back his ring. He begged her to listen, to understand, but she refused. He was angry at me, but he couldn't seem to take his eyes off of my stomach. It was like it was finally real to him, just like I'd hoped it would be."

"So he married you?" Aimee asked, still trying to understand.

"Not right away, but being the gentleman he was, he put me up in a small hotel in town, and took me to see the local doctor. The doctor confirmed my due date, although I still like to believe he'd never doubted it was his baby. I'd been there for a couple of weeks before he finally asked me to marry him and move here permanently. Of course I said yes."

"It sounds like it should be a happily ever after, so where does stealing someone else's baby come in?" She knew she sounded snappy, but this still didn't answer any of her questions, and she was growing impatient.

"Aimee, I know you're angry with me, and I understand that, but I want you to fully comprehend what I was going through. In order for that to happen, I have to explain the events that led up to it."

Aimee folded her arms across her chest, and swallowed the unkind words she wanted to shout. "Go on, I'm listening."

"He wanted the baby to be born in North Carolina, so we decided I would rush back to San Francisco, quit my job, pack my apartment and get back as soon as possible. Your father wasn't able to come with me because of work. It took me a little longer than expected. The day I was scheduled to leave, I had an accident. I fell down the stairs outside of my apartment building. I was rushed to the hospital. Our little girl didn't make it. I'd lost the baby."

"I'm sorry." And she genuinely was.

"I was distraught. I was convinced that now that there wasn't a child between us, he wouldn't marry me. I just couldn't live without him." Her mother closed her eyes and attempted to take a breath. "I couldn't help myself; I was pulled toward the nursery on my way out of the hospital." Her mother looked away from her and stared at her hands. "I watched a nurse place you in one of the bassinets and walk away. I know it was wrong. It felt like I was out of control of my own body. I walked inside, picked you up, and walked you out."

Aimee knew her mother expected her to agree with her decision, to fully understand she'd taken her with the best of intentions. She couldn't do that. More than her own pain, she'd seen the pain her mother's selfishness had inflicted on others.

"I appreciate you telling me the truth." Aimee could feel her chest tightening as she struggled to control her urge to cry. "I'm going to let you rest." She closed the shades again, hoping to hide the emotions she knew were written all over her face. She turned to leave.

"Aimee . . ." her mother called, her voice strained.

"I'll check on you later." She choked as the damn began to break. Without turning back around, she rushed from the room.

Chapter 26

Aimee skimmed her feet across the grass, lifted them, and let the tire swing. She leaned back and swung her legs again to gain momentum. It all felt so surreal. For twenty-eight years she'd believed she knew who she was, and where she came from. Today, she felt lost, alone, and somehow misplaced. The fact that her mother had done it for the love of her father was not a comfort. It didn't change the fact that she'd stolen another family's child. That she had stolen Aimee.

She recalled the years of striving to win her mother's approval. The time she finally came to the conclusion that nothing she did would ever be viewed in a positive light. Was it all because she was a constant reminder of her mother's greatest sin? Or was it simply because she didn't belong to her?

She turned when she heard a car rolling slowly up the long driveway and smiled when she realized it was her Uncle Bob. Not really her uncle, but he'd been her father's best friend for as long as she could remember, and a major person in her life.

He stopped the car and got out when he spotted her. In his mid-fifties, he still had the boyish face of a man in his early thirties. His dark hair was slightly grayed, giving him a distinguished air. He was tall, close to six foot three, and carried himself with confidence combined with a carefree attitude. The combination was magnetic. Aimee had no doubt that women all over North Carolina were swooning in his charismatic wake.

He beamed as he approached her. "Hey there, Buttercup, I heard you were home again."

She slid out from the hole in the tire swing and spread her arms. "Uncle Bob."

He pulled her into his arms and lifting her from the ground, swung her around in a tight bear grip. "I've missed you so much." He set her back onto the grass, and placing his large hands onto her shoulders, studied her face.

"You've been crying." He squeezed her shoulder in comfort. "I can't imagine how you must be feeling. Having just lost your father, and now having to say goodbye to your mother as well."

She could only nod her head as her chest tightened, threatening the tears would start again.

"How is she doing?" he asked.

"Not very good, I'm afraid. I can't believe how much she has worsened in only three weeks."

"Three weeks? Were you home three weeks ago? Why is it the first I'm hearing of it?"

She wanted to lay her head on his shoulder and just spill her heart to him, to tell him everything that happened. She was unsure why she felt the urge to protect her mother from his disapproval, but she remained silent.

"I was only home for a day and had to leave." She said, trying to avoid actually lying to him. The truth would come out soon enough.

She could see his confusion, but he didn't press her any further. "I came to check on your mother as well, but I really wanted to check on you. Are those tears caused by your mother's weakened health, or just by your mother?"

She chuckled. "Both."

Bob had never hidden the fact that her mother wasn't his favorite person, and that he disapproved of the way she treated Aimee. "Don't you worry, Uncle Bob is here and will make sure she's on her best behavior . . . or else."

He turned, and placing one arm protectively over her shoulder, began to steer her toward the house.

She couldn't go in yet. She wasn't ready to paste a fake smile on her face for Joan or her mother, and she wasn't ready to say the words she knew her mother was waiting to hear.

Without looking up, she reached up and squeezed his hand. "Do you think we could take a walk before we go inside?"

"I would love nothing more."

Arm in arm, they turned from the house and walked down the long drive in comfortable silence.

The tree's overhead bowed toward each other, causing a canopy to filter the bright sunlight. "It's been a long time since I've walked this route." She turned to look at him. "I remember when Dad and I would walk this road almost every night after dinner."

"He loved those times with you. When you drove off to college, he showed up at my place, trying to hold it together and babbling about how he wasn't ready to let you go. I remember having a moment of jealousy . . . that he was your father and I wasn't." He laughed. "I'd had those moments over the years, when I realized I would never be a father, and seeing how much joy you brought to his life."

"You would have made a terrific father." She leaned her head against his arm.

"I'd like to think so. But I've always felt blessed just being your uncle. You've grown into a fabulous, successful woman. You made your dad proud every day of his life."

Aimee wiped a tear from her cheek, and snuggled in closer. "Do you think he was terribly unhappy with Mother?"

He kicked at a rock in the road, and pushed his other hand into his pants pocket. She could feel the deep breath he took, and realized he was struggling to answer her.

She stopped in the road, and turned to face him. She felt a sudden urgency to know. She placed her hands on his arms, forcing him to face her. "Was he?"

His eyes searched hers, and he expelled another breath. He bent his head down in silence for a moment, and then looked at her again. "I wouldn't say he was unhappy, and I know he never regretted having you girls, but I think . . . Oh, Aimee, I don't know how to answer this question."

"You think he would have been happier if he could have married the woman he loved instead of the woman who came up pregnant."

Bobs mouth hung open and his eyes relayed his shock. "How? When? Who told you?"

"I only learned recently." She stepped back beside him, tucked her arm into the crook of his elbow, and began to slowly walk again. "Dad never said a word about it. Well, Dad never would. He never had an unkind word to say about anyone."

"I don't understand. Why would your mother tell you this? Why now? Is she looking to tarnish your father in your eyes, or somehow make herself a victim? It doesn't make any sense to me." She could feel his body tense, and knew he was angry.

She didn't want to tell him the whole story yet. She just wanted to know if her mother had ruined her father's life with her lies. "I just want to know if he was happy."

He pulled his hand from his pocket, and laid his arm across her shoulder. "The sun rose and set with you, Aimee. Even if his marriage wasn't what he pictured for himself, and your mother not the woman he had originally chosen, he was one of the happiest men I knew. He was happy because he had you."

She laid her head back against him. She felt comforted in some small way, but she couldn't help but wonder if her father would have been happier in the life he'd planned for himself before her mother brought her home as a trap. She fought the urge to scream, cry, and rage at the unfairness of it all. She wanted to vent, to tell Bob everything. She couldn't. Now wasn't the time.

As they strolled up the driveway closer to the house, they heard screaming. Bob looked at her puzzled, and they both hurried their steps.

"I know she's here! Get out of my way, you little tramp!"

Joan was trying to close the front door in the face of a clearly unwanted guest. "I said she isn't here! Get the hell off my porch before I call the cops!" she screamed in reply.

"Go ahead and call the cops. I have no doubt they know exactly who you are, with as many times as they've taken your picture. And if by some miracle you've discovered the ability to tell the truth, then I can have you arrested for stealing her car. Would it be easier if I called them for you? It must be difficult to dial with those never-worked-a-day-in-your-life fingernails." The man on the porch turned around and pulled a cell phone out of his pocket.

"Luther?" Aimee ran toward the house and flung herself into his arms. "What are you doing here? How did you know where to find me?"

Luther pulled back and looked down at her. "I spoke to Emily. She told me what was going on, so I jumped on the train. Why didn't *you* call me?"

He looked hurt she hadn't. "I was going to call you today. Honest. I only arrived this morning."

He pulled her into his arms again, and held her tightly. Whispering into her ear so only she could hear him, he asked, "How did it go? Are you all right?"

With one last squeeze, he stepped back and peered into her eyes with concern. She felt her control begin to slip, and the tears threatening to spill. She could only nod her head.

Luther reached around her, and stretched out his hand. "Uncle Bob, it's nice to see you again."

Bob shook his hand and slapped him affectionately on the arm. "Glad you're here, Luther. I think our girl could use a real friend with a strong shoulder right now. She's had a rough day."

They all turned when they heard the door snap shut behind them.

"Now we've gone and pissed off the Wicked Witch of the East," Luther said.

"When have you known Joan not to be pissed off about something?" Bob replied. "I suppose this is my cue to sacrifice myself and go see what Joan's all worked up about this time. I'll check on your mother as well, so you two take your time and catch up. I'll see you inside after a bit."

After Bob left, Aimee turned to Luther. "You have no idea how glad I am you're here. It's been a very emotional day and I need to talk to someone without the web of secrets I keep finding myself trapped in."

He took her hand and led her to the swing on the far end of the porch overlooking the yard. "I take it you've seen your mother already today. Did you get a chance to talk to her?"

She nodded her head. "She believes she was justified in what she did because she didn't want to lose my dad." She replayed the conversation for him, leaving nothing out. It wasn't until she'd finished that she realized she was crying.

"I'm sorry this is happening to you. It isn't fair and you don't deserve it." He pulled out his handkerchief and waited in silence while she dried her eyes. "Did she tell Joan?"

A sarcastic cackle ruptured from her throat. "Are you ready for this one? She told Joan I'd been adopted. I suppose she believed that would explain my running from the house three weeks ago without her having to take responsibility for what really happened."

Luther's lips pressed together in a straight line, his eyes mere slits. His voice was lethal as he said, "I can't believe the balls on that woman." He threw his hands up in obvious frustration and jerking off the swing, began to pace the end of the porch. "She's created this massive mess. She's completely altered the lives of multiple people, lied and cheated. However, she decides that it would be better for her if she continued this charade with everyone else so she doesn't appear to be the horrible person she truly is. She then dumps it all in your lap so she can die with a clear conscience, leaving you to deal with this disaster after she's gone."

"That about sums it up. Luther, what am I supposed to do? I couldn't even tell Bob because I knew how he would react."

"Are you seriously still protecting her?"

Aimee hung her head. She was unsure of where to proceed

from here. He was right, this was a huge mess. She was allowing her mother to lie to everyone, and in the last three weeks had discovered she was capable of it, too. If it turned out that Emily was in fact her birth mother, she would have to try to explain why she'd started their relationship with dishonesty. Then there was Mark. She knew that relationship was irreparable and it broke her heart to know it was her own fault.

Luther stopped pacing, knelt down and pulled her chin up. "You need to talk to her again. Make her tell them the truth. You shouldn't be the only one who knows and be left to handle the aftermath because she's a damn coward."

She stood up. "You're right. This is her mess and she should clean it up, not me. Will you promise to stay if I go talk to her?"

"I'm not going anywhere. It becomes clearer each day that you can't handle life without me." He kissed her forehead. "Don't let her off the hook. Remember, you are the innocent in this. Be strong and kick some ass."

He turned her around and swatted her butt, giving her a little nudge. She walked purposely across the porch. Before she reached the door it swung open and Joan came barreling out.

"Mom's bad. She says she has to see you."

Chapter 27

Joan's face was wet with tears when Aimee blew past her on her way toward the stairs. Bob stopped her with a gentle hand.

"Aimee, I'll be right here if you need me. I hope you'll tell me what's really going on. I know it must be big. Joan just told me that you were adopted, and I know firsthand that's not true. You can tell me anything, Buttercup. I hope you know that."

"Thank you." He patted her hand in reassurance and stepped back so she could mount the stairs.

Her palms were sweaty, and her heart was racing. She tried to formulate what she would say. Her mother had lied to her and treated her poorly, but she was still the only mother she'd ever known, and she was dying. She loved her, but she was a stranger. What was she supposed to feel?

She stopped outside the bedroom door and hesitated. Tears rolled down her cheeks. Her jaw clenched and her heart pounded. Opening the door, she walked toward the bed.

Her mother's eyes fluttered open and she looked intensely at her. "You do understand, don't you?"

She took a deep breath and pulled the chair over to the side of the bed and sat down. Did she just let it go and tell her mother what she so desperately wanted to hear, or tell her the truth? Looking back into the eyes of the woman she'd always believed was her mother, she replied, "No, I don't understand. What you did was wrong, not only legally, but morally. You never thought of anyone else, just yourself. What makes me the angriest is you still are. Why would you tell Joan I was adopted?"

She scooted back in the chair, needing to put some distance between them as she tried to calm herself.

"I didn't want her to hate me, too," her mother replied in a whisper.

"I don't hate you, I just don't understand." She blew out a breath of frustration.

"You've always hated me. It was like you didn't have enough love for both of us, your dad and me."

"That's not fair," she snapped. "It was you who didn't have enough to share. Or maybe it was just with me because I wasn't your child." She stood from the chair and began to pace. Why had she just said that? She didn't need to confess how unloved she'd always felt, not now.

"I was jealous."

She froze. Slowly, she turned around and gaped at her mother. "Jealous?"

"Your father loved you so much. He never once looked at me the way he did you, with his heart in his eyes. It hurt me to see you two together. It was a constant reminder of what I'd never have with him."

Her stomach clenched. She threw her hands into the air in frustration. "I was a child!" she yelled. "How could you possibly blame me for that? You treated me like crap for twenty-eight years because you were jealous that he loved me? You were the one who gave me to him. You trapped him into marrying you. Do you really wonder why he didn't love you the way you wanted him too?" All the rage she'd been fighting to control broke loose. "You should be ashamed of yourself. How do you sleep at night?"

She turned to leave, fighting the urge to flee.

"Aimee, please don't leave like this," her mother pleaded in a weak voice. "I understand that you're angry, but I need to know you forgive me. Please don't let me die with you still hating me."

Aimee turned around and sat back in the chair beside the bed. Her rage spent, she said calmly, "I do forgive you. I have to—for both of us. But you need to fix this. At least tell Joan the truth."

"I will. I'll tell her if that's what you need me to do." Her mother reached over and touched her arm. She was surprised by the strange sensation. She couldn't remember her mother ever touching her with affection. "Can I ask you something else?" She continued when Aimee nodded her head. "What's she like? Your birth mother."

She furrowed her brow. It was a strange question and not one she expected. She thought about it for a moment before responding. "Broken."

Chapter 28

Aimee came down the stairs and looked into three curious faces. "She's sleeping."

Joan let out a deep breath in obvious relief and rose from the couch. "I'll go sit with her." She leaned in toward Aimee and added, "I hope your friend isn't planning on staying. He is a vile man and not welcome here."

"Yes, he is welcome here, and yes, he's staying."

Joan jerked back as if she'd been slapped. "Oh, so my feelings don't matter to you?"

"Not at all."

Aimee turned from her sister, surprised by her new voice. It felt good to be honest, to finally say what she wanted to. Both men pumped their fists in the air when Joan stomped from the room mumbling under her breath.

"I didn't know you had it in you." Bob's smile stretched ear to ear.

"Nicely done, and not just because I don't have to sleep in your car, but it's about time you put that girl in her place." Luther held his hand up for a high five slap.

The men scooted to the side and Bob patted the seat between them in invitation.

"What's going on?" Bob asked.

She could tell his patience was beginning to fray.

"This is not going to be a short, nor happy, conversation. Would anybody other than me care for a glass of wine first?"

"Now we're talking my language," Luther said, jumping from the couch.

"I would love a glass." Bob stood up and led the way to the kitchen.

Handing Luther the bottle and corkscrew, Aimee reached into

the cupboard for three glasses. No one spoke, but even the silence was filled with questions.

"Have you eaten today?" Bob stepped behind her and rubbed her shoulders.

She turned her head and nodded. "Joan made me a salad earlier."

Bob snickered and opened the refrigerator, pulling out the makings for a sandwich. "Luther, are you hungry? I could easily make three."

"Starved." Luther walked over and began to unscrew the lid on the mayonnaise jar.

"Not for me, thanks," Aimee said, sitting down at the table and pouring three glasses of wine.

"You need to eat something, Aimee, no arguments."

She suddenly understood. Bob didn't believe her. Joan had never done a nice thing for her in her life. The laughter began slowly, and before she knew it, she was bent over, tears streaming down her cheeks, holding her stomach and unable to stop. The weight of the day exploded and the laughter turned to tears, which turned to painful sobbing. She was aware of the two men standing in front of her, each of them obviously unsure of what to do with a hysterical female.

She could hear them both whispering her name and repeatedly asking her if she was okay. She couldn't speak. The tears wouldn't stop. She took a deep breath and tried to calm herself down. She let it out slowly, and pulled more air into her lungs, holding it for a second before letting it blow out again.

"I'm fine," she finally managed to whisper.

Luther silently handed her his ever present handkerchief and didn't utter a word while she dried her face and attempted to pull herself together.

Looking up into two very worried faces, she spoke again in a stronger voice, "I'm fine, honest."

They both pulled up a chair at the table next to her, all talk of sandwiches forgotten, while they waited silently for her to continue.

"It hasn't been a very good month." She snickered at her own understatement, and then squeezed her lips together to ensure she wouldn't start another episode.

"Just the same boring month in the life of Aimee," Luther shrugged his shoulders.

His sarcasm was exactly what she needed and she could feel her moment of panic subsiding. "Joan really did make me a salad today, with fresh bread, the works."

Both men's jaws dropped, their mouths agape, the disbelief clear in their eyes. Another bubble of amusement escaped, and she clasped her hand tightly over her mouth to trap it inside.

Luther slapped the table. "Shut up! You're not serious? Are you going to tell me you can turn water to wine next?"

"She really did. But then you have to remember, she was worried that I'd been traumatized by this adoption news." She sipped from her glass. "Although, she was extremely happy to realize I wasn't really her sister, something about my not being able to help being uptight. She was also relieved to know the reason Dad seemed to favor me was because he felt sorry for my lot in life. It can't be easy for a girl to discover her parents didn't want her and all."

Luther grunted and rolled his eyes.

Bob finally snapped his mouth closed. Reaching over for his glass, he sipped and leaned back in his chair. "What is going on? Why would your mother tell Joan you'd been adopted?" He fidgeted in his chair. His brow creased, his eyes locked with hers. "Three or four weeks ago, you're here for a day, then just gone, which is completely out of character for you, especially with your mother in this condition. Joan said something about you working in San Francisco for someone else, when you own your own business. Not to mention you completely freak out over a sandwich. Aimee, what the hell is going on?"

She took a deep breath. "A little over three weeks ago, mother told me she'd taken me. That she'd kidnapped me from a hospital in San Francisco."

Bob's face was unreadable, and for a moment he didn't utter a sound. Slowly, bright red crept into his cheeks, his jaw clenched, and his eyes became slits. Abruptly, he stood from his chair, sending it clattering to the floor. "That bitch! That conniving . . . deceitful . . . heartless . . . bitch!"

He turned and began marching from the room. Aimee knew he was going to confront her. Jumping from her chair, she ran after him, catching him just a few stairs up.

"Uncle Bob, please don't. I know you're angry. She hurt your friend and he never even knew it happened, but please, for me, don't do this now."

He turned to her and she could see his anger begin to subside. "I'm sorry. I saw red and didn't stop to think how my confronting her would affect you." He stepped down the last stair and pulled her into his arms. "It's not just that she hurt my friend, she hurt my little girl. I'm so sorry, Buttercup."

She clung to him for a moment longer. Stepping away she took his hand and led him back toward the kitchen. "You only know half of the story. There's strong evidence that I'm currently working for my birth mother in San Francisco."

"I need a drink, a strong, stiff drink. Then I need to sit down, so you can fill me in from the beginning."

"I'm already ahead of you," Luther said when they walked into the kitchen. He motioned toward an already open bottle of whiskey and three glasses.

"Let's take this conversation outside," Aimee suggested. "I can't be sure if mother has told Joan the truth yet, and I think it has to come from her. I don't want to risk her overhearing us."

The three of them grabbed their glasses and headed for the front porch. Luther suddenly stopped, and holding up a finger, ran back into the kitchen. "We might need this." He smirked, and continued walking onto the porch carrying the entire bottle of whiskey with him.

Aimee told Bob everything that happened, from the leather case, her trip to San Francisco, the mistaken identity, the interview, and the web of lies she'd trapped herself in. After catching Bob up on the last three weeks, she told them both about the conversation she had with her mother today.

They sat in silence for a moment. Both men seemed to be processing the information.

Bob was the first to break the silence. "This Mark guy, what's going on with you two?"

Aimee's eyes grew wide, and she stuttered her response. "No . . . Nothing, we work together, well kind of. Why would you think something was going on?"

Luther grunted. She turned to glare at him.

"You're lying, but we can get to that later." Bob turned to Luther and nodded his head. She got the feeling an entire conversation just happened in a single nod. "Why haven't you told them who you are?"

"It's complicated." She threw her hands up in frustration. She looked over at Luther for help, but he simply bowed his head and concentrated on the ice in his glass.

"Is it complicated? Or are you making it complicated?" Leave it to Bob to get to the root of the situation.

"Both," she answered honestly. "I only have circumstantial evidence right now. I don't have any real proof and she's been hurt so much. I don't want to be wrong. At first I just wanted to meet her, and to know if it were true, would she want to know."

"And now?"

"Now, I've trapped myself in lies and if I tell her my suspicions she probably won't believe me, and it could hurt her. Besides, I don't have any proof. I'd look like another con artist after her money."

"You'll have proof sooner than you think," Luther muttered into his glass.

"What do you mean?" Aimee felt her heartbeat increase, and the blood rushing through her veins. "Luther?"

He looked up at her, his face a mask of innocence. "Don't be mad."

She swallowed hard. "Luther, what did you do?"

He looked away from her again. "I wanted you to know for sure, so I got some proof." He shrugged his shoulders.

"What kind of proof?" She raised her voice.

"I had a DNA test done. Well, it's being done. You should have the results sometime next week. Did you know they can do that from a simple piece of chewing gum? It's amazing how far technology has come," Luther said looking directly at Bob.

"Chewing gum?" she asked, stepping into his line of sight so he couldn't avoid her. "How did you get it?"

"Yours was easy, due to the fact that you still chomp and smack it like a first grader. I've been taking gum from your mouth for years. Emily was another story. It seems classy ladies don't chew gum, but my, you-simply-must-try-it voice, and my incredibly hard to resist charm, worked. I felt a little foolish being all pushy over a piece of juicy fruit, but she's such a nice lady, she humored me and chewed away. Judging by the look on her face, she wasn't a fan, so the minute she excused herself I followed closely behind her and picked up the wrapper when she quickly discarded it." He actually seemed proud of himself. "You owe me six hundred bucks by the way."

"Why would you do that?" she shouted. "You had no right! It's none of your business!"

"Aimee," Bob said softly. "He was only trying to help."

Luther stood from the swing and placed his glass on the porch rail. He stood in front of her with compassionate eyes. "I knew you wouldn't do it, even though it made sense. You wouldn't do it because you're scared of the results. I watched you with her, you already love her. You've spent your whole life looking for a connection with your mother. But you were looking at the wrong woman, so you weren't finding that relationship. It's like Emily said, mothers and daughters have a bond, and you already feel it. Now you're afraid it won't be real."

She stepped forward and laid her head against his chest. Looking back up at him she smiled appreciatively as he reached over to wipe the tears from her cheeks. "How is it that you know me so well?"

"Years of research, my dear." He pulled her against him again, and kissed the top of her head. "You're not alone, Aimee. You never have been."

Chapter 29

"Have you heard from her?" Mark asked Emily as they crossed the yard.

"No, not yet, but I left a message on her voicemail."

He was going crazy. That was the only explanation he could come up with. Aimee had walked into his life less than a month ago and somehow she was taking over his every waking thought, which was a better part of a twenty-four hour period, now that he could no longer sleep.

So what if she didn't come back, he kept telling himself. She was Emily's assistant, nothing more, and she could be replaced. He was attracted to her, and that was it. He'd been attracted to women before, and would be again. Hell, she'd only been gone two days.

"I hope she's okay," Emily said, cutting into his thoughts.

"I'm sure she's fine. Probably has a lot going on."

"Why does your tone not match your words, Marcus?" She smiled up at him in that knowing way of hers. "She'll be back."

"Of course she will. She seemed quite competent in her work and I can't see her leaving you stranded at this point."

Emily made a small rumbling noise and didn't respond.

He stopped at the seating area of the rose garden and held his arms out in a ta-dah gesture. It was finally complete, the fountains were in, and roses, in full bloom, exploded in an array of bright colors.

"It's absolutely beautiful and exactly what I wanted." A smile lit her face.

"My boy always had a way with flowers," said a voice from behind.

They both spun around.

"Mom!"

"McKenzie!"

"I can't believe what you two have done to this place. It's amazing." She walked over and threw her arms around them.

Emily couldn't believe how much she'd missed her best friend. She squeezed her again for confirmation before stepping back to get a good look at her.

"You look happy," she told her, taking in the sun kissed skin, the long, ebony hair that lay softly over her bare shoulders, and the new sparkle in her eyes. She hadn't seen that look in her friend's eyes for years. So long, she wasn't sure at first she remembered what it meant. She gasped. "Oh my god, you're in love."

McKenzie blushed, and looked down at the ground before looking up at Emily. "I don't know about love, but I've met someone, yes."

With a girlish squeal, Emily grabbed her hands and tugged her toward the seating area. "Who is he? Where did you meet him? Tell me everything."

"I will, I will. But first, I need to catch up on what's going on with you two."

Emily looked over at Mark, realizing he hadn't uttered a sound. Watching his face, it was clear he was processing this new information, and didn't seem quite as happy with the news as she was.

He walked over and kissed his mother on the cheek. "It's good to have you home, we've missed you. I'm going to leave you two giggling girls to catch up while I help Mimsey get your room ready. I expect to hear all about this mystery man over dinner."

As Mark walked away, Emily said, "I think he's missing Aimee. He's been in a bad mood since she left."

"Let's walk. I want to hear all about this girl who's got my son so worked up," McKenzie suggested.

As they walked down the brick path and through the spacious grounds, Emily told McKenzie all she could about Aimee.

"She's lovely. I believe she has feelings for him as well, but it seems he is doing his best to hold her at arm's length. Peter is also smitten with her and is finding a million reasons to stop by. I'm selfishly grateful for it, because it makes Mark jealous, although he'd never admit it."

McKenzie shook her head. "That boy is so damn stubborn. He'll spend the rest of his life here with us if we let him. I would be the happiest woman in the world if he would settle down with a nice girl who made him happy. Besides, I'm ready to be a grandmother, surprising as that sounds."

Emily didn't speak. She couldn't stop the flash of envy that coursed through her. She'd always wanted to be a grandmother, too. To chase her grandchildren around the yard, walk along Fisherman's Wharf and lick ice cream cones, fly kites on the beach beneath the Golden Gate Bridge, and create necklaces out of macaroni noodles and bright colored yarn.

"Emily? Are you okay?" McKenzie reached over and touched her arm.

Nodding her head, she replied, "Sorry, my mind wondered for a moment. I'm not at all surprised you're ready to be a grandmother. Mark's thirty, and you and I aren't getting any younger. Although no one would believe it to look at you, you look absolutely fantastic."

"Well, thank you very much. I think it's the South Pacific sun, more vitamin D or something." She gasped as they rounded the far end of the house. "It's beautiful. I can't believe how a few bushes, a couple of trees and a simple fountain can transform an entire yard. It's like a national park for the rich and famous."

"Mark has done a great job. I can tell him what I envision and he makes it come alive. He's far surpassed my expectations."

"My boy's a genius. He gets that from me, of course."

"Of course, and speaking of the man he didn't get any of his good traits from, he came to see Mark this week."

The color drained from McKenzie's face. "What? Did Mark speak to him?"

Emily nodded her head. "It seems Jacob had a near-death experience. Heart attack, I believe. He wanted to try to set things right with Mark. They spoke, but judging from Mark's sullen attitude the following day, I don't think it went well."

"The bastard doesn't have a heart so we know that attention-getter was bullshit."

Emily watched emotions run across McKenzie's face, before it finally settled on rage. "Why won't he just leave it alone? Hasn't he hurt that boy enough?"

Emily knew this wasn't just about Mark. The pain McKenzie endured was never forgotten, and clearly, had never been forgiven. She'd never be able to fully understand what McKenzie had gone through, but she did know how fleeting life was.

"Do you think it's possible that maybe he truly wanted to make things right?" Emily asked hesitantly.

McKenzie froze, years of pain and anger etched in her eyes. "Are you kidding me? Are you seriously buying into his bullshit? The man is a snake and he doesn't deserve anything from his son, especially not his forgiveness."

Emily flung her hands into the air in a show of surrender. "You're right. I know he doesn't deserve it. He was the worst kind of predator. But I can't help but wonder if Mark might find some peace if he could let some of it go."

McKenzie shook her head. "I can't talk about this." She started to walk toward the house before stopping and whipping back around. "It's just like that son of a bitch to do this now. I finally step outside of my comfort zone and let somebody in, carve out a moment of possible happiness for myself, and he rises from the pits of hell to make sure I never forget what evil, people are capable of doing in the name of love."

Emily was shocked by the anger radiating from her friend. This was not the way she envisioned her homecoming. Attempting to change the subject she asked, "So when are you going to tell me about this dream man you've met, and why am I only learning of it now?"

"Can we talk about Paul later?" McKenzie looked defeated. "I can't think straight. I'd like to lie down for a bit before dinner. Mark didn't look exactly thrilled with the news that I'd met someone, and I'm expecting an all-out interrogation over dinner."

"Of course, go rest and we can talk later." She reached in to hug her. "I'm really glad you're home."

Chapter 30

Aimee pulled her car into the parking lot and turned off the engine. She stared up at the sign over the door that read Mahn Real Estate. What was she doing here? This visit was pointless; it wouldn't accomplish anything. Still unable to shake her curiosity she opened the car door and stepped out.

On the short drive to Raleigh, she'd gone over what she'd say a million times, but she still sounded crazy. It'd been almost thirty years, what did it matter now? But she knew somehow, it did matter. She'd offered her mother her forgiveness, but had she truly forgiven her? She knew she must, for her own sake more than anything, but she needed answers. How much damage had the backlash of her mother's action caused other people? It was the one question that continued to haunt her.

She tugged on the bottom of her jacket to straighten it, and pulled up her purse strap. She leveled her shoulders, took a deep breath, and pushed open the door.

"Hello, may I help you?" the chipper receptionist asked.

"I called this morning. I have an appointment with Camille Mahn."

"Of course Ms. Morrison, please have a seat. I'll let her know you're here."

Aimee smiled nervously and folded herself into one of the straight back chairs along the wall. She fidgeted with the strap of her purse while questioning her right to be here. Deciding she shouldn't be, she stood to leave.

The office door opened, and a tall, elegant, red haired woman in a trim black suit walked toward her. Aimee stiffened, her heart rate picking up speed.

The woman smiled and reached out her hand. "Ms. Morrison,

I'm Camille Mahn. Come on in."

Aimee shook her hand and tried to form a sentence. She was utterly speechless. Camille closed the door behind them and motioned for her to take one of the open seats in front of the large wooden desk.

Sitting across from her, Camille pulled out a blank sheet of paper and picked up a pen. "So how can I help you?"

Aimee stuttered, all the things she wanted to say flew out of her head.

"Are you looking to buy a home, or sell?"

"Neither," Aimee was finally able to say.

Camille maintained her professionalism, and continued. "Then how can I help you?"

Aimee folded her hands in her lap and stared at them for a minute. She looked up at the beautiful woman her father had loved and planned to marry. "You're going to think I'm crazy. I shouldn't even be here."

Camille's expression portrayed her curiosity. "Why are you here?"

Aimee blew out a breath. Her nervousness increased as she realized exactly how insane it was that she was here. Her mouth twitched. "I know you don't know me, but . . ." She looked imploringly across the desk. "Have you led a happy life? I . . . I mean, well . . ."

Camille's brow creased. "You're right, that is an odd question to ask someone you don't know. The fact that you made an appointment with me to ask that question, I find even stranger. With that said, why don't you tell me why it is you're here?"

Aimee was surprised by the calmness in her tone. She didn't seem angry, or even afraid, only curious.

"Did I mention that this is crazy?" Aimee chuckled when Camille nodded her head and raised her eyebrow. "Do you remember Robert Morrison?"

Camille's eyes grew wide, and Aimee could hear her sharp intake of breath. It was her turn to stutter. "Aimee Morrison? You're . . . are you . . .?"

"I'm his daughter."

Both women silently watched each other. Aimee wasn't sure what to say next, and was relieved when Camille spoke first. "It's been close to twenty-five years since I've seen your father. You were only a little girl. I heard about his passing, and I'm sorry for your loss."

Aimee mumbled a thank you.

"I think I'm even more confused now that we've made our introductions."

"I've only recently learned of you. Well, your past with my father."

"That was a long time ago," Camille said in a somber tone.

"I know. It's just . . . I understand that you loved each other, and I wondered . . ."

"Wondered what?" Camille asked.

Aimee shook her head. "I don't know. If you were happy, I guess." She nervously straightened the edges of her jacket, staring down into her lap.

"Are you wondering if I was happy without him?" Camille asked.

Aimee nodded her head.

"He was the love of my life, the one man that you never forget and always ask yourself what if. He'll always hold a special place in my heart, but to answer your question, yes, I was happy. I was married a few years later and raised three sons with my husband. I've lived a good life." She walked around the desk and sat in the chair next to Aimee.

"So, no regrets?" Aimee studied her face, searching for any sign that she meant what she said.

"I don't think I understand exactly what is going on," Camille said. "I think something has happened to you or someone you love and you're searching for answers. Or maybe it's as simple as you wanting to know more of your father."

"Maybe a bit of both," Aimee admitted.

"You were about three or four years old when I first saw you. You were at the carnival with your father and I was volunteering at one of the game booths. It was the first time I'd seen Robert since I'd given him back the ring. I could tell he was uncomfortable, but more than that, I could tell he was still feeling guilty about how we ended. We spoke for a bit while you tossed rings onto the bottlenecks." Her tone softened and her eyes grew distant. "We were both happy with our lives, and that was all that mattered. He lit up like the sun when he talked about you. I thought I was a princess when I was a little girl, but I think you stole my crown."

Aimee blushed. "I must admit to being a bit pampered by him."

Camille chuckled and patted her hand. "I'm still not sure what you're looking for, but I can tell you, I'm happy. I will never forget your father, nor will I regret a moment of the time I had with him. I'm a firm believer everything happens for a reason, even if we don't understand it. Your father was the most amazing man I've ever known, and he was happy. That's what I was grateful for above all else."

Aimee let the tears fall as she thanked her for meeting with her and being so honest.

Camille handed her a business card and told her to call anytime, day or night.

"I hope you find what you're looking for," Camille said, holding the door for her.

Aimee turned around. "Not everything happens for a reason. Sometimes life is altered when it shouldn't be."

Camille smiled reassuringly. "Maybe, but then it's up to you to find the happiness in your new direction."

Chapter 31

"Where have you been? I've been worried sick," Luther scolded, as Aimee walked through the front door.

"I'm sorry to worry you, Daddy," she answered sarcastically.

"Very funny." He smirked. "But you could have let someone know where you were going."

"I'm sorry, it was a last minute decision and I left early."

"I miss the uptight Aimee. This new impulsive you is causing me to worry, and if I wrinkle prematurely, I will never forgive you." Luther pouted.

Aimee kissed both of his cheeks. "Nothing will ever happen to this face." She pinched his cheeks dramatically. "You spend too much money at the Saks makeup counter for that."

Luther slapped her hands away and turned his back to her, crossing his arms defiantly.

She stifled a giggle, cleared her throat to make sure it wouldn't surface, and stepped in front of him. "I'm sorry if I worried you, I didn't think you'd be up much before noon and thought I'd be back."

"You're forgiven. This time." He uncrossed his arms and let them fall to his side. "Joan is driving me crazy. She's running around the house looking for you. She's upset about something, but I don't think it's a broken fingernail like I'd originally thought. She got really pissed when I asked her if that was her problem. She thinks I'm lying about knowing where you are. She won't stop her damn squawking. She's like a seagull at a picnic."

"Aimee," Joan called from the kitchen. "Aimee, come here? I need to talk to you."

Luther waved his arms in the air like a bird. "Squawk, squawk."

Aimee playfully swatted at him, and walked into the kitchen.

She couldn't see her sister, but she could still hear her. Her voice was coming from the garage.

Joan was sitting on the floor with her head resting on her knees, calling Aimee's name.

"What are you doing? Why are you in here?" Aimee asked, standing in front of her.

"Where have you been? I've been looking all over for you." Joan slowly rose from the floor. Black mascara streaked her cheeks and dotted her white t-shirt.

"What's wrong? Is it Mother?" Aimee asked anxiously.

"Yes, it's Mom," Joan snapped. "She's lost her mind. She's so far gone that she's a complete lunatic. I don't know what to do. Should I call someone? Is it her medication? Should I call the doctor? What do you think?"

"Come into the kitchen and tell me exactly what happened. You're not making any sense," Aimee said, calmly leading her sister to the door.

Joan hurried her step and walked in front of her like it was a first grade playground line up. She sighed and let her sister have the lead. By the time she'd reached the kitchen, Joan was already seated in a stool at the breakfast bar. Aimee didn't know her sister could move that fast. She must have wanted that particular seat badly. Aimee snickered.

Joan scowled. "I don't know what you could possibly find so funny right now."

Climbing onto the stool next to her, she asked, "So what happened this morning that has you so upset?"

"Mom's talking crazy, and then breaking into tears. She's mumbling about the will, and ladybugs, and not making a lick of sense. I don't know what to do. She's—"

"Tell me exactly what she said, Joan."

Scowling at being interrupted, she snapped her reply. "She said that she kidnapped a baby wrapped in a ladybug blanket and that she needed to talk to the lawyer about the will before it's too late. What should we do?"

Aimee wasn't sure how to handle this. Her mother had told Joan the truth as she'd promised, but she hadn't considered the possibility she wouldn't believe her.

She took a deep breath and turned to look directly at her sister. "Mom's not crazy. She doesn't need a doctor."

Joan jerked her head up and glared at her. "How can you say she's not crazy? Did you hear a word I said?"

"Do you remember when Mother told you I was adopted?" She had her sister's attention. "I wasn't. That wasn't the truth. Three weeks ago, she told me she'd taken me from a hospital when I was a baby. She stole me."

Silence settled around them as the tension built.

"You're a liar!" Joan quickly jumped from the stool and stepped back. Her face was blood red beneath the streaks of makeup, and her eyes were small slits as she glared at her sister. "She would never do such a thing!" Her voice cracked. "Why would you even say something like that? Do you really hate her that much? You're evil, that's what you are."

"Please, listen to—"

"Listen to what? Your lies, you're disgusting lies? You've always hated her and now you're trying to make me hate her too. You're evil . . . and mean . . . and . . . and . . . a bitch! That's what you are. A bitch!"

"That's enough." Bob walked into the kitchen, his eyes focused on Joan. "I understand you're upset, justifiably so, but this isn't getting you anywhere."

"Did you hear what she said?" Her voice spiked, sounding like nails on a chalkboard. She threw herself into his arms. "Why is she saying those things?"

As Joan lay sobbing against his chest, Bob looked over her head at Aimee, and mouthed, "You okay?"

She nodded her head and then shrugged her shoulders. How

was she going to make Joan understand any of this? She felt like she was having an out of body experience, and none of this could actually be happening. But seeing her sister bawling, Luther leaning on the kitchen door jam, with worry lines creasing his forehead, and Bob watching her with intensity, she knew it truly was.

In a soft, calming voice, Bob suggested, "Why don't you both go upstairs and talk to your mother together?"

"You can't be serious," Joan said in disbelief. "I won't let her upset Mother. I can't. She doesn't deserve this."

Aimee opened her mouth to speak then closed it again. It wouldn't make a difference if she reminded her that Mother had already confessed the truth. Joan had taken it as mindless rambling, and nothing Aimee could say would change that.

Bob stepped back from Joan, placed his hands on her shoulders and looking very serious, said, "I think it's important."

"Oh my god, you believe her!" Joan took a step back from him. She turned in a circle, looking at one, then the other, before stopping to stare at Aimee. The corners of her mouth twitched, forming a sneer. "Of course you do. It's sweet, perfect, innocent, little Aimee. If she said it, then it must be true. Aimee would never tell a lie. She's never done anything wrong in her entire pampered, perfect, life."

Luther stepped out of the doorway and crossed the kitchen to stand next to Aimee.

Bob took a few steps, until he was standing directly in front of Joan. Without taking his eyes from her, his expression softened, and his tone seemed distressed. "It's true, Joan. Your mother told me herself. If you'd take a moment to think about it, she tried to tell you as well."

Joan stood there with tears streaming down her face, shaking her head, and mumbling, "It's not true. It's not true."

"I'm so sorry," was all Aimee could say.

"I don't believe you, any of you. I'm going to talk to Mom and figure out why you're all saying these horrible things." She turned to Aimee, her eyes a mixture of anger and hate. "I don't know what game you're playing." She pointed a long red fingernail at the ceiling. "That woman gave you a home when nobody else wanted you, when your own family tossed you away. Instead of being grateful to her, you spread terrible, vicious, lies. You may have fooled all of these people, but I've known you're malicious for a long time."

"Joan, that's enough," Bob snapped. "Go and talk to your mother, but I recommend you calm down first. You will need the ability to listen if you're going to hear the truth."

Joan glared at him. Without another word, she stomped from the kitchen and ran up the stairs.

Aimee collapsed onto the stool. Her entire body felt drained.

Before anyone had the chance to react to the scene they'd just witnessed, Joan came barreling back into the kitchen. Her face was twisted with pain, and wet with tears. The three of them flocked around her, trying to make out the words she kept whispering repeatedly.

Aimee felt her legs give out and grabbed Luther's arm to stop herself from falling. She began to weep. The woman she'd grown up believing was her mother was gone.

Chapter 32

Mark crossed the hallway and picked up the ringing phone. There was a long pause on the other end of the line. It sounded like someone was crying.

"It's Aimee." Her voice choked when she spoke.

Mark couldn't remember ever having felt as helpless as he silently listened to Aimee fall apart. He wished she wasn't so far away and he could hold her.

Emily walked into the room, apparently having heard the phone ring. He put his hand over the receiver and told her he believed Aimee had lost her mother.

She motioned with her hands.

"Aimee, hold on a second, Emily wants to speak to you."

He couldn't make out Aimee's response. He told Emily she was in bad shape when he reluctantly handed her the phone. Their conversation was short as he listened to Emily say "I know" and "I'm so sorry" and "Don't you worry about that right now." It was clear Aimee had been able to stop crying long enough to get out a few sentences.

His heart soared when he heard Emily say, "You take your time, and we'll see you when you get back." That meant she was coming back. The relief he felt was surprising, and a bit frightening.

Emily handed him back the phone, and covering the receiver, she said, "She's really having a hard time, let her cry if she needs to."

He frowned at her. "I'm not a complete bastard, you know."

"No you're not. Just pig headed." She smiled sweetly and walked from the room, closing the door behind her.

"Are you still there?" he asked Aimee hesitantly.

She spoke softly that she was, the crying beginning to cease. "I didn't mean to fall apart. I heard your voice, and . . ." She blew out a breath. "It's been a long day." She inhaled again. "Joan shut herself in her room, leaving all the funeral arrangements to me, which I strangely appreciated, as I cope better when I stay busy. I finally find a moment to sit down and return Emily's call, and . . . well . . . maybe I shouldn't have stopped moving yet."

"I wish you weren't going through this."

"It's been a horrible couple of days." There was another long pause before she continued. "So much has happened."

"Do you want to talk about it?" he asked.

"Yes."

He could hear her crying again. "I can be a very good listener." He scooted back in the chair.

In a very soft voice she whispered, "I wish I could. Talk about it, I mean."

He assumed she was too upset to talk. "I'll be here, whenever you're ready."

There was another long pause. "I'm sorry."

"Sorry, for what?"

"I'm sorry for falling apart on you. I'm sorry for the way I left. I'm sorry for . . ." He could hear her sigh again.

"Please don't apologize." His tone softened. "You just lost your mother, so I think you deserve to fall apart. As for the way you left, you received an urgent call and you had to rush out, I get it." He cleared his throat. He knew he needed to say something about the last night they'd been together, and why he'd pushed her away, but he didn't know how to put it into words. Hell, he didn't even completely understand it himself. "I'm the one who should apologize. I . . . I . . . Well, I didn't handle things very well. I was so upset with my father and his attempt to sweep the past under the rug that . . . that I lost myself for a moment. I didn't mean to hurt you." He ran his hands through his hair.

"There's no need to apologize. I understand."

"Yes there is." He stood up and began to pace. He could tell by the tone of her voice that she clearly didn't understand. The look of hurt she'd worn that night was still etched in his mind. "It was wrong of me to take advantage of your friendship. I mean . . ." He took a deep breath and plopped back into the chair.

"Let's forget it happened, okay?"

"I'm not sure I want to forget it happened." He smiled at the memory of her lips parted beneath his. "But if you insist, I will remove myself from the jackass of the year nominations. I was beginning to believe that I was finally going to win an award."

The sound of her soft laughter touched him and he knew that she didn't think he was a complete ass after all.

Something shifted in him, and he realized how much he wanted to hear her laughter, and know he'd been the one to cause it. He wanted to pull down the wall he'd so meticulously constructed and let himself believe again.

Taking a deep breath, he asked, "Do you think after you get back, you'd let me take you dinner?"

Chapter 33

The sun beamed down on the small group wearing all black, as they filed slowly across the grass, past the headstones, and took their places beside the casket blanketed in white roses.

Aimee stood between Luther and Bob, staring blindly at the casket before her. It'd been two years since she'd stood in almost this exact spot and buried her father. She'd been inconsolable that day. She could still remember the way the breeze caressed her wet cheeks, the way the birds sang, and the smell of the cut grass. She remembered the anger she'd felt that he wasn't beside her feeling the same breeze, and hearing the same sounds.

As much as she still missed him, a part of her was grateful he hadn't lived to discover her mother's betrayal. She knew it shouldn't matter, he would have been her father regardless of the fact that it wasn't by blood. But the lost feeling she currently suffered from would have been easy for him to see. It would have hurt him deeply.

She tried to hold onto the happy memories of him. To cling tightly to the stories she'd been told over the last couple days of how happy he'd been with her. If she'd brought him a fraction of the happiness he'd given her, she was glad she'd been a part of his life, regardless of the circumstances.

She prayed to feel the same emotions now. That feeling of sadness and loss that she'd felt then. She wanted to know she could feel that way about her mother. No matter how deep she searched, she couldn't find them. She felt a loss, but the pain her mother inflicted was hard to forget. The lives she'd destroyed weighed heavily on her heart.

Luther nudged her in the side with his elbow. She turned and looked in the direction he motioned. Her hand flew to her chest, and her gasp was audible to those beside her. Mark and Emily stood watching her silently from the other side of the casket.

"Did you know they were coming?" Luther whispered into her ear. She looked up at him and shook her head.

Aimee felt a moment of joy that they'd come all this way to be with her. That moment didn't last long when the reality of the situation fully hit her. Her stomach churned and a large knot formed in her throat. The woman she believed was her birth mother was standing beside the casket of the woman who'd quite possibly stolen her baby.

She didn't realize she was crushing his hand until Luther yelped. She turned to him and apologized before squeezing it again. "This is so right, and so wrong, all at the same time." She said to him through gritted teeth. "What should I do?"

He looked at her with pity and shrugged his shoulders.

Bob took her other hand and pulled her slightly toward him and whispered in her ear. "That's her isn't it? Oh my god Aimee, she looks so much like you. What's she doing here?" Without waiting for a response, he continued. "Is that the guy you're hung up on? Is that Mark?"

Aimee could feel herself blush as she watched the men flanking her on either side, sizing up the new arrivals. All the whispering captured Joan's attention and she turned to glare at them.

Aimee felt like there was a tennis ball wedged in her throat. She grasped both of their hands and squeezed before whispering, "Don't say anything. Please don't let Joan know who they really are, not before I figure out how to handle this."

Both men nodded their heads reassuringly. She caught Mark's eye as the pastor began to speak, and she tried to show her gratitude for his presence without speaking.

She leaned against Luther for support as the pastor introduced Joan and invited her to speak. Standing there in a short, tight, sleeveless, black dress, she looked like she was heading out to a nightclub instead of a funeral. She turned and stared longingly at the large picture of her mother, and began to sob.

The small group waited patiently for her to continue. She wiped her eyes and mouthed the appropriate "Thank you" and "I'm so sorry" as she looked shyly at the tops of her shoes. She cleared her throat and began.

"We all knew this day would come, but for me, it's still much too soon." She paused, and covered her heart with her hand. "Linda Marie Morrison was a wonderful mother, and my best friend." She turned and locked eyes with her sister. "She was giving, even to those who didn't deserve it, and never asked for anything in return. She wasn't always treated with fairness, but she never complained." She stroked her hand lovingly over the casket. "She's where she will always be happy. Standing next to the man she loves, looking down from heaven on all of us."

"Does anyone else feel inclined to applaud her performance?" Luther whispered.

Bob snickered, and tried to cover the sound with a cough.

Aimee glared at both of them, nudging them with her elbows.

The pastor turned his attention to Aimee and invited her to say a few words. All ability to speak escaped her. She looked over at Emily, a woman who'd been so hurt by her mother's selfishness. She glanced over her shoulder at the granite headstone marking the years the earth had been blessed with her father, and turned her gaze to Mark. She would never agree with what her mother had done, but as her heart filled with longing for the life she'd never have with him, a part of her wondered if she somewhat understood the desperation her mother had felt to hold onto the man she loved.

Aimee cleared her throat. "It's never easy to lose someone you care for." She looked over at Emily and Mark and felt her chest tighten. "Since my mother became ill, I've learned many things about her that I'd never have discovered had we not known her time was short." Her eyes welled with tears as she struggled to find the words. "I don't think anyone truly understands the impact they have on the lives of others. How they can completely alter another's life by the decisions they make. If I've learned anything from our last days together, it's the importance of honesty, selflessness, and, above all, forgiveness. She only wanted one thing in this life, and that was to be with my father forever. She has that now and can rest in peace."

The pastor said a few closing words and the mourners each stepped forward to place a single rose on the casket as it was slowly lowered into the open earth. Aimee buried her head in the crook of Bob's neck and let him comfort her.

"Beautifully worded, and those who know the truth will respect your honesty." He smiled down at her with obvious pride.

She turned when she felt a gentle hand on her shoulder. Emily smiled at her and pulled her into her arms. "I'm so sorry for your loss."

She stepped into her arms and closed her eyes, letting the comforting feeling seep into her. Stepping back from Emily, she looked up at Mark standing directly behind her. Her pulse raced when he stepped over and took her hand. No words were spoken, but his eyes told her what his words could not.

"I can't believe you're here." Her eyes darted between the two of them in awe.

"We wanted to be here for you," Emily said. "These are hard times, and I've discovered that when you're surrounded by people who care about you, it makes them a little easier." She smiled sympathetically. "We may not have known each other long, but I've already come to care for you. I wanted to see for myself you were holding up okay."

Aimee felt uplifted by her sentiment, and had to admit that having them here was comforting. But the minute she thought any further than her own needs, she knew it was wrong they were.

Aimee made the introductions between Bob, Mark, and Emily. Luther planted a kiss on each of Emily's cheeks and gently placed her hand into the crook of his arm to escort her to the cars waiting to take them back to the house.

Mark stepped in beside Aimee and softly rested his hand on her lower back as they walked across the grass.

The remainder of the day went by in a blur as well wishers came and went. By late afternoon, Aimee was glad to close the door behind the last guest. Luther had reluctantly left her to return to New York. Joan had, once again, locked herself in her bedroom, leaving Aimee with the responsibility of cleaning up. Mark and Bob were picking up discarded coffee mugs and paper plates, and Emily was wrapping leftover food and placing it in the refrigerator. It was surreal to see Emily standing in the kitchen of the home she'd grown up in. Her relief in having her there was still in constant battle with her deep rooted knowledge of how wrong it truly was. She'd be almost relieved when the results of the DNA tests came back.

"How are you doing?" Mark asked, walking up behind her.

Startled, she turned at the sound of his voice. She wasn't sure how long she'd been standing there staring into space. "I'm okay. Just a little tired. I don't know where to begin to thank you for all you've done today."

"You can take me for a walk," he said, wrapping her sweater around her shoulders and leading her to the front door. "I think we could both use some fresh air."

She smiled appreciatively at him, and silently walked into the fading sunlight. He took her hand in his and walked beside her down the long driveway. They didn't speak. He left her to her own thoughts, and she was grateful he somehow knew that was exactly what she needed.

She fought the sadness that cropped up knowing this time with him was only temporary. Even as she told herself to enjoy the time she had, she wanted more.

He stopped at the end of the driveway and bending over, picked a white lily that grew wild along the side of the road. He handed it to her, studied her face, saying nothing. Unsure of what to make of the gesture, or the look in his eyes, she could only gaze back at him. He reached up his hand and gently brushed his thumb across her cheek. Her head bent to the side, drawing her closer to his palm until her cheek was cradled there. He stepped closer, and moving his hand slowly to the back of her neck, he pulled her in and lightly brushed his lips across hers.

The world began to spin as his body moved in closer, pulling her tightly against his chest as his lips applied more pressure. His teeth softly raked her bottom lip as a soft moan escaped them. She wrapped her arms around his neck and gently ran her tongue along his lower lip. He deepened their kiss, both of them breathless but refusing to pull back for air.

A passing car broke through the quiet, startling them both as they leapt back and turned toward the sound.

"I totally forgot the attorney was coming today to read the will." She looked up at him, wanting to crawl back into his arms.

He stood there for a moment, saying nothing, and she wished she could read his thoughts. The clouds lifted from his eyes when he finally spoke. "Emily and I are staying at the Ritz-Carlton tonight and flying out tomorrow. Will you be alright?"

She nodded her head. She didn't want him to go, but she knew she couldn't ask him to stay.

"Come on, I'll take you back."

They turned and headed back to the house. She lifted the lily to her nose and drew in its light scent. She buried her smile into its soft petals when he gently took her hand in his once again.

Chapter 34

After everyone left, Joan emerged from her room and sat quietly next to her sister at the kitchen table. Louie Smith sat across from them and opened the file in front of him. He perched his glasses on his nose and looked down. He looked up again, a terrible sadness filling his eyes as he focused on Aimee. Louie had been their family's attorney for as long as she could remember. Her mother had sat in the same spot when he'd read her father's will.

Assuming he was saddened by their mother's death, both girls encouraged him to continue, affirming they were ready.

With one last pained look at Aimee, he looked down and read one sentence. "I, Linda Marie Morrison, being of sound mind and body, leave all of my worldly goods to my daughter, Joan Marie Morrison."

The room was silent. The ticking of the old grandfather clock in the hallway sounded like the banging of a drum. Aimee looked over at Joan. She looked triumphant, her shoulders erect with pride. Aimee felt as if she'd been slapped when Joan actually uttered, "Ha!"

Louie was scowling at Joan, his disapproval clear. He turned to Aimee, his tone conveyed his concern. "Aimee, your mother left me a very desperate sounding message that she wished to change her will. She passed before I was able to meet with her, but I believe she was adding you as a beneficiary. If you choose to challenge this, I will testify to my belief as well as to the call I received from her."

She reached over and placed her hand over his. She smiled at him reassuringly. "Thank you, but that won't be necessary. I have no plans to contest the will."

Joan glared at him. "She wouldn't win in court and she knows it. She shouldn't get anything. She doesn't deserve it. They weren't her parents and she has no appreciation for the years they cared for her anyway."

Aimee could feel her calm slip. The room seemed to heat up, her teeth clenched, and her heart felt like it had stopped beating. She stood, feeling like she was moving in slow motion. Resembling a sound through a tunnel, she could hear Joan still speaking, her long red fingernail pointed at her, her eyes filled with hate. Joan rose from her chair, and stepped closer to her, her words coming through like a radio in need of tuning.

". . . never wanted you."

Aimee stepped back.

". . . just a burden."

Aimee pulled back her hand and slapped her sister with all the pain and anger she'd buried inside. Her hand stung, yet ached to strike again. She clenched her teeth, fighting for control. She inhaled deeply, her eyes locked with Joan's. Her sister's eyes were wide with shock, her hand impulsively covering her now reddened cheek.

Joan lifted her hand. Aimee reached out and grabbed her wrist, her eyes narrowed with warning. As she let go, Joan slowly lowered her hand.

"Don't speak to me again about things you know nothing about." Aimee spoke slow and precise. "I won't contest the will. I have no doubt that mother left you everything because she knew you were incapable of taking care of yourself." She could feel her anger subsiding, and in its place, an odd sense of freedom. "You are the type of woman who has no pride, or self-respect. You have a sense of entitlement that is unrealistic, but you're not intelligent enough to see you suffer from it. You're mean spirited and selfish, yet you wonder why you can't find someone to love you once they really get to know you. I pity you, Joan."

Joan stood there, her mouth agape, her arms limp against her sides. Aimee stepped around the table to an equally surprised Louie.

She held out her hand to shake his. "Thank you for everything. I will make sure your office has the information it needs to reach me if necessary."

He shook her hand before pulling her into his arms for a friendly embrace. "I've known you since you were as tall as my knees. I don't know what's gotten into you, but I have to say, I like it." He looked at her intently. "Be happy, Aimee."

She smiled, kissed his cheek, and walked purposefully from the kitchen and up the stairs. Walking into the room she'd slept in for most of her life, she pulled her suitcase from under the bed and began to pack. She took the teddy bear from her father off the shelf and placed him in the suitcase next to her framed college diploma. She focused on the task, attempting to avoid any remorse for the memories that were surrounding her.

She walked across the hall and into the bathroom she'd shared with her sister. She scooped the bottles into her arms and walked back out, turning off the light. She paused in the hallway and looked at the photographs hanging in wooden frames on the wall. The memories flooded back, another life, another time, someone else's life.

She closed the lid to her suitcase and reached for her purse. Looking up, she noticed Joan standing in the doorway, watching her smugly.

"I can understand you're angry, and because of that I'll forgive you for the hateful things you said about me, and about my mother. Now that everything belongs to me, I'm giving you my permission to take a token or two if you want."

Aimee didn't respond. She brushed past her, stopping again in the hallway. She looked around for the last time, her eyes lingering on the closed door of her parents' room. She set her suitcase down and walked over to open the door, her sister directly on her heels.

She walked straight to the dresser and picked up the silver framed photograph of her father on the beach. She walked over to the bookshelf on the opposite side of the room and slid out the photo album containing all of her baby pictures. Tucking the items under her arm, she walked out, and picked up her suitcase.

She turned around and faced her sister, knowing there was nothing left for her here. "Goodbye, Joan."

She walked down the stairs and out the front door for the last time.

Chapter 35

Mark took a sip of his drink and kicked his feet up on the ottoman in front of him. He was glad he'd come, glad he'd been able to be here for her when she needed him. But now, seeing her as a daughter, a friend, outside the position of assistant, or neighbor, he felt even more drawn to her. He couldn't get her out of his mind, and he knew he was in for another sleepless night.

The hotel phone rang. Startled, he jumped, spilling part of his drink down the front of his shirt. Cursing, he set his drink down, and discarded his shirt before picking up the phone.

"Yes, hello," he snapped in irritation.

"We're sorry to bother you Mr. Lee, but there is an Aimee Morrison at the front desk wishing to see you."

He sucked in a breath and shook his head as if to clear it. He glanced over at his glass, trying to determine how much he'd actually drank.

"Aimee Morrison is here? In the lobby?" he stuttered.

"Yes sir."

"I'll be right down."

He hung up the receiver and threw a clean shirt over his head. He wondered what she was doing here. He certainly hadn't expected to hear from her again tonight. His palms felt sweaty as he walked over to the mirror above the dresser. He ran his hands through his hair, and straightened his t-shirt. He was acting like a silly teenager at the simple mention of her name. "Get it together. She's only a girl, and a complication you don't need," he told his reflection.

Grabbing his room key, he headed to the elevator and down to the main floor. The minute the door opened, he saw her. The weight of the day showed on her face. She looked sad, lost. She was holding onto the handle of her suitcase, nervously tapping the toe of her shoe. He could feel the butterflies kick up in his stomach, as he walked toward her.

Spotting him, she froze, looked down at the floor and then turned to him. "I'm sorry, Mark. I'm not sure exactly why I'm here. I wanted to go back with you and Emily to San Francisco tomorrow." She swallowed, hung her head, and resumed staring at the floor. He could see she was trying not to cry. "I probably should have just called to find out what time you were leaving, but I needed to get out of that house." She looked up at him again, unshed tears pooling in her eyes. "I . . . I don't want to be alone tonight."

He reached over and grabbed the handle to her suitcase with one hand, and wrapped his other arm around her shoulders. Without saying a word he pushed the button for the elevator.

The metal doors slid open on floor eight. Neither uttered a word as they walked the long hallway to his room, or when he slipped his card into the lock. He held the door for her to enter, watching her face intently.

When she smiled at him, he felt the earth shift. Her heart was in her eyes, and he was certain in that moment, her heart belonged to him. He tried to identify the feelings coursing through him at the realization. Fear, hope, and uncertainty, those three were clear. But there was another feeling that was harder to understand, almost impossible to put into words. He caught a glimpse of his own reflection in the mirror behind her. His eyes replicated hers. It was only then he understood what these new feelings truly were. He was in love with her.

He fought the urge to run from the room as she stood in front of him, watching him curiously.

"Mark, are you all right?" she asked, reaching out to touch him.

He nodded his head, unwilling to test his ability to speak. This was nothing he'd ever experienced, and nothing he wanted. He knew the pain loving someone brought. So why did he feel the need to pull her closer when he should want to push her away?

He could sense her uncertainty as she stood silently before him. His need for her was growing with each minute that passed. Stepping forward, he slid her purse strap from her shoulder and set it on the chair beside him.

Never taking his eyes from hers, he ran his fingers through her hair and pulled her closer. When her eyes fluttered closed he lowered his mouth to hers. Forgetting his fears and giving into his longing, he kissed her with everything he felt. She moaned beneath his kiss, causing the beating of his heart to increase its pace. Her arms came around him, pulling him in, closing the final inch that separated them.

Her mouth grew more insistent, her tongue exploring his. His fingers locked onto the zipper of her dress and he slowly lowered it, letting his fingers run down the length of her back as each inch was exposed. She lifted the edge of his shirt, her hands gently stroking his bare back.

Tearing his mouth from hers, he stepped back. Her eyes were still closed. Reaching over, he turned off the overhead light, leaving only the soft light from the lamp next to the bed to illuminate them.

Her eyes fluttered open, watching him, her desire evident. He reached over and slid her dress from her shoulders. It fell effortlessly to the floor. His breath caught as he took in the vision of her in only black lace and high heels.

She slipped out of her shoes and stepping forward, reached over to slip his shirt over his head, running her lips over the contours of his chest. She traced his pecks with her tongue, and nibbled gently on his nipples. Her hands roamed freely, softly caressing his back, his sides, and running slowly along the waistband of his slacks.

His control slipping, he grasped her hands in his and stepped back enough to stop the sweet torment her hands were bringing his body.

"I want to see you. All of you," he said breathlessly.

Her eyes locked on his and the corners of her mouth curled up in a seductive smile. She reached behind her and he instinctively reached over to stop her. He shook his head. She stood still as a statue, her breath coming out in little wisps as he laid one hand on her shoulder and slowly circled around her.

Standing behind her, he ran his hands softly from her shoulders, stroking the length of her back. He ran his hands up again, unclasping her bra. He ran his fingers under the straps, over her shoulders and down the length of her arms, pulling it from her. He let if fall to the floor. Stepping closer, he rested his chest against her back and ran his hands slowly along the curve of her hips, over her stomach, and along the sides of her breasts.

He felt her breath catch and lowered his head to nibble the side of her neck. His hands roamed down again, and her head rolled back exposing more of her neck to his kiss. Slowly, he ran his hands back up and cupped her breasts. He rolled her nipples gently between his thumb and forefinger. She moaned.

He slid his hands down her stomach, around to her sides and slid his thumbs into the waistband of her lace panties, slowly lowering them over her hips. She shook her hips to help him, sending shocks of electricity through his body.

He turned her quickly to him and molded his body against hers, covering her mouth possessively with his. She returned his kiss with force, her own need in every soft moan. She lowered her hands, clumsily working the fasteners on his pants as her need for him grew more evident. As the last barrier between them fell, he crushed her against him.

Lifting her from the ground, he laid her across the bed, never taking his lips from hers. Her body arched, demanded. He ran his hands over every golden inch of her, drowning in the sensation as her body quivered beneath his touch.

His heart pounded like a jackhammer as she slid out from beneath him, rolled him onto his back, and straddled his hips. Her mouth kissed him everywhere, her breasts brushing gently against his chest as she moved over him. Unable to bear the exquisite pain a moment longer, he wrapped his arms tightly around her, and rolled her back onto the bed. Looking down at her, her blonde curls fanned out across the bedspread, her cheeks flushed with pleasure, he knew she was the most beautiful woman he'd ever seen.

She reached up her arms to him, her eyes begging him for more. He grasped her hips as she rose to meet him. She buried her hands in his hair and pulled his lips to hers as she met his hips, thrust for thrust. He heard her sharp intake of breath before he felt her body tense and explode. She shuddered beneath him, snapping the last of his control. He closed his eyes, exhaled, and followed her over the edge.

Chapter 36

Aimee had never before been in a private jet and for the first time in her life she found herself more interested in the view inside the plane then out the window. She felt like a little girl on her first trip to Disneyland as she kicked her feet onto the reclining portion of the plush chair she sat in and drank champagne from a crystal flute.

It was apparent that Emily and Mark had flown this way a thousand times and she felt anxious to share her experience with someone who would understand how much control it was actually taking her not to run down the long stretch of thick carpet between the cockpit and the rear of the plane. She wished Luther were here.

"Aimee, are you all right?" Mark asked, looking at her peculiarly.

"Yes, I'm better than all right," she replied, unable to mask her excitement.

She shrieked and ran her hands down the arms of her seat. "How can you remain so still and unaffected while riding on this beautiful plane?"

Mark laughed at her.

Emily turned her attention from the paperwork she was reviewing. "You're right, Aimee. How sad that after all these years I've forgotten the exhilaration of floating over the clouds and sipping champagne."

She smiled, signaled for a glass of champagne from the stewardess, and tucked her paperwork into her briefcase.

The next few hours went by in a whirl of clouds, girlish laughter and empty champagne bottles.

They arrived at the house late in the afternoon. Mimsey threw open the door the moment they'd reached the porch. She placed her hands on Aimee's shoulders and looked sympathetically into her eyes. She shook her head and pulled her into a warm hug.

"I'm so sorry for your loss. How are you holding up?" she asked, rubbing her back.

With a final squeeze Aimee pulled back. "I'm fine, thank you, Mimsey. It's been a long week, and I'll be glad to get back to work."

"You work too hard. You need some time to recover from a loss like you've had." Mimsey clucked her tongue.

"I like to work, it keeps my mind occupied. Besides, the auction is right around the corner and there is still so much to do."

Mimsey batted the air with her hand in dismissal. "Speaking of the auction, you had two deliveries this week. I put them both in your cottage. One is from New York." She winked at her. "The other is from Peter."

The room grew silent. Mark's expression was unreadable, but Aimee noticed the color rising on his cheeks. The unreasonable, childish, side of her prayed that his reaction was caused by the mention of Peter. A little jealousy wouldn't hurt him a bit.

"Oh, and Mark, a man dropped off an envelope for you as well," Mimsey added. "All three of you go get unpacked and cleaned up for dinner. You've got about ninety minutes. I've outdone myself, so don't be late."

Like obedient children, the three of them scurried to grab their suitcases and headed to their respective quarters.

Mark was silent as they walked across the yard. He'd insisted on carrying her bags but was walking steps ahead of her. At this point, she'd have to jog to catch him.

He waited patiently on her small porch for her to unlock the door. She swung the door open and walked inside. Mark stepped in behind her and set her bags down. On the table inside the door was a large box and sitting next to it was a beautiful arrangement of flowers spilling out of an etched crystal vase. She bent over the table to inhale their sweet scent. She plucked the card from amidst the blossoms and opened the envelope. Peter had sent his condolences and asked if she'd be willing to join him for dinner after she'd settled back in.

She set the note down on the table and reached over to open the box. Mark walked into the kitchen and peered into the refrigerator.

"Can I get you something to drink?" he asked with his back to her as he reached in for a bottle of juice.

"No, thank you."

Walking out of the kitchen, he leaned a hip against the counter, crossed his ankles, and took a large swig. "So, I take it the flowers are from Peter."

Aimee didn't look up. Still fumbling with the tape on the box, she mumbled an "ah-huh" as nonchalantly as possible.

Mark didn't say anything else, but his grunt spoke volumes. She struggled to mask her pleasure in discovering he was jealous.

She worked the tape loose on the box and squealed with glee as she pulled out the contents. The handbag she'd designed for the auction was everything she'd imagined. The fabric was a deep blue with an intricate silver chain for the handle. Colored jewels covered the clutch, shimmering in the light, and the clasp was a single diamond like stone.

"Have you been catalog shopping?"

She turned to him, and placed her hand on her hip. "No, I haven't been catalog shopping. This is an original, one of a kind, Amore' Handbag, designed especially for the Preston Talbot Foundation auction."

"It looks like a purse."

She glared at him, trying to keep in mind that he didn't know it was her creation he was insulting. "It's a work of art, and should bring in a nice sized donation for the foundation."

"Really?" he reached over and snatched it from her hand for a closer inspection.

"Don't sound so surprised." She pried open his fingers and gently lifted it from his hand. "Be careful with that."

He looked at her curiously. "You sure seem all worked up over a purse."

She growled at him. "Wait until you see Emily's face when she sees this. You are obviously a man with little taste for excellence." She wrapped the handbag back in the tissue it was packaged in and set it tenderly back into the box. "I'm going to unpack and shower. I, for one, have no intentions on being late to dinner. Mimsey scares me a little."

He laughed and grabbed her suitcase from the entry and walked across the room to lay it on her bed.

She walked in behind him. "That was very chivalrous of you."

He crossed his arm in front of his waist and took an exaggerated bow. "At your service, madam."

He straightened and stepped to her. His eyes appeared unsure, so taking it upon herself, she stood up on her tiptoes and kissed him tenderly.

"You are definitely welcome." His eyes twinkled with mischief. "We could be late for dinner, you know. I could make it worth your sacrifice."

She stepped back, standing just out of his reach and placed her hands on her hips. "I don't know what kind of you girl you think I am, Marcus Lee." She mimicked a southern belle accent. "But I will only allow your hands to roam freely over my body after said body has been properly nourished. Go and unpack before Mimsey tans us both."

He shook his head and headed out of the room while she pretended to busy herself with unpacking. Stepping closer to the wall, she used the mirror to watch him leave. Just as she suspected, he stopped, looked over his shoulder, and lifted the note from Peter, before placing it back on the table exactly where she'd left it.

*

Mark walked into his cottage and set his bag down. The emotion he was feeling was a new one, and he didn't think he liked it. His stomach churned, and not from hunger. He paced the floor, recalling Peter's hand on Aimee's back as she climbed into his girly, little Jaguar. Her head tilted back in laughter at something he'd said, and the memory of Peter's armed wrapped around her in an embrace. Even knowing it had been merely a friendly goodbye didn't ease the anger raging inside him.

He had no right to feel this way. They'd slept together, not declared their undying love for each other with a vow of exclusivity. So why did he feel she belonged to him in some way? He cursed aloud his frustration. Mark knew she felt something for him. He'd seen it in her eyes when she'd come to him last night. He'd felt it in the way she kissed him. He hadn't imagined that. But would she go to dinner with Peter?

He needed a beer, not the juice he'd gulped down earlier to keep his hands busy. Hell, he needed something stronger than a beer. His hands itched to rip Peter's card to shreds and throw the flowers into the trash. Walking into his kitchen, he saw the large envelope lying on the table.

He stared blindly at the latest reminder of why he had no right to ask Aimee to stay away from Peter. He lifted the envelope. The weight of it was heavy, but he knew it was more than the number of pages it held. It was the representation of his inability to trust. How could he say, even to himself, that he'd fallen in love with Aimee, and hold an investigators report in his hands?

A war was raging inside him as his heart battled his head. He told himself he could read it, if only to confirm that she wasn't hiding anything from him, and never question her again. He knew the simple act of requesting the report, of needing that proof, already posed a problem. His heart knew that breaking the seal would be a complete act of betrayal.

His decision made, he stood up and walked purposely to his

desk in the corner, yanked open the bottom drawer and dropped the envelope inside.

Chapter 37

"Mark's in love," McKenzie sat down in the open chair beside Emily. "I'd about given up hope that would ever happen."

"I noticed it, too." Emily kicked off her shoes and pulled her legs beneath her. The rose garden was quickly becoming her favorite after dinner hangout.

"His smile reached his eyes, and the way Aimee returned his smile leads me to believe she returns his affections."

"I was beginning to believe he'd never find her." Emily sipped from her tea. "It seemed unlikely when he hardly dated, and the ones he did date were brainless."

"I think he did that on purpose. As a way to protect himself from meeting someone he could find himself caring for." McKenzie turned to her friend, her head tilted to the side, worry lines etched in her forehead. "Emily, this girl, is she one of the good ones? No games? No hidden agenda? No tattooed boyfriends waiting in the wings for her to cash out and bail?"

"You really need to watch less cable." Emily shook her head. Her expression grew serious and she placed her hand over her friend's in reassurance. "I think she is one of the good ones. I've been fooled before, so maybe you shouldn't trust my gut instincts as much as your own, or as much as Mark's, but I'm drawn to her. I don't know how to explain it." She stood up and lit the candles around them. McKenzie sat quietly, waiting for her to continue. "Simply being in her presence makes me happy. That sounds so strange when I say it out loud, but there is something about her. I feel like I've known her forever."

"She certainly seems to have had an undeniable impact." McKenzie seemed to search for her words. "Something has changed around here. The entire house feels transformed. It's brighter, happier, and almost more peaceful." McKenzie turned to Emily. "You're different, too. I can't explain it, but you are."

Emily smiled. "This year seems a little easier than last, and the year before that. Maybe I'm getting better at handling things in my old age."

McKenzie didn't laugh. Instead, her eyes welled with tears and her voice faltered. "You're always so haunted at this time of year. It's like you're reminded of the life you should have lived, as you talk with the ghosts of the people you should be surrounded by."

Emily reached over and placed her hand on her friend's. "It's not quite that bad. Not anymore. I won't lie and say this time of the year isn't hard for me, because it is, but I'm living a great life. I'm happy."

They both turned their heads toward the sound of laughter that penetrated the air. The bits of dialogue they were able to decipher told them Mark was in the process of threatening to throw Aimee into the pool. Apparently in her favorite Jimmy Choo heels. That would be cause for retaliation in ways that no one could fathom.

"She reminds me a lot of you when you were younger," McKenzie said.

"I'm not the only one around here that would kill over her favorite pair of Jimmy Choos." Emily tilted her head back and laughed at her own joke.

"It's more than that. It's something in her mannerisms. The way she processes things before she speaks, the way she blushes so easily. Like you, she doesn't complain, or show weakness. I mean, she just lost her mother, and she's completely focused on the auction. I think it's less a strong work ethic, and more an escape. Again, a lot like you." McKenzie grew silent for a moment, then continued. "There is something so familiar about her. I feel like I've known her forever and it's only been a couple days. I just have a feeling, one I can't identify."

Emily looked at her curiously.

McKenzie smiled and the seriousness in her eyes only a moment ago dissipated. "Her love for accessories is admirable, but not exactly what I meant."

"Mimsey told me the same thing the other day, although I think she was only trying to flatter me," Emily said. "She said she thought Mark had finally found the girl he couldn't resist because she was so much like me." She smiled. "The flattery worked. I gave her a raise at lunch."

They both laughed.

McKenzie tipped her head in the direction of the pool as the sound of a loud scream followed by a large splash, shattered the silence of the night. "Now we have to pray that she has your patience and strength. She's going to need it with Mark."

Chapter 38

Aimee awoke curled up next to Mark. The early morning sun streamed in through the partially open curtains, painting his face in muted gold tones as he slept. She slipped quietly from the bed to avoid waking him.

Her dress lay in a puddle on the floor, in the exact place it'd landed when Mark undressed her after her fully clothed dip in the pool. Not really a dip. More a plunge taken against her will. She was grateful he'd valued his life enough to take off her favorite shoes before he threw her in.

She'd just pulled his discarded t-shirt over her head when his phone rang. She impulsively reached over to answer it. She pulled her hand back quickly when her mind finally caught up with her reaction. She wasn't sure if that was something he'd approve of, or that she had a right to do.

Mark ran his hands over his face, and smiled at her. "I like the way you look in my shirt. You should wear it more often." He grinned mischievously. "On second thought, I prefer you without it."

She could feel the heat rise on her cheeks as his eyes seemed to look through the thin cotton. He didn't take his eyes from her as he reached to pick up the phone with a mumbled hello.

His brow furrowed, and he sat up stiffly in bed.

"When? How bad is he? Yeah . . . okay . . . I'll try . . . thank you."

By his grim expression, the news being relayed to him wasn't good. She sat on the edge of the bed and reached out to take his hand. He hung up the phone and leaned back against the headboard. He didn't speak, and she didn't push him. He clenched his jaw, raked his hand through his hair, and sighed.

"Are you okay?"

He shook his head.

"What happened?"

He reached up and stroked his forehead like he was trying to ward off a headache. "It's the donor. That was the hospital. He had another heart attack."

It took her a minute to understand his chopped statements. His father was in the hospital. And they called him. It must be serious.

Unsure what to say, she squeezed his hand. He looked up at her. His eyes flashed with anger, then with sadness. "Why did they call me? Do they expect me to go racing over there?"

"Is that what you think you should do?"

"Hell no!" Throwing back the covers, he shot out of bed. Rummaging through the heap of discarded clothing, he roughly shoved his legs into a pair of jeans. "The man has been absent my entire life. He destroyed my mother, and abandoned us both." He raised his voice, and began to pace. "He comes walking back into my life almost thirty years later, with a lame ass apology, and now I'm supposed to take up the role of the dutiful son who sits beside his hospital bed?"

"Maybe there was nobody else to call."

"Maybe he should've thought of that before he made the decision to be the world's largest prick."

Mark was picking up speed as he paced back and forth. She wanted to tell him the importance of forgiving his father. Not for his father's sake, but for his own. She wanted to hold him, and stroke his brow, and erase all the ghosts from his past.

She knew better than anyone that he would never understand the decisions his father made. He couldn't. But, as she'd come to learn more about him, she also knew he wouldn't be able to live with himself if his father died and he'd denied him forgiveness.

"You don't have to sit dutifully beside his bed, but maybe you could stop by and check on him," she said carefully.

His cheeks grew red. The veins on the side of his neck pulsated.

"Are you serious? You really believe I should rush off to the hospital? I don't remember seeing him at the hospital when my appendix ruptured or when they took out my tonsils. Why should I, because nobody else will?"

"Because even if he doesn't deserve to be, he's still your father." She rose from the bed and faced him. "And you may not get another chance to do the right thing where he's concerned."

"I did the right thing. I let him walk out of this house with all of his limbs intact, when he had the audacity to show his face here. I even let him have his say. It was more than he deserved, that's for damn sure."

He stormed from the bedroom. She could hear the sounds of mugs banging against the counter, beans grinding, water running, and cupboards slamming.

Giving him a few minutes to calm down, she busied herself with wrapping her wet clothes in a towel, running a comb through her hair, and using her finger as a toothbrush.

She didn't know what the right words were, but she knew she loved him enough to try and find them.

Walking up behind him, still wearing his t-shirt, she wrapped her arms around his waist and kissed his back. She could feel the tension in his body as she ran her hands along his hard chest.

He turned around when she stepped back, and handed her a steaming mug of coffee. Thanking him, she blew on it, and took a small sip.

She looked up when she felt him watching her. His eyes were stormy, a vision of the battle raging inside him. She stood on her tiptoes and gently kissed his lips.

"I have something I need to say, and then I promise I will stay out of this." She scooted up onto the counter, letting her legs dangle and took another sip of her coffee. "We think parents should be a certain way. Unconditional love for their child shouldn't be something they work at, but something that simply is. For some parents, it's impossible to grasp that such a level exists, therefore, it's not even something they work at."

She looked at him, trying to gauge if he was still listening. He tipped his head to the side and looked at her from beneath the hair that hung over his eyes. For a moment, she saw a glimpse of the hurt little boy trapped inside of him.

"In the saddest of cases, a child is something that just is. It's someone that, at some point in their lives, they take out and dust off, like a book on a shelf. They cling to hope that the past can be forgotten, never fully realizing that their neglect of that child is now deeply imbedded under emotional scars. They apologize for the wrong things said or done, and expect that it'll only be a matter of time before things are the way they want them to be and their conscious is cleared."

He glared.

"I didn't say it was right." She leaned back dramatically, like he was going to slap her if she stayed in reach.

"This is more than my daddy didn't love me enough." He paused as if searching for the words. "He was a con man. He used my mother for her money. Hell, he used me for her money. He cashed us in like chips in a casino. He never looked back."

She looked away from him, her eyes brimming with unshed tears. She wanted desperately to tell him the truth, to purge herself of this heavy secret. "I understand more than you know, how hard it is for you to forgive your father."

"How could you?" He walked over to the sink and poured out his remaining coffee. He leaned against it and stared out the window. "I didn't even know how hard it would be. It was never an option."

"And now?" she asked.

"I don't think I can."

Sliding off the counter, she stepped in front of him and caressed his cheek. "I hope you're wrong."

Chapter 39

In the empty ballroom of the Civic Center, Aimee sat at a large round table, staring blindly at the floor plan for the auction, trying to work out the seating chart. She couldn't concentrate. Even with the awe-inspiring list of attendees, she hadn't written one name down. She was already a week behind, and she still had to make changes in the floral order, get the final head count to the caterer, and confirm the linen order. The main room wasn't set up, and the silent auction items couldn't be delivered until the showing room was set.

Her mind kept spinning back to the look in Mark's eyes this morning. The internal battle he fought between old anger and necessary forgiveness.

Before she'd left for the center, she'd watched his car drive out the gates. She hadn't been able to see who was behind the wheel from the window of her office, but she knew it was him simply by the car. She'd heard it before she'd seen it, the powerful purr of a classic American muscle car. The black and chrome 1969 Mustang, with white stripes running up the hood and down the trunk was in pristine condition, and all Mark.

She could see herself riding beside him, winding along the coast, the wind whipping through the windows, the stereo blaring, and his arm wrapped over her shoulder.

She didn't know where he was headed this morning, but she hoped it was to the hospital. She wondered what he'd say if he saw his father. She knew how hard it would be for him, the forgiveness, the possibility of having to say goodbye. Picturing her final days with her own mother, and understanding the torment he must be feeling, she wished she were with him. More than that, she wished he would have wanted her with him.

The weight of a hand on her shoulder startled her. She jumped in surprise. She whipped around to find Peter standing behind her. His eyes were filled with sympathy as he silently watched her.

"I didn't hear you come in."

"You were off in another world." He squeezed her shoulder. "I was so sorry to hear about your mother. Are you doing okay?" He sat in the empty chair beside her.

"I'm fine, thank you. It helps that it wasn't sudden. You have some time to mentally prepare yourself, or at least as much as possible." She nervously tapped her pen against the table. "Thank you for the beautiful flowers. You didn't have to do that."

"I wanted to. I wanted you to know I was thinking about you." He took her hand in his. "Did you get my card?"

Looking away from him and down at the table, she nodded her head.

"The timing may have been selfish on my part, but I can't stop thinking about you." He placed his finger underneath her chin, forcing her to look up at him. "I mean it, Aimee. You're taking over my thoughts constantly. Will you have dinner with me?"

"I can't . . ." her voice cracked. "I . . ." She had no idea what to say.

"Are you seeing someone?"

She looked up into his handsome face. He watched her intently, almost as if he were holding in his breath.

Nodding, she replied, "I am."

His brow creased and his voice became agitated. "It's Mark, isn't it?"

Surprised by his reaction, she hesitated before responding. "Yes, it's recent, but I am seeing Mark." She watched his face, wondering why he appeared angry.

He inhaled deeply and let his breath out slowly, his lips in an exaggerated pucker. When he looked at her, his eyes were now filled with sadness. "You are aware that you're going to get hurt, aren't you?"

She was beginning to feel like she was being scolded. "What makes you say that?" she asked defensively.

"Mark is a nice enough guy, don't get me wrong, but . . ." He looked up at the ceiling, like he was searching for the right words.

"But what?" she snapped.

"Maybe I've overstepped. If so, I'm sorry. I just don't want to see you get hurt."

"How can you be so sure I'm going to get hurt?" Her stomach churned, and her palms grew sweaty. She knew he was right, she would get hurt. It was inevitable they both would.

"Mark isn't a one woman guy. From what I've witnessed, no girl has gotten past date three. You don't seem to be the three date maximum type."

She stood up and gathered her paperwork from the table.

"I offended you. I'm sorry." He stood as well.

"No, you didn't offend me." She decided to leave out the fact that he'd hit a nerve. "Peter . . ." She placed the guest list inside her briefcase and turned to face him. "You're a wonderful man. Under different circumstances . . ." she trailed off, wondering if she truly meant what she was about to say. Where her heart was now, she couldn't imagine anyone else or any different circumstances.

He smiled reassuringly. "As hard as this is for me to say, I care enough about you to hope you're the one to break the cycle. I hope you get whatever it is you want with Mark, and that he appreciates how lucky he is."

He pulled her chair out and waited for her to sit back down. Pulling the paperwork back out of her briefcase, she smiled thankfully at him.

"Catch me up, and let's make this auction a money making success."

After spending three hours going over the final details with Peter, Aimee pulled into the Nathan Talbot Hospice House and parked her car.

She was surprised how homey the building looked for one so large. There were brick paths wrapping around the sides of the building leading to cozy seating areas spaced throughout the gardens. There were fountains and bird feeders, and everywhere you looked, brightly colored flowers blended with vibrant green bushes and trees. Somehow she knew Mark had done the landscaping.

She walked into the bright reception area expecting to see something resembling the inside of a hospital. She didn't. Cozy chairs and small couches clustered together around wooden tables topped with green plants, inviting small conversation circles. There were stunning fish tanks, bookshelves offering the latest bestsellers, and children's books. Painted castles and pirate ships welcomed the children to come inside through small doors and let their imaginations run free.

The reception desk itself was large, but instead of the tall, white, wall-like feel of a hospital desk, it allowed the visitor to sit at a normal wooden desk, face to face with the reception nurses. It felt friendly, and open, nothing like the cold, intimidating feel of a sterile hospital.

"Can I help you?"

Aimee smiled at the friendly face behind the desk. "I'm looking for Emily Sinclair. She asked me to drop off some papers to her."

"You must be Aimee." The friendly young redheaded girl smiled, exposing a mouth full of braces. "She asked me to bring you back when you arrived. Follow me."

Aimee followed obediently behind the young girl. It wasn't until she'd entered the hallway that it became clear this was still a medical facility. But even with the machines, the nurses, and the medical charts, it felt homey and comfortable. It was apparent how much love Emily had put into its design.

"She's right in here. She's expecting you."

Aimee opened the door, thanked the girl again and stepped inside. Emily was seated next to a hospital bed talking with a pale young woman. Her head was covered in a bright red scarf and her arms were wrapped around a sleeping baby. Another young woman with a pixie face and a contagious laugh sat beside her, and the nurse, a pretty red head, stood across from them. The four of them were laughing at something one of the women said. They hadn't spotted her, and not wanting to interrupt, she stood back.

Looking around the room she was again amazed by the little details. The room was a cheery yellow and the bed sat at an angle allowing the occupant a clear view of the gardens through the window. White wicker chairs with yellow and lavender throw pillows sat beside the bed. Instead of thin hospital blankets, the bed was covered in a colorful lavender quilt, and the television wasn't mounted to the wall but settled inside a white oak armoire.

The petite brunette was talking about her brother. It seemed he was a "tall and dashing police officer" who didn't date much and she was telling Emily she should take him out.

"He's young enough to be my son." Emily shook her head, a slight blush rising on her cheeks. "Lexie, I promise you that I will go out on a date, right after you do."

"Well there goes that idea, Lexie." The girl in the bed laughed and suddenly began to cough and choke.

Aimee watched as Emily gently lifted her forward and helped her sip from a water glass. The nurse walked over and made an adjustment on the IV machine, and the brunette lifted the sleeping baby from her arms and laid him into a small basinet before heading to the sink to refill a water pitcher.

She spotted Aimee. "Hi, can I help you?"

All eyes turned to her before Emily rose from the edge of the bed. "Aimee, you made it. Come on in, there are some people I'd like you to meet." Emily placed her hand on the small of her back and escorted her toward the bed. "Girls, this is Aimee, my new assistant, life preserver, and friend. Aimee, this is Maggie, our favorite guest, and my dear friend."

She held out her hand to the frail woman in the hospital bed. She was weak, and her skin was transparent, but her eyes were vibrant and full of life. Aimee liked her immediately.

Emily pointed at the petite brunette. "This is one of my favorite volunteers, Lexie Wayne. She is a lousy matchmaker, but has the Midas touch around here."

Lexie shook her hand, and leaned in closer, whispering loudly. "I'm her *very* favorite volunteer. She's mad I won't start dating so she has an excuse to go out with my devilishly handsome brother." She leaned back, and scanned Aimee up and down. "Wait a minute. I don't see a ring on your finger."

"Leave her alone, Lexie." Maggie raised the bed, pulling herself closer to the conversation. "You make Jordan sound like a charity case. He doesn't need you to set him up. Besides, judging by Aimee's choking, she's not married, but she's not single either."

Emily laughed and shook her head. "And this is Marissa. She is one of my best nurses. I don't know what we would do without her around here."

Marissa was still working the buttons on the IV machine, but looked up and smiled. "It's nice to meet you, Aimee. We've heard a lot of good things about you."

"I'm sorry to interrupt you. I was dropping off some papers for Emily. It was very nice to meet all of you."

"I'll walk you out." Emily headed for the door ahead of her.

"She seems so young," Aimee didn't realize she'd spoken aloud.

Emily nodded her head. "She is too young. She's barely twenty-four, and her son will lose his mother before he sees his first birthday." She took a deep breath. "Cancer is the worst evil. It hits where and whom it wants without any regard for age, gender, health . . . Or with any concern for the good people it takes, or for the people it leaves behind aching from the loss."

Emily stopped at the front desk, and waited for Aimee to pull out the papers that needed signing. Aimee wasn't sure what to expect when she'd walked into the hospice house, but she hadn't expected to feel pulled to step in, to help. Seeing the companionship of the women, seeing the difference they made to the patient, and the genuine joy on each of their faces, she wanted to be a part of it, to make a difference.

Emily handed her the papers and thanked her again for bringing them by. "We're always looking for volunteers," she said in that knowing way of hers.

Aimee smiled and nodded her head. It was no wonder Emily was so respected and revered. It wasn't her money or her status, it was her heart. She gave every part of her to the people who needed her most.

Aimee swallowed down the lump in her throat.

Chapter 40

The tapping of Mark's boots echoed down the quiet hallway of San Francisco General. He hesitated at the door. He took a deep breath and pushed it open. A blue drape was pulled closed around the bed. The sound of beeping machines reverberated through the room.

He'd turned to leave when the curtain suddenly slid open and a nurse shuffled out, writing something on her clipboard.

She looked up, appearing startled to find someone there. Her bright blue eyes lit up. "You must be Marcus." She held her hand out to shake his. "Your father has been asking for you."

He wasn't sure how to process the fact that his father was waiting for him. He hadn't been sure he'd come at all. He'd spent the morning driving along the coast, trying to untangle his thoughts. He kept getting stuck on the things Aimee had said to him, and when he turned his car around to go home, he knew what he had to do.

"Can I go in there?" Mark motioned at the closed curtain.

"Of course. He's sleeping now, but I think he'd be happy to wake up and see you there." She held back the curtain for him to enter before leaving the room.

Mark walked to the side of the bed. The mountain-like readings of the heart monitor continued their repetitive beeping. His father lay motionless, his hands above the covers, an IV line taped to his arm. He looked pale against the white sheets. Frailer than he'd been the last time he'd seen him and nothing like the villain he always pictured.

He struggled to identify the emotions that raced through him. Jumbled pieces of sadness, resentment, worry. He'd always held tightly to his anger. It was only now he realized it had been a shield, a way to keep him safe from the alternative. Hurt wasn't an emotion he was comfortable with.

His father shifted, his eyes drifting open. Mark could identify the moment he spotted him. His eyes grew wide with surprise, before his face settled into a soft smile.

"You came," he said in a raspy voice.

"How are you feeling?" Mark sat in the chair beside the bed.

"I'm hanging in there. I didn't think you'd come."

Mark couldn't answer him. The reasons he'd come were unclear in his mind. He replayed the words Aimee said. Was it possible that his father didn't have anyone else? The fact that the thought made him sad didn't sit well. He'd asked to be alone. He walked out on his family and never looked back.

"I'm not sure why I did."

His father was quiet for a moment. He opened his mouth to speak, and then closed it again.

"Why did you ask me to come here?" Mark finally asked, rubbing his hands down the length of his thigh.

"I needed to see you." His father watched him. "I needed to talk to you, to try and bridge the distance between us."

His anger boiled to the surface. "What would lead you to believe that's even remotely a possibility?" He stood abruptly from the chair.

"Hope."

The word was spoken so silently that it took Mark a moment to process it. Again, he thought of Aimee. She seemed to have a strong understanding of the situation. He wished she could tell him how he was supposed to deal with it.

He sighed and sat back down, lowering his face into his hands.

"Mark . . ."

He could feel his father's eyes on him. He looked up but couldn't speak.

"I know there is nothing I can ever do or say to make up for all the wrong things I've done. The fact that I hurt you and your mother, deeply, is something that I will have to live with for as much time as I have left."

He scooted up higher on the bed and cleared his throat. "Even returning the money to your mother couldn't erase the damage that was done—"

"What are you talking about?" Marks voice rose above the machines.

His father looked away, hiding his face. "I only meant I understand it wasn't about the money for either of you."

"But you made it sound like you gave the money back."

His father turned to face him, his eyes growing wide. "She never told you?"

Mark shook his head, struggling to understand why he felt like breathing a sigh of relief.

"That part doesn't matter. It was the right thing to do, but it could never undo the wrong that had already been done."

The curtain opened and the same blue eyed nurse shuffled in.

"Good, you're awake." She smiled brightly at both of them. "How are you feeling?"

Mark stood to leave.

"Please stay." His father pleaded.

He wanted to walk away, to bury himself in the familiarity of his anger. The look of fear in his father's eyes stopped him.

"I'm going to grab a cup of coffee. I'll be right back."

Mark stopped outside the door and leaned against the wall for support. He was surprised by the fact that his father had returned the money. He was stunned that his mother hadn't told him. But more than anything, he was astounded by the fact that he could physically feel small pieces of the wall around his heart falling away. He was petrified of the yearning taking its place.

He walked down the hall and into the waiting room, taking his place behind the man currently filling a coffee cup at the vending machine.

The man turned and smiled cynically. His eyes were red from crying, his face ashen from an apparent lengthy run with no sleep. "I recommend the triple caramel macchiato with extra whip cream."

Mark laughed, "Must be some vending machine."

"It's been a long night, and a longer day. I've had so much of this sludge that I've resorted to fantasizing that it tastes good."

"I only come here for the coffee. Well, that and the incredible ambiance of the place."

"You need to get out more." The man raised his paper cup in a mock salute. "I hope whoever you're visiting today gets home to you soon."

Mark nodded his head and took a swig of the bitter coffee. "You too, and be careful, this stuff alone could guarantee you a room here."

Mark headed back down the hall, and was stopped by his father's nurse and another doctor as they left his father's room.

"I'm Dr. Olep, your father's cardiac surgeon." He held out his hand to shake Mark's. "We've scheduled your father's surgery for nine o'clock tomorrow morning. I think he's strong enough, but it's still a pretty serious procedure."

Mark lowered his head in embarrassment. "What's the procedure, exactly?"

If the doctor was surprised by Mark's lack of information, he didn't let it show. "We're going to perform a triple bypass. It's fairly common, but no less serious. Our concern is the stress on his heart so soon after his last heart attack. The damage from the prior two is significant." He reached over and placed his hand on Mark's shoulder in reassurance. "We're confident this procedure will repair the damage."

Mark nodded his head and mumbled his thanks before stepping back into the room.

"You're still here," his father said, his tone one of surprise, as Mark walked through the curtain.

"I told you I would be."

"I know, but . . ."

The room grew silent, the tension crackling between them. Mark searched for something to say. He'd spent years trying to understand how his father could betray him so heartlessly. Now he had the opportunity to get answers to every question he'd ever had, and he couldn't bring himself to ask one. Was it fear of the answers? Or was it easier to hold onto the anger without them? He wondered at what point in his life he'd become comfortable with his anger and mistrust.

Not sure he was ready to evaluate himself, he asked, "Are you nervous about tomorrow?"

His father looked stunned by his question. "A little bit I guess. Don't like hospitals much." He grew silent again, but Mark could see he was about to say something. "I'm really glad you came today." He swallowed hard. "But why did you?"

Mark turned and looked out the window. He watched a cloud float gently across the face of the sun. He thought again of the words Aimee said. "Because it was the right thing to do, and even if you don't deserve to be, you're still my father."

His eyes filled with tears. "I don't deserve to be, and you deserve so much better." He turned his head away, and slowly turned it back, looking at Mark intently. "I have very little I'm proud of in this life, but you, you make my time here worth something. I wish I would have realized it then, before I messed everything up between us."

Mark didn't realize he'd been holding his breath until he went to speak and it burst from his lungs. "I don't know if I'm ready to do this now."

"Does that mean you might be ready to talk about it later?" his father asked, his voice pleading, his eyes filled with desperation.

Mark stood up and tossed his empty coffee cup into the trash can. "What time are they rolling you out of here tomorrow?"

"I think they said a little after eight." His eyes asked the question that his mouth didn't.

"I'll see you then. Get some sleep."

He didn't turn around as he left the room, but he could hear his father crying softly behind him.

Chapter 41

The following weeks went by in a blur of activity. The final arrangements for the auction were complete, and Aimee had even managed to get her handbag designs for the upcoming season mailed off to Luther in New York.

Aimee was happier than she could ever remember being. She spent every night with Mark, either at his cottage or hers, and she was enjoying every minute of their time together. He was like a new man since the night he'd returned from visiting his father. The surgery had gone better than expected and he'd spent a lot of time with his father since he'd been released from the hospital.

Her relationship with Emily had grown as well, and she knew if the results came back negative, that she'd feel a tremendous loss. When she'd started working for her, she hadn't been prepared for the emotions it would stir up. She wanted to belong to her. If she were to be honest with herself, she already felt as if she did.

Slipping her foot into the strappy silver heel, she turned to see herself in the full length mirror. The red dress clung to her body like a second skin. Her hair was pinned up, with a few scattered blonde curls falling around her face. She'd decided to forgo any jewelry, and chose instead to wear only simple diamond studs in her ears, letting the dress speak for itself.

She hadn't heard Mark come in, but she turned when he let out a soft whistle.

"You're stunning." His eyes scanned her from head to toe. "Are you sure you want to go to this thing? I can think of a few other things we could be doing."

She smiled at him, her heart racing. "And lose the opportunity to show you off? I don't think so." Wearing a simple black tuxedo, he took her breath away. "You look like you were born to stand on a red carpet."

Walking slowly toward her, his scent enveloped her, causing her mouth to water, and the look in his eyes making her knees weak.

"I prefer jeans, but putting on this monkey suit is a small price to pay to see you in that dress." He bent over and kissed her exposed neck. "Now all I want to do is get you out of it."

She moaned, closed her eyes and leaned her head back to give him better access. "You promised me a dance."

"That was before I'd seen you in this dress. I don't know how much control I'll have, holding you close to me. The room will be filled with people, I might embarrass us both. I think we should avoid any possibility of a scandal and stay in." He ran his mouth up her neck, slowly nibbling on her ear lobe.

She moaned again, and ran her hands along his shoulders, finally burying them in his thick hair. "Emily would be so mad at us," she mumbled breathlessly.

"It might be worth it." He brushed his hands over her bare shoulder.

"We're going to be late. We have to go." Goosebumps rose on her arms. "But I want you to remember exactly where you are at this moment. I expect you to pick up in this same spot after the auction."

He exhaled in frustration and laid his forehead against hers. "I don't wanna go." He pouted.

She smiled and stepped back, holding out her hand for his.

"Okay, I get it, responsibility, blah, blah." He took her hand, lacing his fingers with hers.

She laughed, grabbed her small silver bag, and headed to the main house.

The others were waiting for them in the entry when they came through the back.

"Emily, you look amazing," Aimee said, as she took in the floor length emerald gown they'd picked out together. Her hair was pulled back in a classic French twist, a thin line of perfectly square cut emeralds hung from each ear, emphasizing her long neck.

"Oh Aimee, the dress is perfect. You're a vision." She took her hands, holding them out between them to get a better look at her. "Is that the silver bell Amore' clutch? I'm so jealous. It's perfect."

Aimee felt the color drain from her cheeks. Speechless, she was again reminded of her dishonesty.

McKenzie stepped over to them. "What am I, chopped liver?" All eyes turned to her as she stood with her hands on her hips. She was draped in a deep blue gown the same color as her eyes. It wrapped behind her neck, leaving her shoulders and arms bare, and dropped to the floor in a small pool at her feet. Her dark hair hung down her back in a silky sheet, her olive skin glowed.

"I'd say you looked stunning, but that's an understatement," Aimee said honestly.

"I knew I liked you," McKenzie said with a wink.

Aimee hadn't noticed the other man seated on the chair until he rose. "We should get going. We don't want to be late."

Her breath hitched. She couldn't move. Her eyes were glued to him. It was Nathan Talbot, a few years older, but it was him. The man who could possibly be her father had stepped out of a photograph and currently stood in front of her.

She didn't notice the curious eyes on her until McKenzie reached out and laid her hand on her arm. She leaned in and whispered in her ear. "It's not a ghost. Just breathe."

McKenzie made the introductions. "Preston Talbot, this is Aimee Morrison, Emily's assistant. Aimee, this is Preston Talbot, Nathan's twin brother."

After the appropriate handshakes and nice to meet you-s, the group climbed into the awaiting limousine outside.

Aimee was surprised when McKenzie leaned in again, and whispered, "Are you okay? That must have been quite a shock."

She smiled reassuringly, and nodded her head. It was almost as if McKenzie understood the real reason she'd reacted the way she did. Aimee watched her as she chatted with the others. When McKenzie looked back at her there was no accusations in her eyes, no evidence of distrust, only a genuine smile of acceptance. Aimee dismissed her brief moment of insecurity.

Stepping out of the limo, Aimee felt transported to another world. Beautiful women in elegant gowns and successful men in black tuxedos spilled onto the sidewalk, all awaiting their turn to enter the center. She recognized famous actors and actresses, smiled at politicians she'd only seen on the news, and shook hands with grateful cancer survivors helped by the foundation. Everyone knew Emily's name, and they all stopped their conversations when she neared them, turning all of their attention to her.

She watched in awe as Emily smiled, mingled, greeted, shook hands, and still managed to keep their group moving forward through the masses.

Inside the door, Emily paused, her face lighting up with delight. She walked over and wrapped her arms around Lexie and Marissa, the women she'd met at the hospice.

"I am so glad you two came." She held each of their hands in her own. "You two are what make the foundation what it is."

"We wouldn't have missed it for the world," Lexie said. "And someone mentioned an original Amore' handbag on the auction list."

"That's true, and it's beautiful. You both remember Aimee, don't you? She's the woman responsible for getting her hands on it." Emily wrapped her arm around Aimee and gently tugged her to stand at her side.

Aimee shook their hands, "It's nice to see you again."

With final hugs, Emily and Aimee made their way into the ballroom to search for the rest of their group.

As they stepped into the main room, Aimee could barely contain her pride at the results. Round tables filled the room, each surrounded by elegant, tall backed chairs. In the center of each table sat a long, round, silver bowl, spilling over in a white combination of orchids, roses, Asiatic lilies, and mixed with different green leaves. The arrangements sat low to the table, to ensure each guest's visibility, and were surrounded by multiple candles glowing in crystal holders.

Servers walked through the crowd balancing trays topped with champagne flutes or bite-sized appetizers. The staff was directing the guests toward the silent auction room before showing them to their assigned seats. She excused herself and made her way back.

The bids were increasing steadily, the contributors seeming eager to one up each other in the bidding wars. She looked over her shoulder to see if anyone was watching her before taking a glance at the bids for her custom designed handbag. She could barely control the urge to clap her hands with glee when she saw how high the bids reached.

"I think you're a success."

"It seems to be going well." She turned and smiled at Peter. "I couldn't have done it alone these last few weeks. Thank you again for all your help."

His eyes roamed over her, his appreciation clear. "It was my pleasure. And may I say you look amazing. You take my breath away."

"Why, thank you." She glanced around the room at all the heads turning in his direction. "You look pretty sharp yourself. You're having quite the effect on the women in the room. They will all need a chiropractor to work the kinks out of their necks."

Without looking away from her, he replied, "I was only trying to get a reaction from one of them."

"Hey, Peter." Mark walked up behind him and patted him on the back. Hard. "Placing your bid, are you?"

Aimee watched as the two men spurred each other while still wearing the false expressions of friendly acquaintances.

"Mark, it's so good to see you." He shook Mark's hand and squeezed, his knuckles turning white with the effort. "I was telling our girl how beautiful she looks tonight. She always looks amazing, but tonight she's spectacular."

"I'm the luckiest guy in the room, that's for sure. *My* girl is nothing if not breathtaking." Mark walked over and placed his arm possessively around her.

"I understand you two are seeing each other. Congratulations, you've found yourself a terrific girl here." Peter smiled but his eyes sparked with challenge. "Is this your second or third date?"

Aimee didn't miss Peter's dig, even if Mark did.

"What was the name of that lingerie model you brought last year? Wasn't it Bambi, or Destiny? Something like that?" Peter asked with a fake smile still pasted on his face.

She could feel Mark tense. "I believe Destiny was the name of your date."

Aimee stepped away from Mark's grasp. "If you two Neanderthals will excuse me . . ."

Entering the main ballroom, McKenzie fell into step beside her.

"Nicely done." She nodded, her lips tilting up in an approving smirk. "Looked like they were about to set up a time to meet outside after school."

Aimee laughed at the sparkle of humor in her eyes.

"I don't think I've ever seen Mark like this. Not even in high school. It warms a mother's heart." McKenzie grabbed hold of Aimee's arm. "Let's go find our seats. Along the way we'll try to find a handsome movie star for you to flirt with and send Mark right over the edge."

They approached the table, and took a glass of champagne from the tray of a passing waiter.

"The room looks wonderful. You've done a great job," McKenzie said, scanning the room while taking a sip of her champagne. "I can't believe you were able to pull it off with all your other deadlines, and the not to mention your mother's passing."

Aimee looked at her curiously. "Other deadlines?"

Before McKenzie could respond, the others arrived at the table and the conversation shifted back to the auction. Emily couldn't contain her excitement, or her nervousness. She was talking fast, her sentences running together in a long string of chatter. Her hands moved as fast as her words, and every time she sat in her chair, she would shift, cross her legs one way, then the other, only to stand again.

Aimee put her hand on Emily's arm. "It's going to be okay. In fact, it's going to be fantastic. I'll check on the kitchen, and then make sure the auction items are in order. Relax and try to enjoy yourself." She smiled reassuringly before turning to leave.

"I'll go with you." Mark stepped up to the table as she began to walk away and hurried to catch up with her. They walked in silence for a while, before he mumbled, "Sorry about earlier. He was basically undressing you with his eyes, and it pissed me off."

"Obviously."

"He was acting a bit childish, don't you think?" His tone was defensive.

"You were both acting childish."

"Maybe," he sighed. "I don't know where this thing between us is going, but I do know I don't like other men drooling all over you."

"Oh, Mark, you say the sweetest things." Her voice dripped with sarcasm.

"Well, you know what I mean. I . . . Well, I . . . Damn it, Aimee, I don't like him hanging all over you. I can't stand the thought of him touching you."

She stopped outside the kitchen door and turned to face him. "He wasn't touching me, but I understand what you're saying. I'm having difficulty controlling my own imagination when it comes to you and Bambi."

He laughed. "Her name wasn't Bambi, it was Delilah."

She pushed him back with a small shove. "Delilah? Are you serious?" She huffed, and pushed through the kitchen door.

The noise inside the kitchen was a barely controlled roar.

Multiple Chefs bustled about shouting out directions while lifting the lids of large pots and stirring the contents, or dipping in a plastic spoon to taste. Crates filled with plates were being carried by waiters and placed at the staging area.

Aimee found Lois, the caterer, double checked the serve time, and verified she had the latest selection list. Satisfied, she walked back through the swinging doors and headed across the crowded ballroom to locate Peter and the auctioneer.

Not realizing Mark was still behind her, she stopped abruptly, causing him to walk into her back.

She jumped, and turned to him. "I didn't see you."

He lifted his hand to her face, cupping her cheek in his palm. He closed his eyes and parted her lips with his. He kissed her until she swayed on rubber legs. He pulled back slowly, sucking on her bottom lip. She left her eyes closed, basking in the feelings enveloping her. Nobody else in the room existed.

"I know you have to get back to work. I wanted you to have something to think about when you see Peter."

Chapter 42

The sun warmed her face as Aimee sat outside her cottage, sipping her first cup of coffee. The evening was a success, raising over three million dollars for the Talbot Foundation. She couldn't help but feel proud that she'd had a part to play in its success.

Just waking up, Mark sat down beside her, his hair still messed from sleep, his face scraggly, his chest and feet bare. She laid her head on his shoulder and felt the butterflies in her stomach begin to dance as she recalled last night. He'd kept his word, and picked up exactly where they'd left off before the auction. She couldn't remember a time when she'd been incapable of keeping her hands off someone. Simply sitting next to him she was mentally removing his clothes.

"Where is your mind this morning? You have the naughtiest look on your face," Mark asked.

"I was remembering last night, and wondering if I could talk you out of working today. I'd really like to climb back in bed and pretend it's not close to noon."

"An offer like that is going to make me change my mind about driving up the coast this afternoon."

She jumped up, her coffee sloshing over the rim of her cup as she bounced up and down with excitement. "Like a drive in the Mustang up the coast? Like, only you and me, sunshine and loud music?"

"I take it you no longer want to go back to bed?" He bowed his head and stuck out his bottom lip.

Grabbing his hand, she pulled him up and threw herself into his arms. "I'm so excited." She kissed him soundly on the lips. "Hurry and get dressed, we're wasting the day away."

An hour later they were zipping down the highway, the wind billowing through the open windows, both of them singing along to the radio. It was everything she'd imagined the moment she'd first seen him behind the wheel of his car.

Pulling up at a public beach, he parked the car, and held open the door for her to climb out. He grabbed a blanket and a picnic basket from the trunk before they headed down the path and onto the beach.

Reaching the sand, Aimee pulled off her shoes and tossed them down. Unable to resist, she ran toward the water, waving her hands in the air, beckoning for him to join her. The water was cool against her bare legs. She dug her toes in the sand letting the waves roll in and bury her feet.

She felt her lungs empty with a whoosh sound when Mark picked her up and threw her over his shoulder, taking her deeper into the ocean.

"Mark, don't you dare!" she yelled, slapping him playfully on the back. He pulled her forward like she weighed nothing at all. Balancing her on his arms, he held her away from him, dangling her over the waves. "Don't!" She tried to sound stern, but laughter bubbled from her throat.

"Or you'll what?" he said and dipped her closer to the water.

She reached down and cupping her hand, she splashed him, getting more water on herself than him.

He narrowed his eyes. "Why'd you have to go and do that? Now I have no choice but to toss you in."

He swung her forward and she knew he had every intention of following through with his threat. She grabbed his neck and held on, throwing him off balance, and sending them both into the next wave.

She shot up, wiping the salt water from her eyes and combing the wet hair from her face. "I can't believe you did that," she sputtered.

"I can't believe you made me do that."

"I certainly did not," she replied, placing her hands on her hips. His eyes clouded over and his amusement abruptly stopped. Eyeing her up and then down, he stepped over to her. Crushing his mouth to hers, he ran his hands down her back, grabbing her at the waist and pulling her body to his.

He tasted like salt water and peppermint. Every nerve in her body seemed to surface in reaction to his sudden change in mood. She dug her hands into his wet hair and pulled his mouth closer, burying herself in his kiss.

He pulled back, and leaned his forehead against hers. "Follow closely behind me. I want to be the only one eyeing the winner of this wet t-shirt contest."

Looking down at herself, she crossed her arms over her chest. "Today was the wrong day to wear white," she mumbled.

He kissed her again, before taking her hand and walking with her back to the beach. Standing like a shield in front of her, he grabbed their belongings and led her up a steep path that jutted out from the beach.

They passed a No Trespassing sign and he informed her Emily owned the property they were on. "It's more of a hill, but it's private up here and the view is incredible. We spent a lot of time here when I was young."

Aimee continued to climb, happy there were wooden boards creating stairs at some of the steeper points. "Why would Emily buy a hill?"

He laughed. "Nathan bought it for her right after they were married. I think it was meant to be one of those quirky romantic gestures he was known for. Supposedly, he told her that if he couldn't buy her the beach he'd make sure she had a great view of it."

What an understatement that turned out to be. Aimee's jaw dropped open as they came to the crest of the hill. The ocean surrounded them on three sides, and the direction the shore veered off, hid any sign of the public beach below, making it feel like they were alone on a deserted island. Seagulls flew overhead, and the smell of salt water perfumed the air.

There was a hammock to the left, positioned between the only two trees, and a fire pit had been dug into the ground, surrounded by sand. She turned to Mark and watched him spread out the blanket.

"It's so beautiful."

"So are you." He walked over to stand next to her.

She kissed him, and spun around in a slow circle, taking in the view again. Spotting something in the sunlight, she walked over to the trees holding the hammock. She ran her fingers over the heart carved into the bark. Inside it were the initials, ES and NT.

Her eyes filled with tears. "Emily and Nathan?"

Nodding his head, he reached into his pocket and pulled out a pocket knife. He placed the blade against the bark of the tree, and seemed surprised when she reached out her hand to stop him.

"This is their tree."

He smiled and kissed her sweetly. "You're right, it is their tree." Walking around the hammock he stopped in front of the other one. "This one is ours."

Her heart soared as she watched him lovingly carve a heart into the bark, and write ML and AM inside. She knew this day would be forever etched in her memory like the initials in the tree.

Her love for him had grown beyond anything she'd ever imagined. The thought of living without him wasn't something she could comprehend. She needed to tell him. In fact, she'd started to tell him a million times, but in the end, decided to keep it to herself until she was positive of the truth. Luther told her she'd receive the DNA results any day, so she chose to simply enjoy the time she had with Mark until then. Now, she could only hope he loved her enough to understand why she'd waited.

Pulling her into his arms, he kissed her again. She shivered and leaned in closer.

"Let's get you out of these wet clothes." His eyes sparked with desire.
He gently laid her down on the blanket and removed her wet clothes, brushing his hands along her skin. She reached up to remove his shirt. Grasping her hands, he moved them over her head, pinning them against the blanket and holding them securely in one of his larger ones. His eyes roamed over her body. She wasn't sure if the goose bumps rising on her skin were caused by the cool air hitting her wet skin, or the look in his eyes.

Once he'd removed her clothes, he continued to watch her while he slowly discarded his own. Leaning over her, he brushed a loose curl from her forehead and bent down to kiss her lips. "I've imagined you here, just like this, since the first time I kissed you."

"I think I will remember us here, just like this, for the rest of my life."

She wrapped her arms around his neck and pulled him down to her, running her hands along the smooth crevice of his back, her hands memorizing every inch of his body. Her excitement grew as his muscles flinched at the gentle touch of her fingertips. Feeling his restraint slipping, she arched her back in breathless anticipation. Never taking their eyes from one another, they made love in the warm sunlight.

Chapter 43

Aimee yawned, and stretched. Feeling luxurious, she kicked her feet out from underneath the covers and lifted her arms above her head. Smiling peacefully, she rolled over to cuddle up to Mark. He was gone. She sighed, and picked up the note he'd left on his pillow telling her he was playing in the dirt this morning and he'd see her at lunch.

Rolling onto her back, she watched the rising sun create colorful splashes on the bedroom wall. She closed her eyes recalling the feel of the sun on her face as she lay snuggled against Mark in the hammock at the beach. It felt like they were alone, on their own little piece of the world where nobody else existed. She was beginning to wonder if it was illegal to be so happy. Reaching over, she pulled his pillow to her chest and buried her face into the soft cotton, inhaling his scent. No, it wasn't illegal, but it was temporary.

It was only a matter of days before she'd have the results and know the truth. Rising from the bed, she pulled his discarded T-shirt over her head and wandered into the kitchen for a cup of coffee.

What would happen then? She wanted it to be true that Emily was her birth mother, but what about Mark? What would that do to her relationship with him? Would he ever forgive her for not telling him? Would he even try to understand? Would Emily be glad her daughter found her way home after all these years?

She sipped her coffee and walked to the window. She spotted him across the yard, shoveling large piles of soil to a nearby wheelbarrow. He bobbed his head and then threw it back, dramatically belting out the next note of the song playing on his iPod.

Her heart fluttered when he turned in her direction like he sensed her watching him. She raised her hand to wave at him.

Amusement bubbled from her throat when he bent at the waist and took a bow. His eyes seemed to grow serious for a minute before he blew her a kiss, and turned back to dig out another shovel full of dirt.

She placed her mug back into the sink, made the bed, and scooped up her clothes before dashing the short distance to her cottage. Her cheeks flushed when she heard him whistle. Reaching behind her with her only free hand, she tugged at the t-shirt riding up her legs and ran around the last bush between her and the front door.

She spent the next four hours finalizing the details for the birthday party. It was coming together perfectly, and she felt confident Emily would love the final results. She needed to spend some time with Mimsey this afternoon and work through the appetizer menu. She'd actually insisted on doing all the food preparation herself, using her own recipes and a staff of helpers she chose personally.

"Nobody else knows what Ms. Emily likes but me. It will only be perfect if I do it, so there is no more discussion," she'd snapped when Aimee had insisted they hire a catering company.

Aimee tried repeatedly to remind her she was supposed to be a guest at the party and not working, but Mimsey only held her hand up and turned her face away, dismissing any further conversation.

Crossing the foyer, she headed toward the kitchen to fix some lunch for herself and Mark. She could hear McKenzie's laughter and Mimsey scolding her.

"How do you think you're ever going to find a good man if you can't even boil water?" Mimsey clucked her tongue.

"That's why they invented the microwave. So that spoiled, pampered, rich princesses can boil water for themselves," McKenzie replied. "Besides, if he's truly the man for me, he will be a fabulous cook and I won't have to worry about it."

Mimsey picked up the bowl she'd been adding ingredients to, and began to stir vigorously, mumbling under her breath with every circle of the spoon.

"Is this a bad time?" Aimee asked as she walked into the mine field.

"Don't be silly. Come sit by me." McKenzie pulled out the stool beside her. "Mimsey and I were discussing the importance of a good man knowing how to cook."

Mimsey scowled. "Part of the reason our Marcus is so happy is because Aimee knows how to cook."

"Is that so?" McKenzie straightened her back and placed her hands on the counter before turning to her. "Aimee, do you believe that your cooking is the reason for Mark's happiness and wellbeing? Do you think if you suddenly stopped cooking he'd break off the relationship? Do you think if you never entered the kitchen again you would spend the rest of your life alone?"

Aimee stuttered, not sure if she was actually supposed to answer the question, or the questions, being asked.

"I wouldn't leave her if she didn't cook, Mother." Mark slinked into the kitchen, with a smirk accenting his dimples and brightening his eyes. "But I would leave her if Mimsey would stop playing hard to get and finally agree to run away with me." He kissed Mimsey on the cheek and reached around her, dipping his finger into the bowl.

Mimsey's cheeks turned red and her scowl instantly changed into a smile. Batting his hand away, she said, "Marcus Lee, behave yourself." She moved the spoon faster through the batter in the bowl. Looking up, she added, "Isn't it true that the way to a man's heart is through his stomach?"

McKenzie rolled her eyes and Aimee rested her chin on her palm feigning total interest in his response.

"I'm completely outnumbered here and they have me surrounded. Why would you put my life in jeopardy by asking me that question, Mimsey? I thought I meant something to you." Mark placed his hand over his heart and bowed his head dramatically.

"What question is that?" Emily asked as she walked into the kitchen and climbed onto the stool on the other side of Aimee.

"Mimsey thinks I haven't had a man because I don't cook," McKenzie informed her.

"Then she asked Mark if the way to a man's heart is actually through his stomach and we're still waiting patiently for his response," Aimee added.

"Oh, this ought to be good." Emily leaned her chin on her palm, copying Aimee's waiting pose.

"I can't win this one. So I'm going to take the honesty route. I don't think the inability to cook is a deal breaker, but I think a home cooked meal, especially made for you, carries some weight in gaining a man's attention, especially if it comes with wine and candlelight."

"The wine and candlelight I can do," McKenzie said. "And if the meal on the table is good take out, he'll never have to know you didn't get red sauce on your favorite blouse or flour under your fingernails."

Mimsey frowned and shook her head again.

"There has to be one meal you can make," Aimee said, trying to come to McKenzie's aid.

"Nope, not one. Can't sew, either. But I did learn the whole boiling water in the microwave thing a few years ago and I make a mean cup of tea."

Mimsey sighed. "McKenzie, I've neglected you somehow. I can't let it continue now that I know the seriousness of the situation. You must learn at least one meal to make, and today is your son's favorite so it's a good place to start. Grab the apron from the pantry and come around here."

Aimee and Emily tried to stifle their giggles as McKenzie reluctantly rose from her stool.

"You're not seriously going to let her ruin my chicken and biscuits are you, Mimsey?" Mark said, panic in his eyes. "My mouth has been watering all day in anticipation."

Mimsey shushed him and moved aside when McKenzie stepped up to the counter. "You need to spread some flour onto the counter so the biscuits don't stick when you roll them out."

McKenzie dipped the scoop into the flour canister and poured it generously onto the counter creating a large dust cloud.

Mark pretended to choke and waved his hands in front of his face causing Emily and Aimee to laugh uncontrollably.

Without hesitation, McKenzie grabbed a handful of the flour off the counter and threw it at Mark. His eyes grew large in shock as he wiped the flour from his face.

Mimsey tried desperately to regain control of her kitchen as Mark stepped over to the canister and dug both of his hands inside. His eyes twinkled as his mother slowly backed away from him, shaking her head back and forth. He laughed as he dropped both piles over his mother's head.

McKenzie shook her head, sending flour everywhere. Mimsey tried to stop her from going in for more as the two of them played tug of war with the flour canister. They both released their grip at the same time, sending it flying across the counter and spilling all over Mark's boots.

Aimee and Emily both covered their mouths in astonishment before they looked at each other and bent over in girlish giggles. Emily scooted her chair back out of the line of fire, but continued to watch the war erupting in front of her. Aimee felt a comfortable warmth fill her. She watched as Mark reached over and picked up one of the tomatoes sitting in the basket beside him.

McKenzie held up her hands. "Mark, don't you dare. It was an accident."

"This isn't." He pulled his arm back, squeezed the fruit, and sent it flying, hitting his mother in the chest. Red juice splattered her face, the walls, and Mimsey standing beside her.

Aimee and Emily erupted with laughter. Sudden silence filled the kitchen. They both looked up in time to see three menacing smiles aimed at them, two of them armed with tomatoes and one with the remaining flour from the canister.

"Mark . . ." Aimee attempted to smile innocently at him.

"Don't do it," Emily said, trying to sound stern.

"One . . . two . . ." McKenzie started to count off. "Three."

They jumped from their stools a little too late, as one tomato hit Emily on the shoulder and the other hitting Aimee square in the stomach. Mark pelted them with flour as they rounded the counter to arm themselves.

Food flew everywhere as handfuls of biscuit dough sailed through the air, sticking to the walls and the ceiling. Mimsey even picked up her freshly made peach pie and smashed it into Emily's face like an old Three Stooges episode.

Bodies were sliding around the floor, trying to gain their footing as they scrambled to get the upper hand over each other. Mark grabbed Aimee from behind and pulled her down with him as he slipped on the remnants of the peach pie. She scrambled to escape his grasp, her feet sliding across the floor as she struggled for traction.

Laughter surrounded them, and Aimee couldn't remember a time she'd been so happy. She wanted to be a part of the love that filled the room, the friendship and the happiness. Her eyes pooled with tears and she turned her head, trying to keep Mark from seeing her reaction.

He turned her head to him and kissed her gently. "You're even beautiful covered in flour and tomatoes." He kissed her again.

If he'd seen her tears he never let on. "Not sure the dough clumped in your hair is working for you, though."

She punched him playfully in the shoulder. Another piece of peach landed directly on his forehead. His eyes grew serious. He looked into her eyes and motioned to the basket of peaches sitting just out of view from the others.

She nodded her head in understanding. In between their bodies where only she could see, he held up one finger, then another, and as he lifted the third one, she jumped from his lap and grabbed an armful of the fruit, tossing them to him before she armed herself.

They turned and pelted the three unsuspecting women in true team-like fashion.

Chapter 44

The kitchen was clean, the fruit scraped off the cupboards, walls, and floors. Aimee smiled at the afternoon's events as she bent backwards, working the kinks out of her spine from the hour she'd spent on her knees scrubbing the floor. Even that had been fun. They'd all worked together, arguing over the music that played in the kitchen, and who'd won the food fight. Laughter filled the room as they'd picked pieces of fruit out of each other's hair and brushed it off their backs.

She'd watched movies and read books about families like this one, but being a part of it, if for only a short time, had been magical. The four of them were truly connected in every way. It was more than love and commitment, and it was deeper than blood or friendship. Somehow, all of them were connected at a level that very few people could understand. She wouldn't have understood either had she not been standing in the middle of it, watching it from every angle. They were the true definition of family. One built on history, respect, and understanding. She wanted to be a part of it, of them.

"Hello, are you listening to me?" McKenzie snapped her fingers in front of Aimee's face.

"Yes, well no, I wasn't, but I am now, sorry. Lost in thought I guess."

McKenzie laughed, shaking her head. "Would you get them?"

"Now I know I definitely wasn't listening. Get what?"

"The clean kitchen rugs. Upstairs in the big linen closet. Where were you?" McKenzie picked another piece of fruit off her shoulder.

"Sorry. Sure, I'll get them. Where exactly is this closet upstairs?" She removed her yellow rubber gloves and set them next to the sink.

"It's the far end of the hall, right after Emily's room." McKenzie's voice was almost a whisper.

Aimee smiled. "Be right back."

If she were a paranoid person she'd almost believe McKenzie could read her mind. Sometimes when Aimee had lost herself in a daydream about Emily or even Mark, she would find McKenzie looking at her with a knowing smile on her face. It was like she'd walked through her daydream with her and knew all of her secrets, all of her longings.

Reaching the end of the hallway, she discovered door after door lining the walls. None of them resembled a closet. She tried to remember exactly what door McKenzie had told her. Right after Emily's room, she'd said.

Swinging the door open, she gasped and grabbed the handle for support. Tears burned her eyes as she stood frozen in the open door. Instead of a closet, it was a little girl's bedroom.

Tears began to flow unchecked down her face. She knew she should close the door and leave, but something pulled her to step inside. She pictured herself as a little girl lying in the small bed with the delicate white bedspread, while Emily sat beside her reading a bedtime story. Walking to the far wall, she gently ran her fingers along the faded red letters that hung there. Amelia. Was that to be her name?

Drawn by the painted mural that climbed the wall, she walked over and traced the brush strokes of the vine. Studying the ladybugs gathered there, she noticed a group of three that sat sheltered beneath a large leaf. The larger of them had its wings open like arms, embracing the two smaller bugs. Was this the three of them, Nathan, Emily, and their daughter?

She walked to the dresser and lifted the lid of the heart-shaped jewelry box that had once been silver, but was now tarnished with age. It was engraved, *My Princess Amelia, Love Always, Grandma.*

The sobs burst from her chest. Laying her head down against her arm on the dresser she let the tears go. After all these years, their daughter's room stood empty. If she was Amelia, then all this pain had been caused by the woman she'd believed to be her mother.

"It's heartbreaking, isn't it?"

Aimee's head jerked up in surprise. McKenzie stood in the open doorway watching her.

"I'm sorry, I didn't mean to come in here. I opened the wrong door ... then I couldn't . . . I couldn't . . . leave." Aimee fought to catch her breath.

"Every year they would update this room, right before Amelia's birthday. They wanted it to be ready when she got home. Every year, for six years, they would redecorate in preparation for her." McKenzie's eyes grew distant. "That was until Nathan died. Emily couldn't bear to enter this room after that."

Aimee couldn't speak. It felt like her heart was lodged in her throat. Tears continued to roll down her cheeks as she imagined the pain Emily had endured.

"But even when Emily stopped updating the room, she never stopped wishing, never stopped praying her little girl was alive. Wishing she would come home." McKenzie looked intently at Aimee. "I'd like to believe that Amelia would be a bit like you."

Chapter 45

Lifting her legs, Aimee tucked the blanket under her feet before leaning back against the arm of the couch and pulling it to her chin. She was cold. It was still close to eighty degrees outside and she was buried beneath a quilt with her teeth chattering. Even after rushing back to her cottage for a hot shower, she couldn't get warm. All she wanted was a fire in the fireplace and a nap. She was beginning to think she may be getting sick. She didn't want to believe her symptoms were caused by her emotions, or that stepping into that bedroom had affected her so strongly.

She'd just dozed off when there was a soft knock on the door, followed by heavy footsteps.

"Hey, baby, did I wake you?" Mark reached down to kiss her.

"Not really," she answered, sliding up to a sitting position.

He sat next to her feet and laid a box on his lap. His eyes were hesitant, but seemed to glow with anticipation as he looked between the box and her.

"What's that?" she asked curiously.

"I think its Emily's birthday present." He continued to stroke the box.

"You think?" She leaned down trying to catch his gaze. His hands shook as he continued to run his hand over the box.

"Did you buy her stationary?" she asked.

He looked up, locking his eyes with hers before shaking his head. She wanted to reach over and rip the box from him, to throw the cover off and understand why he was behaving so strangely.

"Are you going to tell me, or did you only come over to torment me with my own relentless curiosity?"

His smile reminded her of a little boy hiding his first preschool drawing behind his back before presenting it to his mother.

"I did it," he finally mumbled. "I don't know if I did it right, or if I wasted a lot of time, but I did it." His boyish smile spread from ear to ear across his face.

"Did what?" His excitement was contagious and she found herself bouncing on the couch in anticipation.

Slowly opening the lid, he stared at the box's contents, but didn't speak. He took a deep breath, and handed her the box. Inside, was a stack of typed pages. The top page began, "Once upon a time . . ."

She gasped. "You did it? You really wrote Emily's book?"

He nodded his head, color spreading across his cheeks. "I did." He clasped his hands tightly in his lap and rubbed his thumbs together. "I need your help."

"Of course, anything," she said, still looking at the page on top of the pile.

"I wanted to know if you'd read it, let me know if it's okay, and then possibly create a cover for me. You've doodled on everything since the day we met, and you're an incredible artist."

She reached over and took hold of his hand. His pulse beat rapidly as he continued to look at her nervously. "I would be honored to read it. What is the title?"

He blew out a breath. "I don't know. All the ones I come up with seem so corny to me. Maybe you can help me with that when you read it."

She nodded her head excitedly.

"I would like to give it to Emily for her birthday, but I know how busy you are, so if you won't have time, that's okay." He clasped his hands back into his lap.

Aimee didn't think she'd ever seen him as uneasy as he was right now. "Are you nervous to let me read it, or to give it to Emily?"

"Both." He exhaled the breath he'd been holding. "I don't know many grown men who write fairy tales, and the fact that I kind of enjoyed it worries me a little." He frowned. "I feel like I should be racing to the shed for the power tools, just to prove to myself that I'm the same guy."

Aimee laughed at his nervousness. "The panic on your face is priceless."

"It's not funny! It's bad enough that I'm holed up with a house full of women day after day, but now I'm writing fairy tales, for Christ sakes."

"You're not simply writing fairy tales, you're stepping out of your comfort zone to do something amazingly thoughtful for someone you love." She reached over and squeezed his hand. "You shouldn't be embarrassed. It makes you a better man than most. It's one of things that make me crazy about you."

Marks eyes twinkled with mischief. "So you're crazy about me, huh?" He set the box on the table, and tugged her down on the couch until she was lying beneath him. He struggled to pull the blanket out from between them, his lips burning trails along her neck and shoulders. Unable to pull the blanket off, his head suddenly jerked up, worry etching his brow. "Why are you buried in this blanket? Are you sick?" He reached over and laid his hand on her forehead.

"No, I don't think so, I was just cold."

"Well, in that case . . ." Mark stood up, and pulled the blanket off her, tossing it onto the floor. "I bet I could warm you up."

Sitting up, she reached for the box on the table. "Later you can warm me up. Now, you have to go play with your power tools. I am dying to read your book."

"You're going to read it now, like right now?" His face was filled with anxiousness.

Reaching up her hand, she pulled his face down to hers and kissed him gently. "How about if I fix you dinner tonight, make it up to you?"

"Can we eat dinner naked?" He twitched his eyebrow up and down.

She laughed, and swatted him with the throw pillow. "Out, I want to read."

"This is what I was afraid of. I write one fairy tale and my girl no longer finds me appealing. She would rather curl up with a book than me." He stuck out his bottom lip and bowed his head.

Aimee shook her head, and smiled. "Okay, we can have dinner naked. Out."

Mark let out a loud whoop, kissed her again, and skipped out the door.

Pulling her legs under her, she began to read.

She wiped a tear from her eye as she turned over the last page. He'd written an amazing story. It was a combination of Cinderella and Romeo and Juliet, told from the memories of a young girl in love. He referred to it as a fairy tale, but it was more than that. It was Emily and Nathan's fairy tale, complete with the obstacles they faced disguised as wicked witches and powerful sorcerers. He knew Emily so well, and Aimee was sure she would see this was a fictitious biography of her and Nathan's lives. A story of true love forced to wait out another lifetime to be together.

Aimee walked to the desk, pulled out a plain sheet of paper and began to draw.

Chapter 46

Holding the envelope in her shaking hands, Aimee paced the front room of her cottage. The results were in, and as soon as she worked up the nerve to open the envelope, she'd know if Emily was her biological mother. She pulled the letter opener from the holder on her desk and slid the corner under one side of the sealed envelope. Her hand froze. She took a deep breath and willed herself to slide it forward.

The realization of how her life would change overwhelmed her. If the results proved Emily to be her mother, she truly believed that after the shock wore off, it would be happy news for both of them. She wanted to pull Emily into her arms and tell her she loved her, and she was finally home. She wanted feel the love pour from her as the emptiness faded from her eyes.

She also knew she would lose Mark to her own web of lies and deceit. At the thought of losing him, the envelope and letter opener slipped from her fingers and crashed against the desk.

If the results proved she wasn't her mother, she knew she would feel an immense sense of loss. Never in her life had she wanted to belong to someone the way she did Emily Sinclair. In the months she'd worked for her, she'd grown to love and respect her in a way she barely understood, and never expected.

But she would be able to keep Mark? After she told him she wasn't an office assistant and actually a famous handbag designer. That she'd never meant to lie, she just needed to be sure who she was. That she loved him and never meant to be dishonest. She had no idea how to convince him, how to make him understand.

She sighed again, and walked into the kitchen to pour herself a much needed glass of wine. Her hands continued to shake as she took a sip and let the crisp flavor wash over her tongue. Tonight was the big night. Emily's fiftieth birthday party would start in a matter of hours and she still needed to shower and dress.

Luther was in town for the weekend and would be fighting her for the mirror before much longer. She hadn't told him the results had come in this morning. She wanted to be alone when she opened them. To not be rushed or pushed to do it quickly and get it over with. The longer the envelope sat unopened, the more she regretted her decision. Luther would have already had it ripped open and the contents read aloud.

She needed to pull herself together. The results wouldn't change because she hadn't read them. She walked back to her desk, set her glass down and picked up the envelope. It's like a Band-Aid, the faster you do it, the less it hurts, she told herself. Picking up the letter opener, she quickly slid it along the fold.

Setting the opener back down, she hesitantly reached inside and pulled out the folded sheet of paper. She'd somehow thought it would be more. Like a binder filled with laboratory results, or a long legal explanation that filled ten pages front to back. Instead, she slowly unfolded a single sheet of paper and read from the top to the bottom. She blew out the breath she didn't know she was holding. Tears rolled down her cheeks.

Her head jerked around at the sound of the door opening. She wiped her eyes, trying to hide the tears as Luther strolled through the door, whistling an unfamiliar song, and wearing a smile that stretched from ear to ear.

"I've decided to quit working for you and when you move back to New York I'm going to take over your job here." He brushed a kiss across her cheek and picking up her glass, emptied the contents in one gulp. "I love this place. I have an extremely large crush on Emily. I keep trying to talk her into letting me be her boy toy without the sex. I think I could definitely be a kept man. I don't have a lot of pride to work around, and she can afford to keep me in the lifestyle to which I plan on becoming accustomed. Why aren't you dressed? I hate sharing a bathroom with you. You're such a mirror hog."

Aimee smiled and shook her head. She'd missed her friend and his crazy rants that were impossible to follow. Glad he was here, especially now, she leaned over and rested her head against his shoulder.

"What's wrong? Are you crying? What happened? Was it Mark? He may be bigger than me, but I'm quicker and I think I could do some damage to his pretty little face before I had to run to protect mine. You know how much I treasure my face. It's hard not to love it, don't you think?"

Without lifting her head, she nodded, her cheek brushing back and forth against the soft cotton of his shirt.

"Aimee, what is it? I hate to see you cry."

Lifting her head and stepping back, she handed him the sheet of paper she clenched in her hand. She walked into the kitchen, refilled her glass, and poured another for him.

Walking in behind her, he took the glass she offered him and remained unusually quiet. His eyes watched hers over the rim of his glass, seeming to await her reaction.

"She's my mother," she said breathlessly. "Emily is really, truly, my mother." Tears began to run down her cheeks again.

"I thought this was what you wanted." Luther sounded confused.

"It is. I do. I'm so happy. I really am, I just . . ." She let her head fall forward.

"Is it Mark?"

"This has all been such a double edged sword. Somehow I have to pick between them and it's my own fault. I don't want to pick. I'm in love with him, Luther. In love in a way I never believed existed. But—"

"But Emily's the mother you always wished you had."

She nodded her head. "She needs me. I really think she needs to know it's me. She's waited so long, never giving up hope."

"You have to tell her. Regardless of anything else, you must tell her. She deserves to know. She's a fantastic woman, and so are you. She's going to be ecstatic to see the baby she never knew turned out to be a woman she already loves."

She walked into his arms and let his confidence seep into her. He placed his hands on her arms and set her back to look into her face.

"What are you going to say to Mark?"

"Oh Luther, I don't know what to say. What can I say to make this seem less of a crime? For Mark, this is the greatest of all wrongs. I really want to believe he could forgive me for my deception but I don't know. I've been lying to him since we met. I'm not sure he will ever get past that."

Neither of them heard the front door close.

Chapter 47

Mark slammed his hand on the counter. His mind raced with worst-case scenarios. What was she hiding? What had she lied to him about? He felt like a fool. For the first time in his life he'd let himself believe in someone. He'd let her into his heart, and now the pain had him wanting to rip it out of his chest.

Pounding his fist again, he pushed away from the counter and walked purposefully over to his desk, yanking open the bottom drawer. He pulled out the sealed envelope from the investigator and tore open the flap. His stomach was in knots.

Reading the report, he found himself riddled with more questions. She was also known as Aimee Roberts, and she owned Amore' Handbags? So what was she doing working for Emily? What would have sent her to a temporary placement agency in San Francisco?

He flipped his laptop open and typed in Amore' Handbags. He couldn't see anything that would send her to work at another job. And why wouldn't she say anything? Why would she be working here and not New York? He tried to recall the first day he'd met her, the day of her interview. She'd seemed disoriented, almost confused. He'd believed it was nerves at the time.

He scanned farther down and clicked on a blog that mentioned Amore' and Aimee by name. He read the information posted by a long time customer named Lucy Strand. She'd heard firsthand that Aimee, and subsequently, Amore' Handbags, was in financial difficulty and that Aimee's chance to pull herself out of her situation lay in a secret benefactor in San Francisco.

He clenched his fists, and pulled large gulps of air into his lungs. He could feel his heart physically shredding into tiny pieces. It couldn't be true. He desperately needed her to be who he thought she was.

He picked up the phone and called information.

"Lewis Employment Agency in San Francisco," he said to the recording.

He waited while the computer looked up his request and pushed the button to connect the call.

"May I speak to Janet Lewis please? This is Marcus Lee calling."

The wait felt like an eternity. He paced the room, cursing out loud when he bumped his shin on the table. Leaning against the arm of the couch, he squeezed his eyes shut, trying to block the memory of Aimee sitting beside him, her head thrown back in laughter, her eyes alight with happiness.

"Mr. Lee, how nice to hear from you," said the voice on the other end of the line. "What can I do for you? Is Ms. Sinclair still looking for an assistant?"

The room began to spin. "Still looking?" His heart rate increased, sounding like a marching band in his head. He turned and sat on the edge of the couch, not trusting his own ability to stand.

He could hear the confusion in her voice. "I wasn't sure if she'd gone with another agency. Our candidate had a family emergency and failed to notify us when she'd been unable to attend her scheduled interview. When I called to speak to Ms. Sinclair—"

"Your candidate didn't show?"

"I'm sorry, no. I called Ms. Sinclair's office the minute I heard and offered to send another candidate immediately, but I was informed by her associate that she was no longer looking."

"Her associate?" Mark ran his hand through his hair. Taking a deep breath, he asked, "So you didn't send Aimee Morrison to meet with Ms. Sinclair?"

"I don't believe so. I can't imagine my assistant filling a position and not informing me. Would you like to hold a moment while I check the files?"

"Yes, thank you." Standing up, he slowly paced the room.

The seconds ticked by like hours. When she finally returned to the phone, he felt as if the wind had been knocked out of him. "Mr. Lee, according to my records, Aimee Morrison has never been a client with us. Would you like—"

The phone slammed against the wall, tiny pieces of plastic scattering across the room.

Chapter 48

Aimee knocked. She tried the handle again. It wasn't like Mark to lock his door. When he hadn't shown up to walk her to the party, she'd started to worry.

"I'm sure everything's fine. Maybe Emily needed him to do something and he's up at the house," Luther said, trying to reassure her.

Her paranoia set in the minute she'd made the decision to tell Mark the truth immediately after the party. She couldn't keep the news to herself any longer than that, and she needed to tell him first. She couldn't shake her overwhelming feeling of doom.

"Maybe you're right." Taking his outstretched hand, she followed him to the house.

"Did I mention how beautiful you look tonight?" he said, in an obvious attempt to distract her.

She ran her hand down the mint green cocktail dress she'd had Luther bring her from New York. It clung to her frame like a second skin, leaving her back bare but for a simple silver chain that hung from the neck and landed at the curve of her hips.

"You did, and did I mention that you are a stunning vision yourself?" He'd chosen a cream colored linen suit, worn over a casual peach shaded, button-less shirt. "There are very few men who can still pull off the Miami Vice thing. You wear it so well it could be back in style by morning."

"Let's hope not darling, I very much prefer my originality. Plus, even if they attempt to wear it, they could never wear it like this." He waved his arms up and down the length of his frame.

Entering through the back door, Aimee headed directly for the kitchen, and Luther shot straight to the open bar. The kitchen was bustling with workers taking orders from a very persuasive Mimsey.

"No, place the rosemary around the edge of the tray, Kim. We don't want to overpower the flavors in the chicken bites. It's simply for decoration purposes. Yes, perfect, thank you dear." Mimsey continued to walk from tray to tray, inspecting the job of each of her servers.

"So how is everything going?" Aimee asked, stealing a cube of cheese off a nearby tray.

"Well now, would you look at you," Mimsey said before letting out a faint whistle. "Our Marcus is going to lose his ability to breathe when he gets a look at you."

Aimee blushed, but did a slow spin as directed. "Speaking of Mark, have you seen him?"

"No, I sure haven't. I saw his car pull away a couple of hours ago. I thought he'd be back before now. He's always so punctual."

"He could be back already. He wasn't at his place, so he must be around here somewhere. Everything looks fabulous. Be sure to let me know if you need anything."

Aimee headed toward the main sitting room where the buffet tables had been set up. Everything seemed to be in order. The linens were placed, the chaffers polished, waiting for the hot pans of food to be set inside. Multiple vases of fresh cut flowers were sporadically placed down the long buffet table, and candles flickered atop mirrored squares.

Luther was still at the bar, batting his eyes at the bow-tied bartender. "You must try the pear martini. It's almost as good as the ones they serve at Katwalk in the fashion district."

"I promise I will as soon as I get a chance. Do you have everything you need?" she asked the flushed bartender.

"Yes, thank you, I think I'm all set."

She nodded her head, and tugged Luther a few feet away. "Have you seen Mark?"

"No, I haven't seen anyone yet. You really should try this martini, it's beyond fabulous."

Shaking her head and patting him on the upper arm, she said, "Try to remember that the party doesn't start for another hour or so. Pace yourself."

She left the room and headed upstairs to find Emily. Tapping on the door, she walked inside the master suite. She found her sitting at her dressing table, staring blindly into the mirror.

"Emily?"

"Oh Aimee, there you are, and don't you look stunning." She turned and smiled at her, her eyes misty. "Would you help me with this necklace, I'd forgotten how small the clasp was."

She walked over and took the ends of the delicate chain, connecting them together. "Are you alright?"

Emily reached back and patted her hands. "I'm fine. Feeling a little nostalgic tonight is all."

"Do you want to talk about it?" Aimee stepped from behind her and sat in the chair beside the vanity.

"I'm fifty years old. Can you believe that?"

"Not for one second."

Emily clucked her tongue. "You're flattering me because it's my birthday. Although, I like it, and plan on believing you, at least for tonight." She laughed. Turning back toward the mirror, she tilted her head, inspecting her reflection from a different angle. She appeared wistful for a moment. "I never expected today to be like this. Don't misunderstand me, I'm so grateful for my life, my family, my friends. I'm truly blessed. I just pictured . . ."

Aimee waited for her to continue. When she didn't, she asked, "You just pictured what?"

Emily turned and looked at her. Her eyes filled with sorrow. "Why is it, that when we have it all, we still yearn for what we lost?" Her eyes brimmed with unshed tears. "It truly shows the truth in our selfish existence doesn't it?"

Aimee swallowed down the lump forming in her throat. "I don't think wanting something, or longing for something important to us is selfish. I think it's human, I think it's real."

"You really think so?" Emily reached out for her hands. "I have so much. I'm not talking about wealth and possessions, but look at the people who love me. I'm the luckiest woman alive. Why can't I simply focus on that? Why can't I let go of the ones that aren't here?"

Aimee felt her chest tighten. Her hands began to shake as they clung to Emily's. She wanted to tell her. She had to tell her. She'd decided to tell Mark first, to admit her deceptions, and tell him the complete truth. But the longing on Emily's face was more than she could bear.

Emily gently pulled her hands back and waved them in front of her face. "I swore I wouldn't cry tonight. Yet, I can't seem to pull it together. This is my third attempt at putting on my makeup."

"You look beautiful." Aimee said the words slowly, wanting the truth behind them to be heard. "Emily . . ."

She couldn't seem to form the words. How do you tell someone that you're the daughter they never knew? She inhaled, and cleared her throat.

Emily's eyes clouded over. Concern etched in her expression. "Aimee, what's wrong? What is it? You've gone completely pale."

"I have something important to tell you. I . . ." She bowed her head, praying for the right words to say. "I . . . I'm your—"

The door swung open, the force slamming it into the wall and lodging the handle into the sheetrock. Both women jumped from their seats, startled by the commotion.

Mark strode in, his face filled with rage. His jaw tightened, the veins in his temple throbbed, and his fists clenched. His eyes never left Aimee as he approached her with fierce determination.

"Get out." His voice was toxic, the words each forming their own command. He whipped up his arm and pointed to the door.

Emily stepped between them. "Marcus Lee, what has gotten into you?"

Aimee felt her knees buckle and grasped the chair for support. Tears flowed down her cheeks. He knew. Somehow, he knew. She couldn't speak. Her mouth was moving, but her throat had closed up, striking her mute.

"She's a fraud. She's been lying to us all along." He never took his hate-filled eyes from hers.

Emily looked confused, her head whipping from one to the other, like she was a spectator in a horrible tennis match.

"I'd like you to meet Aimee Roberts, owner of Amore' Handbags in New York City."

"What?" Emily turned to look at Aimee. "What is he talking about?"

She couldn't speak, but she knew she couldn't lie, not any more. She nodded her head, sobs racking her body.

"She was never sent over from the agency. She's just like the others. A liar, a fraud, a money-grubbing—"

"Marcus, that's enough!" McKenzie walked into the room. She faced her son, silencing him with her glare.

Aimee sat down in the chair, her breath coming out in wisps as she tried to control herself. Her entire world had collapsed. She couldn't defend herself. She couldn't speak. Everyone's eyes were on her.

She looked up at Emily, her expression wary, cautious and filled with pain. She tried to speak again, her attempt only producing a quiet whimper as she continued to shake her head. Mark no longer looked at her, he simply looked through her.

Narrowing his eyes, he seethed, "I said, get out."

Emily looked from one to the other, tears rolling down her face. She straightened her shoulders, lifted her chin and slowly began to walk. She'd barely reached the open door before she began to run.

Aimee looked at Mark again, his face filled with fury. She slowly rose from the chair, bowed her head and began to leave the room. As she passed McKenzie, she caught a glimpse of compassion that she didn't understand. Still unable to find her voice, she shook her head no, and mouthed the words, "I'm so sorry," before slowly walking out the door.

Chapter 49

Emptying the last drawer of the dresser into her suitcase, Aimee tugged the zipper around and hefted her bag onto the floor.

"How did things get to be such a mess?" she asked.

Luther grabbed the handle of her suitcase and rolled it across the floor, parking it beside the door. "I'm sorry," he said, walking back into the bedroom.

Looking around, the reality that this would be her last time coming home to the cottage hit her. Hangers still swung back and forth on the rod from her haste in ripping down her clothes. Some of the drawers hung open, and the books she'd recently purchased on roses sat unread beside the bed.

She walked over to the garment bag hanging from the closet door. She slid the zipper down slowly and pushed back the heavy plastic. She stared at the red dress hanging inside. She recalled dancing across the floor in Mark's arms, and the sound of his laughter. She heard the clinking sound of champagne glasses as she toasted the success of the auction with Emily and McKenzie. She pictured the day she first saw the dress, draped on a model while she shopped with her mother; the woman who'd rushed from her room, less than an hour ago, crying because of her dishonesty. Emily was her mother and she'd ruined any chance of being a part of her life.

Luther sat on the bed and hung his head. "I'm sorry," he said again.

"Why are you sorry? I'm the fraud."

She felt the tears well up again. She didn't think she had any left to spill. She walked into the bathroom, and looked around at the bottles still sitting on the counter. "I don't have room to take all of this stuff back with me."

She leaned on the counter, her body shook with the force of her crying. She looked at her reflection in the mirror. Her eyes were swollen, black streaks ran down her cheeks, and her hair had fallen from its pins.

"Are you sure you want to leave like this?" He walked up behind her and rubbed her back in support. "Don't you want to talk to him, to try to make this right?"

"He hates me. I've never seen so much repulsion in someone's eyes before." A croak erupted from her throat. "Oh, Luther, what could I say? I messed it all up. He'll never believe me now. I think it's best if I leave before I make it worse."

Grabbing her purse from the counter, she headed for the door.

"Wait for me in the car. I'm going to do a quick check to make sure you didn't forget any essentials."

She nodded her head and walked through the front door, closing it behind her.

She hadn't seen the envelope fall from her bag, but Luther had. Walking over to where it landed on the counter, he picked up the envelope containing the DNA results.

Stepping into the bedroom, Luther pulled down the forgotten case from the top of the closet shelf. Opening the lid, he gently laid the envelope on the top of the faded baby blanket. Running his hands over the soft cotton, he said a quick prayer and closed the lid.

Pulling the garment bag from the closet door, he tossed it over his arm, turned out the light and closed the cottage door behind him.

Chapter 50

Mark burst through the double doors, McKenzie right on his heels. Scanning both hallways, he reached back for her hand and pulled her to the left. Their shoes clicked along the linoleum, as they all but ran up to the counter outside the emergency room.

"Emily Sinclair?" he panted. "We're here to see Emily Sinclair."

Behind the counter, the woman smiled, her eyes roaming from the top of Mark's head, down to the tips of his black dress shoes.

McKenzie stepped in front of him, blocking the woman's view. The woman inhaled, envy registered in her eyes as she stared at the woman in silver sequins. "Where is Emily Sinclair?" she demanded. Her impatience was clear in her tone, and the woman quickly moved her mouse around on its pad.

"She's been moved to ICU. It's on the eighth floor. Elevators are down the hall, first right," she answered, still staring open mouthed at them.

They said their thanks and ran for the elevators. Mark knew under different circumstances he would have laughed at the familiar reaction the woman had to his mother. Her beauty had a way of striking people mute, even while they rushed to do her bidding.

The door slid open on the eighth floor and they both rushed out. Mark rushed to the desk and again, asked for Emily.

The nurse behind the counter looked up briefly and then back at her computer screen. "Are you family?" she asked in a monotone voice.

"Yes. No. Well, sort of. We're all the family she has. The hospital called," Mark said, his voice winded, and his control slipping. "Can we see her? Is she going to be okay?"

"The doctor is in with her. I will let him know you're here. He will fill you in on the details. You can have a seat in the waiting room."

She tipped her head in the direction of the small room across the hall. McKenzie took a seat in one of the straight backed chairs while Mark paced back and forth. She had to be okay. He tried to avoid picturing the last time he saw her, rushing from her own party, tears pouring from her eyes as if her heart were breaking all over again.

His anger surged again. What was Aimee's game? He couldn't quite figure it out. She'd never asked for anything, or done anything to make him suspect her. Other than lie, of course. He squeezed his eyes shut against the memories of her, but he could still see her smile, feel her hair against his cheek, and feel his heart split open.

"This is all her fault, you know." His eyes flashed with rage.

"This is all whose fault, Mark?" McKenzie asked. Her eyes filled with concern and confusion.

"Who else?" The rage in his voice made it clear who he was referring to.

"It was an accident. How can this be Aimee's fault?" She rose from the chair and approached him. "Please try to remember that we don't know what really happened, or why she lied. Maybe there is a simple explanation for all of this confusion."

His eyes narrowed and his jaw clenched. "Simple explanation? Are you serious? She's been lying to all of us for months. How is that going to only require a simple explanation?" He stuffed his hands into his pockets to keep himself from punching the wall. "She owns her own company so why is she working for someone else?" Mark picked up his pace, his mind spinning, his anger building, as he continued to talk aloud, but mainly to himself. "Why didn't she say anything? How did she know about the job interview? What was she after?"

"Mark, come and sit down for a minute. You're burning a hole in the linoleum."

He spun around, momentarily forgetting his mother was there. "When are they going to tell us what is going on? Why won't they let us see her?"

As if on cue, the doctor walked into the room. "You're Marcus Lee?" he asked.

"I am. This is my mother McKenzie." The doctor shook each of their hands. "How is she? Is Emily going to be alright? Do you know what happened?"

"She had a pretty serious car accident. The police are still investigating but it seems she crossed into the path of an oncoming car and overcorrected, causing her vehicle to roll over an embankment."

McKenzie gasped, and covered her mouth with her hand. Tears spilled down her cheeks as Mark wrapped his arm around her shoulders and pulled her in closer.

"A piece of glass lodged into her thigh severing a major artery. She's suffered massive blood loss and requires a transfusion. Emily has an extremely rare blood type. We have none on sight, but we're in the process of contacting other hospitals in the area, as well as our donors on file. Our records indicate she has no living family members. Is this accurate?"

Mark nodded his head. Looking at his mother, he paused a moment, confused by the uncertainty that showed on her expressive face.

"That's unfortunate. In these situations, it is normally our safest bet, as well as our fastest option to test the family members first. Rest assured, we're doing all we can." He pulled his clipboard against his chest and looked directly at Mark. "She's strong." He turned to look at McKenzie. "We have her sedated, but if you'd like, I can take you, one at a time to see her now."

"Mark, you go ahead." McKenzie attempted to smile.

He hesitated, surprised when his mother walked to the other end of the room and pulled out her cell phone.

"Ready?" the doctor asked.

Mark nodded and followed him out of the room.

Chapter 51

Mark stood quietly beside the bed, holding onto Emily's hand, careful to avoid the IV line taped to the top of it. Her beautiful face was marked with cuts and scrapes, and her complexion was pale as she laid against the stark white hospital sheets.

Today was her fiftieth birthday. She was supposed to be laughing and toasting with her friends, not lying motionless in a sterile room. She'd experienced so much pain in her life already, it seemed unjust she would be here. Presents sat unopened, trays of her favorite foods uneaten and open bottles of champagne would be poured down the drain.

He thought of the rare rose bush he'd secretly planted this morning. The Bride's Dream was already blooming; its delicate pale pink buds had cooperated in his plan to surprise Emily on her birthday. He hadn't had the chance to show her. Instead, she lay sedated in a hospital bed.

He gently set her hand back onto the bed and began to pace. He hated hospitals. The smell, the beeping machines, the fear. Why was this happening to her? He knew he was being somewhat unreasonable, but he couldn't help it, he blamed Aimee. He had to, it made it easier. How could he have been so foolish? He'd let this girl get close to Emily, and crawl under his skin. Emily had paid the ultimate price for his negligence. He'd failed to protect her. Again. He'd let his heart overtake his common sense. A mistake he swore to never make again.

Growing agitated he clenched and unclenched his fists. He knew he should have handled the evening differently. He'd been so angry when he'd found Aimee in the room with Emily that he'd reacted without thinking. The fact that his heart had lodged itself in his throat when he saw her standing there in that dress hadn't helped his mood. He had to give it to her, she was definitely a beautiful woman. Then again, some people found cobras or black widow spiders beautiful.

He sighed. The sound erupted like an explosion in the silence of the room. He knew he should step out, take a moment to calm himself down. Besides, his mother was waiting to see Emily. Walking over to the bed he placed a kiss on her forehead.

"I promise she won't hurt you again. Nobody will."

He closed the door quietly behind him and walked down the long hallway toward the waiting room. Peering through the window of the double doors, he froze, his feet cemented to the floor. How dare she show up here. He could hear the blood pumping through his veins, the sound like a bass drum in his ears. Clenching his teeth, he remained rooted, paralyzed in fury, as he watched Aimee speak to the nurse behind the counter.

McKenzie came out of the waiting room and headed over toward her. Heat climbed up his chest, spreading across his cheeks as he watched his mother pull her into her arms. Willing his feet to move, he burst through the door toward the scene unfolding in front of him.

Aimee had her back to him and his eyes uncontrollably followed the chain down her back and took in the soft curves of her hips. His involuntary reaction to her fueled his rage, and propelled him forward. Increasing his speed, he marched toward her and grabbing her arm, spun her around.

He was pleased to see the look of fear cross her face.

"Get out of here. Now!" His voice shook with barely controlled anger. "Or I promise you, I will personally throw you out."

"Mark, that's enough." McKenzie pulled his hand from Aimee's arm and stepped between them, her eyes pleading with him.

The doctor came through the doors, apparently having been alerted to the disturbance. His voice was full of authority when he turned to

Mark. "Step back. Calm down or I will have to ask you to leave."

Aimee could see Mark fighting for control. She knew him well enough, and was certain he wouldn't calm down as long as she was in the building. Her heart was beating fast, her palms sweaty, and her knees weak as he took a step back from her, his eyes never leaving hers. Maintaining his silent accusations, he crossed his arms, and clenched his jaw. Over Mark's shoulder she could see Luther standing in the doorway of the waiting room, protectively watching her, disbelief and sadness shining in his eyes.

She turned her attention back to the doctor. "I would like to give blood for Emily Sinclair." She straightened her shoulders and tried to hold her head up high, but she wasn't able to bring her voice above a whisper.

He studied her for a minute. "Ms. Sinclair has an extremely rare blood type. Although we appreciate your concern, the chances of your being a match—"

"I'm AB negative."

Relief registered on the doctor's face. Mark uncrossed his arms and took a step closer. His eyes narrowed, cutting through her.

She caught McKenzie's encouraging glance, urging her to continue.

Looking back at Mark, she searched for any sign that he still cared for her. She felt a piece of her die away as she understood that all that remained was the hatred filling his eyes. She knew she couldn't fix this. She'd lost him and no amount of truth would take back the lies she'd told or the secrets she'd kept.

She needed to concentrate on saving Emily. She took a deep breath and tried to speak. "I'm . . ." She cleared her throat and looked back at Mark again. Overwhelmed with regret, tears escaped beneath her lashes. Looking into his eyes, she finally muttered, "Please let me help. I'm . . . I'm her daughter."

Chapter 52

"You're a fool, but you'll figure that out. Might want to work on your apology speech, you're going to need a miracle to talk yourself out of this one."

Mark replayed the words Luther whispered into his ear at the hospital over and over again. He wished he could understand what he'd meant, and why the words bothered him so much. It made sense that Luther would stick up for Aimee. But why had he spouted off about Mark being a fool? Common sense would have him simply slipping out the back door. Was he referring to his foolishness for falling for Aimee? Or was it something else? And why did he care so much?

He'd been surprised when she actually played the lost daughter card. Even after discovering she was a liar and assuming that was her game, he'd been shocked when she said it. It was a common pattern, so why would she be any different than the others? But he'd truly believed she was different. So different that he'd fallen in love with her. Luther was right, he was a fool.

What didn't make sense, or possibly made her that much better than the cons that came before her, was how she knew Emily had a rare blood type. Not only that, but the doctor had informed them later she'd been a perfect match and had actually saved Emily's life. He'd told himself it was all an impressive coincidence.

He pulled next to the fountain and parked his car. It'd been a long night. After they were sure Emily was going to pull through, his mother had insisted he grab an hour of sleep and a shower. Needing to clear his head, he hadn't argued.

Walking through the front door, he headed toward the kitchen to update Mimsey. She was standing at the counter with a large bowl resting against her hip as she stirred vigorously. Normally in a tidy bun, her hair was wild, falling around her face in knotted clumps. Her eyes were swollen and red, her apron covered in batter and dusted with flour.

"Mimsey, are you alright?"

Whipping her head up in surprise, it seemed to take a moment for her to register he'd spoken. She let go of the spoon, then the bowl. Hitting the floor, the bowl shattered, and batter sprayed across the kitchen. She ran to him and threw herself into his arms.

"Marcus, how is she? Please tell me that Ms. Emily is okay. I can't tell you how worried I've been."

"Emily is going to be fine. She's weak and sleeping a lot, but it sounds like she'll be home in a few days."

"Oh thank goodness. I was so afraid." She stepped in and snuggled into his arms. "Yesterday was supposed to be a celebration. I can't understand how it could all go so wrong."

"It's all okay," he said, cooing in her ear as if she were a small child. "There's nothing to worry about anymore."

She rested against him quietly for a few minutes. Suddenly, her head whipped up and she abruptly stepped back. "Did you say she'll be home in a few days? Look at this place . . . Look at me." Running her hands through her hair, she tugged some of it back into the band. She looked down at her apron, then over at the mess on the floor. "I have so much to do. I've got to clean this place up. Will she be able to climb the stairs or should I set the reading room up for her? Can she eat normally, or will she need softer foods? I have to go to the market, and oh, I should make her favorite—"

"Mimsey, breathe."

Her cheeks grew red and she smiled awkwardly. "Sorry, but I do have a lot to do." Her smile faded and her voice became a whisper. "Is Ms. Aimee going to be returning?"

"She will not be returning." His tone was filled with disdain.

"In fact, if you happen to see her anywhere near this property, call the police immediately."

She nodded her head in acknowledgement, but Mark noticed the single tear that fell from her eye. He turned and left the kitchen. His mind reeled with the reality of how much an impact Aimee had on the women in the house. How had she become such a fixture in such a short period of time?

He headed for the back of the house and noticed signs of an abandoned party in each room he walked through. Small tables were still set up, with half-filled glasses of champagne resting on them, and a table in the sun room was stacked high with un-opened gifts. He saw one of the gifts laying on the floor and set it back on the large pile.

Turning around to leave he noticed the framed photo sitting on a small table in the corner. His stomach turned as he drew closer, pulled by its familiarity. He must have walked past this photo a million times, but it was more than that. He'd held it in his hands only recently, yet he knew he hadn't. It was a photograph of Nathan and Emily at a charity fundraiser years ago. Picking it up, he stared closely at the smiling faces, trying to understand his reaction. The wind blew out of his lungs as if he'd been punched and the photo slipped from his hands. Aimee's prom photo. The similarities in the two pictures were impossible to miss. He knew then he'd never seen Aimee's photograph before it came from the investigator, but he'd remembered this picture and confused the two.

He rubbed his hands over his face, trying to understand how this was possible. He hurried from the room, beginning to wonder if he was losing his mind.

He snapped the door closed behind him and stopped to pull fresh air into his lungs before moving forward. Even walking the path to his cottage he saw her everywhere. His feet stopped outside her door, as if they had a mind of their own. He felt light headed, and he could feel the pressure building behind his eyes.

Telling himself his reaction was simply because he was overtired, he took a few steps back, willing himself to go home.

He shook his head in frustration and let out a breath. He pushed open the door, but remained outside on the porch. Her scent wafted from inside, carried on the breeze. His stomach clenched, and he allowed his anger to engulf him, welcoming it over the sadness.

Walking inside, his footsteps echoed in the emptiness of the room. As if pulled, he walked through the door to her bedroom. He noted the empty hangers on the rod, the drawers hanging partially open, the vase filled with roses he'd clipped for her, and the stack of books beside the bed. His attention was drawn to an old leather case sitting in the middle of the bed.

Sitting down on the edge of the bed, he clicked open the latches and lifted the lid. He lifted an envelope from the top and noted the date on the postmark. It was mailed only a few days ago from New York City. His palms grew sweaty as he pulled the sheet from the envelope and read it. Scanning the typed words, he held his breath. "Based on the scientific evidence we conclude that Jane Doe cannot be excluded as the biological mother of Josie Doe. The probability of the stated outcome is 99.9999%." He stared blindly at the paper in his hand, unable to process the information and what it might mean.

He looked down at the contents still resting in the case and lifted out an old photo album. He gently flipped open the cover, staring at a green eyed baby with cherub cheeks and a kewpie doll mouth. Turning the pages faster, he watched Aimee growing up in photographs. She was tottering toward a dark haired man, his face alight with pride. In another, she was sitting on the lap of a dark haired woman, her eyes bright with love for the person behind the camera. Reaching the final page, he flipped back to the beginning, looking again.

He set the book to the side and carefully lifted out a baby blanket. He gripped it tightly, the pressure behind his eyes building as he fought to control the tears threatening to fall. It was yellowed with age, and the red ladybugs climbing around the edges were now pink, but it was the same. It was the blanket that was lying over the top of Amelia in the only photograph Emily had of her daughter.

Folding it up, he dug deeper into the case. He set aside the pile of newspaper articles regarding the kidnapping, and paused when he reached for the last item. She wasn't a fraud, she wasn't conning anyone. Holding the broken plastic circle that had been cut from her tiny wrist, he knew. Aimee was Emily's daughter. And he'd made her leave.

He felt dizzy as he tried to process the events of the last two days. She wasn't a playing a game, she was real. Why hadn't she told him? He shook his head. He would never have believed her and they both knew it.

Rising from the bed, he held the baby blanket to his chest. He needed to get to Emily. He had to tell her what a horrible thing he'd done and beg for her forgiveness.

As he reached the door, something caught his eye and he walked over to the dining room table. A brightly wrapped gift sat unopened at the edge of the table. Reading the tag, he knew exactly what was beneath the wrapping. It was addressed to Emily, from Mark. His hands shook as he ripped away the paper.

The cover she'd drawn captured his story perfectly. Emily's likeness was incredible, as was Nathan's. She'd drawn them gazing lovingly at each other, Emily standing on a balcony, in a white dress exactly as he'd pictured it when he'd tried to describe it in words. She was holding out her hand for the pink rose being offered to her by Nathan, kneeling on one knee, dressed as a heroic knight. She'd drawn the moon as a giant circle illuminating the scene in the perfect shades of blue and gray, not detracting from the bright pink of the rose bushes in the background.

It was exactly what he'd wanted, and more than he'd expected. It was printed and bound in a genuine hard cover. When he'd brought it to her, it had been untitled. Now, written across the top, it read: *The One*. He ran his hands gently over the story he'd written and she'd improved. The symbolism was impossible to ignore.

Chapter 53

Mark's entire body shook as he lingered outside the door to Emily's room. He could see his mother asleep in the chair beside the bed, still holding tightly to Emily's hand. His heart raced as he anticipated her reaction to what he was about to tell her.

He'd debated the entire drive over as to whether he should be the one to tell Emily, or if Aimee should do it. Remembering the way he'd treated her, he was certain she was back in New York by now, and he wasn't sure she would agree to come back with him. Not that he could blame her.

Looking up, he saw his mother eyeing him curiously as he stood outside the door. Waving her hand for him to come in, he took a deep breath and swung open the door. She frowned at him, looking him up and down.

"I thought you were going to shower." She posed it more as a statement than a question.

"I didn't have time. I needed to talk to Emily right away." He stepped over to the side of the bed, clinging tightly to the baby blanket he held against his chest.

"Mark, are you okay?" McKenzie scooted forward in her chair. "You really need to get some rest. Emily is going to be just fine, you don't have to worry."

"It isn't that." He bit his tongue, hoping the pain would hold back the tears.

McKenzie rose from the chair and came around the bed. "What's going on? What's happened?" she asked with obvious concern.

They were both startled when Emily spoke. "Mark?"

He bent down and kissed her cheek. She reached out her hand to keep his face close to hers. Her eyes darted back and forth, her expression wary as she studied him.

"What is it?" Her eyes were insistent. "Something's up."

Resting his hip on the corner of her bed, he lowered his head, searching for the words.

Emily's voice was weak, but there was no question she was serious. "Spill it, Mark. I'm in no mood to be coddled. Are you ill? Is it Mimsey?" He could sense her growing agitated.

Before he could think of the right way to tell her, he blurted, "It's Aimee. She's—"

"Is she hurt? What happened?" Emily's face revealed the love she felt for Aimee, even after everything he'd accused her of.

He stroked her hand, and gently laid the baby blanket across her lap. He reached into his jacket pocket and slowly pulled out the tiny hospital bracelet and laid it on top.

He watched as her eyes registered shock, then disbelief, and finally a look of complete joy. She slowly lifted the bracelet and stroked it lovingly, tears streaming down her pale cheeks. She didn't speak. She unfolded the blanket, caressing the hand sewn ladybugs, seeming to be transported back in time.

She looked up at him, her eyes filled with hope. She swallowed and tried to speak, her voice emitting a croak, before she swallowed and tried again. Clearing her throat, she finally murmured, "Amelia?"

Mark nodded his head as the tears he'd been fighting finally broke through and ran unchecked down his face. "I think Aimee is your daughter."

Pulling the blanket to her face, Emily quietly sobbed. McKenzie sat on the other side of the bed and pulled her into her arms as she cried with her.

"I knew it." McKenzie beamed. "I knew it was her."

"You did?" Emily's eyes were filled with questions. "How? Why didn't you say anything?"

"I suspected, but I didn't know for sure. There were so many similarities, and she seemed so filled with longing when she was around you." McKenzie took a deep breath. "I didn't understand how strongly I suspected it until your accident. When my first instinct was to call Aimee and ask her blood type, I realized I wasn't surprised it was the same as yours. I know it sounds strange, but I simply felt it."

"How come I didn't? I should have known. A mother should recognize her own child, right?" Emily began to sob.

"How could you? You'd go crazy looking for signs in every young girl you met." McKenzie grabbed her hand. "You loved her. You had a connection with her. Deep down, maybe you sensed it, but after all this time, you can't think you're wrong for not jumping to the impossible conclusion."

"I'm so sorry," Mark finally said, pushing off the bed. Unable to hold still, he paced back and forth. "I made her leave. I was horrible to her. I didn't know . . ."

Emily reached out and grabbed his arm, stopping him midstride. Looking down at her tear stained face he knew he'd never seen a woman happier then Emily at that moment. She seemed to glow from the inside out.

Tugging his arm, she forced him to sit back down, never taking her eyes from him. He couldn't look away. She tried to speak, but seeming unable to control the emotions that erupted from her she began to laugh instead. Mark watched her curiously as she leaned back against the pillows crying and laughing simultaneously.

Suddenly growing serious, she struggled to sit upright. "What are you still doing here?"

Confused, Mark stepped back as if he'd been slapped. "You want me to leave?"

"Yes, I want you to leave. Go get my daughter and bring her home to me."

Chapter 54

Aimee pulled the covers over her head and grumbled at Luther to go away. She didn't want to get out of bed. She didn't want to go to work. She definitely didn't want to hear Luther's chipper voice as he tried to coerce her into resuming her normal routine. She simply wanted to lie beneath the covers and try to pretend the last few months never happened.

She missed Mark. She'd rolled over and subconsciously reached for him as she slowly awakened. It'd taken her a minute to remember she was back in her loft in New York, not her quaint cottage in sunny San Francisco.

She wanted to have breakfast with Emily and talk about nothing, and everything. She wanted to listen to Mimsey humming as she fluttered around the kitchen, and hear McKenzie's quiet laugh as she whispered to her mystery man on the other end of the phone. She wanted to watch the sun setting with Mark's hand in hers.

Burying her head in the pillow, she wept. She didn't think she had any tears left after the hours she'd spent crying last night. Luther insisted on staying with her after they'd arrived home. Not having the strength to argue with him she'd handed him a pillow and blanket before closing herself in her room.

Luther sat on the edge of her bed. "Come on, Aimee. You can't stay in bed forever."

She dug her face deeper into the pillows.

Pulling back the covers, he tried again. "Let's go get some coffee and a bagel with a ton of cream cheese. We'll walk to work and breathe in the smog. It'll make you feel better."

Sitting up, she wiped her hair out of her eyes and glared at him. "I know I can't stay here forever, but is one day too much to ask for?"

Undeterred, he grabbed her hand and yanked her to her feet. "Yes, it is. You won't be happy with only one day. You need to get back to it or you will wallow for weeks." He pushed her gently in the direction of the small bathroom. "You look like hell. I saved you some hot water. You can thank me later."

"I hate you," she mumbled before slamming the door in his face.

Forty-five minutes later, she stood on the sidewalk sipping her latte. She'd done all she could with her swollen eyes, but her heartbreak was evident. Luther continued to try and cheer her up, chatting non-stop beside her, gently leading her through the crowds.

"Listen to those horns, those cursing pedestrians, and the sirens. Can't you feel the energy? Man, it's good to be home." He grabbed her arm to keep her moving forward.

At one time she'd loved the noise, the energy, the endless pace. Today the horns were startling, the cursing was rude, and the sirens made her wonder how Emily was recovering. For the first time since she'd moved to New York, she wanted to be anywhere else.

Her purse fell from her shoulder and her coffee sloshed through the lid she was abruptly bumped from behind. Stopping in the middle of the sidewalk, tears filled her eyes as she watched the man continue to walk on without a backward glance.

"Hey, watch it, asshole!" Luther shouted at the man's retreating back. "You okay?"

She nodded, wiped her eyes, pulled her purse back onto her shoulder and continued in the direction of her shop. Work would make her feel better. She could bury herself in her sketches, check on the new line. Do what she did best. Luther was right, she needed to keep living. After all, this was her life. The dreams she'd come so close to reaching weren't real. She wouldn't live the happily ever after fairy tale. It didn't exist.

*

Mark stood on the sidewalk outside Amore' Handbags and mentally tried to perfect his apology. This was what Luther meant. And when he'd called him a fool, it was for not believing in the woman he loved. He'd made such a mess of things. He cringed as he recalled the horrible things he'd said to her, the way he'd looked at her, the things he'd accused her of. What if she wouldn't forgive him? His panic swelled as he imagined himself walking away from here without her.

He could see Luther behind the counter, ringing up a sale for a grey haired woman in a mink coat. He stretched his neck trying to see over the window display for any sign of Aimee. What if she hadn't returned to New York? That thought hadn't even crossed his mind before now.

He pulled his coat closed against the sudden chill and watched as the lady in the mink coat exited the store and climbed into the back seat of a nearby town car. He jumped when sudden movement caught his attention. Shocked, he looked up directly into the eyes of an angry Luther. He didn't move, his hand stiffly clinging to the sign he'd been about to flip showing they were closed.

He lifted his hand in a hesitant wave. Luther's eyes became slits. He looked over his shoulder, and then marched outside to confront him.

"If you're here to continue your little tirade, you can forget it. She's had enough and I won't let you hurt her anymore."

"I'm not," Mark managed to say.

"So then you finally realized what a fool you've been?"

Mark nodded his head, his cheeks warming with the shame he felt.

"Have you practiced your groveling like I suggested?"

Unable to contain himself, Mark chuckled. "I don't know what it is about you that I like—"

Luther waved his hand in dismissal. "Don't waste your breath flattering me. You need to get your kneepads on. You hurt my girl.

You didn't even give her a chance to explain."

Kicking at a loose stone on the sidewalk, Mark kept his head down. "I know. I really screwed up."

"She wasn't after a damn thing. She only wanted to be sure before she said anything. It wasn't a game to her. She isn't a liar and she doesn't have an ounce of maliciousness in her body." Luther's voice rose as his words flew out with excessive speed. "I may not agree with the way she handled it, but she didn't deserve to be treated that way. And by you! How dare you. I don't know if you're good enough for her. I thought so at first, but now I'm not—"

"I love her Luther, with all of my heart." He looked up, his eyes pleading. "I'm not good enough for her, that much is true, but I want to be. I'm a better man with her, and I know I can't live without her."

"Okay, that's a good start." Luther smirked. "She's in the back. Got your kneepads strapped on?"

Mark nodded his head, straightened his back and inhaled. Luther held the door for him to enter. Inside smelled like leather, and her. Colorful handbags sat on glass shelves and hung from scrolled racks, matching wallets sat on pedestals, and a few crystal and rhinestone belts laid across a display table.

This was her world. She'd created it with her own two hands. Mark felt himself swell with pride.

As if reading his mind, Luther looked around the room and said, "Yeah, she's pretty amazing. Remember that." He pointed to the doorway tucked in the corner and walked to the other end of the store.

Mark unbuttoned his coat, and walked slowly to the door. He stood back and watched her for a minute, as she sat at her desk, head down, and a pencil in her hand drawing on a pad. His breath hitched.

Her head lifted, and their eyes locked. He could see the surprise on her face, and sensed her hesitation. Wiping his shaking hands on his jeans, he took a few steps closer. He could feel his heart beating, even as it poured out to her through his eyes.

"Your mother wants us to come to dinner tomorrow night. She actually wanted you home tonight, but I told her I needed a bit more time to grovel for your forgiveness."

Watching a faint smile move her lips and a single tear roll down her cheek, he saw his love reflected back in her eyes and knew he hadn't lost her.

Chapter 55

Aimee stood outside the large front door. She subconsciously wiped her sweaty palms on the front of her dress. Her stomach fluttered, her pulse raced, and her hands shook.

"I've walked through this door a thousand times." She turned to Mark. "Why do I feel so nervous?"

"Are you nervous or are you excited?" Reaching out, he took her hands into his. "You've waited a long time for this. You know Emily, and she knows you, but it's different now. For all the nerves you're feeling, can you imagine hers? She's waited for her little girl to come home for twenty-eight years. Today, she is."

The tears rolled down her cheeks as she pictured Emily. Her eternal hope in her daughter's return, her heartbreak as one year rolled into the next without her. She knew how blessed she was to be here. To know that on the other side of that door was a woman who'd loved her unconditionally her entire life.

"Aimee." Mark squeezed her hands. "Before we go inside would you take a walk with me?"

"Now?"

He nodded his head. "Humor me."

Taking her hand in his, he led her down the front steps and around the back of the house. The sun was beginning to set, the light softly filtered through the trees. She felt herself unwinding, the nerves she'd felt before beginning to ease. She inhaled the intoxicating scent of jasmine and roses filling the air.

Grateful that he'd realized her need to clear her head, she turned to Mark. Her appreciation never passed her lips. She was entranced by the expression that lit his face. She followed his gaze to see what held his attention.

The rose garden was aglow with candlelight. Hundreds of candles flickered in holders strewn throughout. A few feet in front of her, pale pink rose petals lined the pathway. She turned to Mark again, certain her surprise was written all over her face.

He smiled at her, his eyes filled with childish delight. He squeezed her hand and slowly led her down the petal lined path deeper into the garden.

"Mark, what is all of this?" she asked, overwhelmed by the beauty surrounding her. The sky was splashed with reds and oranges as the sun continued to set. The glow from the candles emphasized the rich colors of the rosebushes surrounding them.

He brushed his lips gently over hers. "I've been thinking about the changes that are going to happen around here now that you've come home."

He took her hand and led her to the small bench seat. She sat down next to him, and turned to face him, her knees gently touching his.

"I can't begin to tell you how happy I am you're Emily's daughter. You're an incredible, loving woman, and I know how much happiness you will bring into her life." He looked down, and rubbed his thumb over the back of her hand as it lay clasped with his on her lap. "To me, though, you're much more than that. I realize I haven't shown you how much you mean to me lately, but I would like the chance to make all of that up to you. I want to show you how much I love you, every day for the rest of my life, and longer, if it's possible."

Her heart swelled as his words began to sink in.

"I want to have children with you. Although, I insist they be born at home and under tight security. I want yours to be the first face I see every morning, and the last face I see each night."

He ran his fingers through his hair, stood up and pulled a box from his pocket. He knelt in front of her and lifted the lid.

"I've already asked your mother's permission, and she's given it, although she mentioned she thought you could do much better than me. Aimee, will you marry me?"

She looked into his eyes and felt her heart soar. "Of course I will marry you. I love you, Marcus Lee."

He lifted the ring from the velvet box and slipped it easily onto her finger. It fit like it had been made for her.

"It's the most beautiful ring I've ever seen," she said, not taking her eyes from it as it sparkled brightly, reflecting the surrounding candlelight.

"It belonged to your mother. It's the same ring that Nathan put on her finger on their wedding day."

Her eyes glistened as she held up her hand to look again. She never imagined she could feel as much love surrounding her as she did at that moment.

They both stood, and he pulled her into his arms. His lips pressed firmly to hers, he spun her around in a circle. Hearing scraping and murmuring sounds behind the large tree in the corner, they both turned their heads.

Crackling sounds were followed by loud whispers. "I can't see, move over."

More rustling sounds were followed by a snappy, "I can't see either, you move over."

Aimee and Mark covered their mouths, fighting the urge to laugh out loud. They bent down and quietly crept toward the sound. Coming up behind them, they stood for a moment and watched Mimsey, McKenzie, and Emily, elbowing, and pushing each other as they strained to peek around the large tree trunk.

"Where did they go? I can't see them anymore, can you see them?" Mimsey asked, leaning farther out.

"I can't see anything but McKenzie's head," Emily snapped, jabbing her elbow into her side.

Aimee began to laugh. All three women jumped in surprise.

McKenzie was the first to speak. She smoothed down the skirt to her sundress, and smiled innocently. "There was a poor cat stuck in the tree." She looked up and lifted her hand to point, exaggerating her shock at finding it gone. "Well, will you look at that, it found its own way down."

Mark laughed again, and walked over to hug his mother. "You three just couldn't wait, could you?"

"We'd have to rely on you to provide all the details. What if you left something out? Forgot an important detail, or something she said?" McKenzie appeared to have convinced herself this was actually an honest justification for spying.

Mimsey and McKenzie stepped from behind the tree, but Emily stood frozen in place. Aimee didn't move, as she stared at her mother. All the things she's wanted to say flew from her mind.

Emily's eyes filled with tears as she tilted her head and smiled at her. Without taking her eyes from Aimee, she stepped from behind the tree and came to stand in front of her.

"I'm sorry for spying." She looked over at Mark, and then locked eyes with Aimee again. "I simply refuse to miss another big moment in my daughter's life."

Aimee wrapped her arms around her mother and pulled her close. Mark walked over, and took her hand to walk her into the house for dinner. Aimee looked at them, surrounded by love and feeling happier than she'd ever imagined possible. A movement caught her eye. She watched as a ladybug landed softly on a nearby rosebush.

A Word About the Author. . .

Debut Author Erin McCauley has always been fascinated by the dynamics that make a family. Be it by blood or destiny, our pasts lead us to become the people we are meant to be and the families we work to form. She enjoys writing about self-discovery and the healing that must take place before true love can be recognized.

Erin lives in the Pacific Northwest with her husband and three children.

"Look for *The Truth*, the second book in this series, forthcoming December 2012."

Visit her at www.erinmccauley.com.

In the mood for more Crimson Romance? Check out *Best Laid Plans* by Eliabeth Palmer at CrimsonRomance.com.

Made in the USA
San Bernardino, CA
20 October 2012